Edge of
MIDNIGHT

Other Police Chief Susan Wren Mysteries

Edge of MIDNIGHT

Charlene Weir

Thomas Dunne Books
St. Martin's Minotaur
New York

This is a work of fiction. All of the characters, organizations, and events portrayed in this novel are either products of the author's imagination or are used fictitiously.

THOMAS DUNNE BOOKS.
An imprint of St. Martin's Press.

www.thomasdunnebooks.com
www.minotaurbooks.com

Library of Congress Cataloging-in-Publication Data

Weir, Charlene.
    Edge of midnight / Charlene Weir.—1st ed.
        p. cm.
    ISBN-13: 978-0-312-34797-0
    ISBN-10: 0-312-34797-9
        1. Wren, Susan (Fictitious character)—Fiction.
    2. Women police chiefs—Fiction.
    3. Police—Kansas—Fiction.
    4. Kansas—Fiction. I. Title.

    PS3573.E39744 E34 2006
    813'.54—dc22   2006046583

First Edition: December 2006

10 9 8 7 6 5 4 3 2 1

FOR BRUCE AND PATTY, MY IN-LAW CHILDREN, A GREAT
BONUS, WHO MAKE THE FAMILY RICHER

$\mathscr{A}$CKNOWLEDGMENTS

Many thanks to Bette Golden Lamb for information on the care and treatment of things medical, and to Leila Laurence Dobsha, who always comes through with the answers when I call and yell "Help."

Gratitude to friends and colleagues Avis Worthington, Barbara Brunetti, Elise Morgan, and Patricia Elmore for encouragement, criticism, and invaluable advice.

Lasting appreciation for my editor, Ruth Cavin, who knows a shaky scene when she sees one and says, Firm up this mess.

Thanks to my daughter, Leslie, for reading the manuscript several times and creating consistency from chaos.

Thanks, gratitude, appreciation, and heaps more thanks to my agent, Meg Ruley, who is absolutely the best. That goes also for Annelise Robey.

Thanks also to Art Gatti, who spotted errors and hard-to-accept time sequences, and threw in a few hellish questions.

Edge of
MIDNIGHT

$\mathcal{P}$ROLOGUE

$\mathcal{L}$ily snapped the camera shutter for one last shot and looked out over the river as she rewound the film. She'd gotten some good ones, worth the time it took to wait until the light was just right. Time! Oh my God! She looked at her watch and realized she'd been out here for over ninety minutes. Brett would kill her!

She sprinted back to the clubhouse and raced to the bar. He sat alone at a table by the window and he didn't look happy. She rushed over and planted a loud, smacking kiss on his cheek.

"Where the hell have you been!"

A row of small round tables ran along the bank of windows that looked out on the river. A red globe with a candle inside sat on each table. The waitress, in midcalf-length black skirt and white blouse, was moving from table to table lighting the candles. The bar was deserted, except for one man at the end, and the bartender, who was polishing wine glasses.

Lily threw herself in the chair across from him. "I told you I was going to go down there and—"

"You said twenty minutes. It's been an hour and a half."

"I'm sorry." And she was. She'd never intended to be gone that long.

"Why do you always do this?"

"Do what?"

"Take those fucking pictures all the time?"

"That's why we came," she said with emphasized patience. "So I could take pictures of Sam and Alley's wedding." She looked around at the nearly empty room. "Where is everybody?"

"They left an hour ago. I've been sitting here with my thumb up my ass while you're out prancing around with that stupid camera stuck to your face."

"Come on, Brett, it wasn't so long. We can go now. I just wanted—"

"It's always about what you want, isn't it? What about what I want? Maybe I wanted to go to the party."

"So, let's go. It's not too late. The party'll be going on half the night—"

"I missed the kickoff."

"Oh my God, the kickoff! He missed the kickoff!" She put her hand on her chest like a Victorian lady about to swoon.

"You're a riot." He shot up so abruptly the chair tipped. He caught it just before it fell, shoved it under the table, and strode off.

With little flicks of anger licking around in her stomach, she stomped after him. "Brett Witherson, stop being such an ass."

"You're always going off with that fucking camera."

"Brett, it's what I do. I take pictures. And I exchange them for money. It's how I pay my rent and buy my food."

"Oh, really? And what does your daddy pay for?"

She tried a conciliatory smile. "So I exaggerate a little sometimes. One day, I'm going to sell them and pay for the rent and stuff."

"Yeah, well, until you learn how to take a decent picture, just throw the camera in the back seat when you're with me."

Decent picture! She'd show him decent! Aiming the camera at him, she said "Smile," and clicked the shutter.

2

"Funny!" He unlocked the car door and slid in under the wheel. "Apologize or I'm leaving."

"Apologize!? You're the one behaving like a jerk! You think you can treat me like some worthless piece of shit? That is some kind of selfish—I only wanted to—"

He started the motor, backed out of the parking space, and stomped the accelerator.

Lily threw her backpack on the ground, put her fists on her hips, and watched the car drive away, laying down rubber as it squealed out of the lot. "Cretin!" she yelled.

So, she'd been gone a few more than twenty minutes and he missed the kickoff. What the hell was so important about a kickoff? She'd show him a kickoff!

Oh hell, had they just broken up? She'd only wanted to take a few more pictures while the fading light was slanting onto the water. The moon, a pale disc that looked paper thin, was biding it's time in a sky so blue it made her catch her breath. With sun shining like the flaming chariot of Helios, the moon was nothing, but when the sun slipped behind the hills, it would be magic.

Well, shit, just how was she supposed to get home?

With a jagged sigh, she dug out her cell phone and pressed a button. Nothing. Damn! Dead battery. She'd forgotten to charge it again. Slinging the backpack over her shoulder, she started toward the clubhouse.

"Need a ride?"

She squinted at the man just coming out the door with the sun at his back. He smiled. "Nice wedding, didn't you think?"

Nothing about him looked dangerous. Dark hair, amused smile—he'd obviously just witnessed that childish fight—dark suit, white shirt gleaming in the sun, and highly polished shoes. Kind of cute, maybe a few years older than she was.

"Do you have a cell phone? I could call a taxi."

"Sorry, I don't own one."

"That's okay, I'll use the phone inside."

"I can take you wherever you want to go."

"The bus station?" There had to be buses, and then when she got back to El Cerrito, she could take a taxi.

"Sure. No problem." He headed for his car and she followed. If it had been a broken-down heap, she might have had qualms, but it was a new—at least newish, she didn't know anything about cars—Toyota. When he opened the passenger door, she hesitated only a moment, then slid in and dropped her backpack on the floor between her feet.

You don't take rides from strangers, but another wedding guest, even if he was someone she personally didn't know, wasn't exactly a stranger. Sam and Alley knew him, that was enough for her.

"I'm supposed to join some friends staying at a condo in El Cerrito" Lily said. "It belongs to somebody's parent. Johnson, I think their name is. I don't know much about El Cerrito. I'm from Palo Alto."

"That's where I'm going. You might as well come with me."

"Uh—yeah, okay, that'd be great." It would save her hanging out in the bus station waiting for a bus back.

"My name's Wade."

"Lily," she said, wondering if Wade was first name or last.

He pushed a button and light jazz floated from the speakers. She relaxed back in the seat, thinking what she'd tell Brett when she saw him. The jerk! How dare he just drive off and leave her! It was dark by the time they got to El Cerrito, she tried to remember the directions that were given to Brett, but she hadn't paid much attention, counting on him to get it all right and get them there.

After several turns up one dark deserted street and down another it was obvious she didn't know where she was going, and equally obvious Wade was getting pissed because she didn't know.

"Just drop me at the police station," she said. "Maybe they can help." She had been to the house once before and thought she'd recognize it if she saw it.

"There are condos on Richmond Street. Let's drive by before we

4

give up." He drove up through hills and down a steep road into a dark wilderness area with no houses. Nerves started prickling the back of her neck. He was sitting very still and stiff somehow. No longer cute. Now he was—kind of scary.

"This couldn't be right," she said. "There aren't any houses down here." She looked out the window. Nothing was here, tangled brush and trees, pitch black everywhere.

He drove past a sign that read merry-go-round with an arrow pointing right and pulled up into a cul-de-sac, bushes scraped against the nose of the car. Putting an arm over the back of her seat, he turned slightly, smiled. This smile was different. He was different, focused, like a bird dog who had just spotted quail. Fear made her chest tight.

"There aren't any houses here," she said.

Wade looked around as though surprised, then nodded. "This will do." He pulled the key from the ignition and shoved it in his pocket. "Lose the clothes."

"What?"

"Get them off!"

Lily fumbled at the door handle. Quick as a snake, Wade backhanded her across the face, grabbed her hair and slammed her head against the dash.

"Stupid bitch!"

"Please, no," Lily whispered. "Please."

"Shut up!" He slapped her again, her head snapped against the door, blood seeped from her nose. Snatching the throat of her blouse, he ripped it open.

I'm going to die, she thought, fingers desperately searching for the door lock. *I'm going to die in this dark place with this creep pawing me.* "Please don't hurt me." Tears rolled down her face, mixed with snot and blood.

"I told you to shut up!" One hand squeezed her throat and the other grabbed for her breast. "You like this? This what you let that stupid boyfriend do?"

He smashed a fist into her face. Pain exploded through her head. "Take off your underpants."

"Yes, okay, just don't hurt me." Focusing only on living through this nightmare, she wiggled around trying to pull down the wisp of nylon under the tight wool skirt.

When she succeeded, he muttered, called her an evil bitch, a stupid whore, and jammed his fingers inside her. She screamed. He punched her face, grabbed her arm, and yanked her closer.

He pummeled her, smashed her face and breasts and stomach. The more she struggled, the harder he hit. Finally, she lay still and he stopped hitting. She was sprawled against the door, her head at an awkward angle on the armrest. He unzipped his pants and flung himself over her. *Please, God. Please, God. Please, God.* She said it over and over in her mind to block out what was happening.

Several seconds before she realized he didn't have an erection. At first she was glad, then he punched her chest. "Do it, bitch!" He squeezed her fingers.

She fought for breath. Screaming and shrinking inside, she touched him.

"Harder!"

Even trying harder didn't help. He groped along the floor, reached under the seat and slid out a hammer. *Oh God, he's going to hit me with the hammer! He's going to kill me!* She tried to curl in on herself, make herself smaller to reduce the area of pain.

Moonlight glinted on his teeth as he smiled. He held the wooden handle out to her. She didn't understand what he wanted. He hit her again with his fist.

"You want me to kill you! Is that what you want? Huh?"

"No! No, please no!"

"Take this and stick it in! Do it!"

He wanted her to put the wooden handle inside herself? *I can't, I can't, I can't. You can,* she told herself. *If that's what it takes to survive, you can. You have to.*

She fumbled with the hammer, dropped it. Enraged, he grabbed it and jammed it inside her. She screamed with pain. The screams made him angrier and he jabbed the hammer harder, over and over.

Every time he rammed it inside, she screamed and scrabbled at him with hands sticky with her own blood. He stopped only to hit her, again and again. The car seats and dash were awash with blood, the windows smeared, the floor mats squishy.

Hang on, a voice inside whispered. *Hang on*. She thought of her father, working so hard to pay the college tuition, her mother, leaning against the dresser watching her put on makeup.

Don't die, she commanded herself. Don't be one of those statistics, woman missing, twenty-two years old. What would he do with her body? She'd rot somewhere, no face, no name, her parents never knowing what happened to her. Why? What had she ever done to deserve this?

Anger brought a surge of adrenaline that let her twist and rip at his face with her fingernails. She'd have his skin and blood beneath her nails. He yelled, dropped the hammer and grabbed her throat with both hands. He shook her head, banging it against the window. She could feel the life leaving her lungs, then his hands loosened and she gasped at air.

He picked up the hammer again. "Turn over!"

She was so battered, she couldn't move. He yanked at her, tossed her around like a half-stuffed toy. When she was face down, he shoved the hammer up her butt. When she screamed, he smashed her head with the metal end.

Cold—she was getting cold. Pain, the pain was everywhere. Her mind stopped its frantic scrabbling and she was drifting, just drifting, riding on the pain into the darkness.

1

Two years later

$\mathcal{N}$othing like firing somebody on a Monday morning to start the week out right. A scratchy throat, sharp pains above the bridge of her nose, and a throbbing earache put Susan Wren smack in the mood. The officer in question, recently hired Ida Rather, had performed an unforgivable sin, disobeyed a direct order from a superior.

Ida—tall and slender, dark, feathery cap of hair, oval face, dark eyes, high cheekbones—stood so stiffly at attention in front of the desk that Susan worried she was in danger of falling like a board in a hard wind. Which, God knew, there was plenty of in Kansas. Jaw clenched so tight any fillings were in danger of shattering, eyes staring straight past Susan's shoulder at the flag behind the desk, Ida bravely waited for the axe.

"Your actions could have gotten Demarco seriously injured," Susan said.

Ida, tightening her lips into an even thinner line, dipped her head the merest fraction to indicate she'd heard.

"You have no experience. No knowledge. You don't think, and you don't listen."

Another small dip of the head.

Susan suppressed a sigh. Ida had finished second in her class at the academy, she was fit, eager, ambitious, smart, and willing. Unfortunately, she was also impulsive, overly self-confident and ready to dive into the fray. Had Ida made even the merest hint of an excuse, Susan would have dropped the axe on the back of that stiff neck. But Ida standing there bravely, expecting to get her career chopped to an end before it had barely begun, made some evil genie in Susan's head hold her tongue.

Maybe she was partly to blame. She shouldn't have partnered Ida with Demarco, who had a problem with women and a *big* problem with women in law enforcement. She should have placed her with Osey. Kind, patient, gentle Osey. The disadvantage there was, at first sight, he didn't command respect. Scarecrow with no brain was the impression. False impression. Except for the scarecrow part. He did look like a scarecrow, but his brain worked like lightning, even if his mouth didn't.

"We'll mark this up to a learning experience," Susan surprised herself by saying.

Ida was so startled her faraway stare fell to Susan's face and a rosy flush spread over her cheeks. "Thank you," she stammered. "You won't regret it. I'll—"

"Save it. Don't make rash promises."

"Right, yes. Shut up. No, I mean myself . . ."

"Back to work." Forgetting about the pain that would occur when she bent her head, Susan gave a gesture of dismissal.

"Yes, ma'am." Ida wobbled out, wilting with shock and relief.

Susan picked up the phone and held it against her left ear, the right one being mostly deaf. When the dispatcher responded, she said, "Hazel, get Osey in and tell him he's responsible for the care and feeding of our fledgling."

"Got it. I thought you were going to let her go."

"So did I. I'm not sure why I didn't."

"Ours is not to see the future. Maybe she's meant for something special."

Susan grunted. "Meantime I hope she doesn't get Osey treed, with the hounds slavering at his heels."

"That image doesn't quite work."

"I'm not at my best today. I've got an errand to run. Anything you need while I'm out?"

"Yeah, you might bring me some coffee filters. I'm tired of chewing on coffee grounds."

"I can do that. Anything else?" Susan swallowed experimentally, hoping to find the scratchiness gone. No such luck. And the pulsing in her right ear echoed like the hollow sounds of an indoor swimming pool. She eyed the listing pile riding her in basket, trying to gauge the time it might take to work her way to the bottom. Many, many hours.

"If you want something in your coffee besides that white powder stuff, you might get some milk."

"Okay." Like the rest of the country, Hazel was suddenly weight-conscious and using milk for the communal coffee instead of cream, much to the irritation of the rest of the troops. Not that Hazel need be concerned about weight, she was five feet tall and thin as a pencil.

"Whole milk?" Susan said.

"Ha."

"Right. Fat-free. I'll be back in an hour or so. Call me if anything comes up?" Hazel had been with this department far longer than Susan and could, no doubt, run it without help.

Susan grabbed her shoulder bag from the coat tree and fished out her keys. With a wave to Hazel as she passed, she plodded down the hallway and out to the parking lot. The heat wave was hitting its third week, the temperature had topped a hundred before nine A.M., and the always-present wind slapped hot air at her face.

The gas gauge in the pickup hovered around empty and she made

11

a stop at Pickett's service station to fill the tank before she forgot again. Besides being tired all the time, lately she was getting forgetful. She never used to forget things.

The Barrington medical building, a square, red brick building, was new, with none of the charm of the old limestone buildings around it, bank, fabric shop, antique shop, and bookstore. She parked in front of the bookstore. Inside the medical building, the air-conditioning prickled goose bumps on her sweaty skin. Taking the stairs had her breathing heavily by the second-floor landing.

"Hi, Holly," she said to the sweet young receptionist as she entered the doctor's office.

"Chief Wren." Holly smiled, a pert smile that showed off her dimples. "Doctor Eckhard will see you in just a minute. Have a seat and I'll call you."

Susan sat, picked up an old *New Yorker* and flipped through, glancing at cartoons. Not as funny as they used to be. Or was it that she'd lost her sense of humor?

"Chief Wren?"

Susan looked up, dropped the magazine, and followed Holly down a corridor and into an examining room where her temperature was taken, her blood pressure checked, and her pulse counted. A minute or two later Dr. China Eckhard came in. Forties, attractive, brown hair held in a clip at the nape of her neck, no-nonsense manner, sharp intelligence.

"Thanks for seeing me at such short notice, China," Susan said. "I think I have an ear infection."

"*I'm* supposed to say that." China stuck an otoscope in Susan's right ear, peered in, then looked at the left. "You have an ear infection." She straightened and put the instrument on a tray.

"You look tired." She stuck a tongue depressor in Susan's mouth and had her say *ah*. "Throat sore? Headache?"

Headache was an understatement, more like agonizing spikes being pounded in her skull.

China snatched a prescription pad, scribbled on it, and tore off the top sheet. "Antibiotics. Not the most broad spectrum, but we need to save the big guns for the big problems. Take them all. If you aren't any better at the end of ten days, give me a call and we'll try something else."

"I can't hear a thing in this ear," Susan said.

"Not surprising. It's full of fluid."

"When will that clear up?"

"Take the antibiotics and wait. Now, get out of here so I can tend to people who are really sick."

Susan got out of there and stopped at the pharmacy to drop off the prescription. "I'll pick it up around seven," she told the pharmacist.

When she came out, she noticed Jen, her fourteen-year-old friend and neighbor, slouching toward the library, backpack sagging on slumped shoulders, arms full of books. Nobody but a reluctant teenager moved that slowly. What was the matter with the child? Jen was a bright energetic girl, always on the lookout for new interests, and this sullen lump of misery wasn't like her at all.

"Jen?"

Startled by the interruption of her thoughts, Jen dropped her books.

Susan bent to help them pick up books. "Are you all right?"

Jen started to shake her head, but switched to a nod.

"Aren't you supposed to be in school?"

"It doesn't start for another week." Her tone said any doofus knows that.

With August coming toward an end, she hadn't been around much, and Susan assumed she was busy winding up studies for her summer classes, and hanging with friends. Physically small and mentally occupied with myriad interests, Jen had been slow advancing to typical adolescent behavior, but maybe she'd simply turned into a teenager. The thick braids that used to hang down her back had been hacked off and now her brown hair was chin-length, with streaks of fuscia.

"Wish we could have lunch, but I have a desk piled high with stuff. You okay?"

Jen nodded.

"You sure? Somebody bothering you?"

She shook her head, thin arms clutching the books closer to her chest. "I need to go."

"Can I give you a ride somewhere?"

Jen shook her head. "Mom's picking me up. She went to see about Grandpa. He got away again."

Jen's grandfather had Alzheimer's and periodically slipped away from the caregivers. "Well, my pickup's over there. Okay, if I walk that far with you?"

Jen blinked and raised her shoulders in a shrug. "I guess."

When Jen trudged up the library steps, Susan turned to the pickup and climbed in. She almost forgot coffee filters and milk and had to backtrack to pick them up.

"Anything happen while I was gone?" She handed the grocery bag to Hazel.

"Injury accident on Post Street."

"Serious?"

"Bad. Kids racing. Tim Baker pulled out of a parking lot to make a left turn. T-boned by one of the speeding kids. Tim's car sent skidding into oncoming traffic. Two cars rammed into it. One exploded and set off the others. All three are toast."

"Jesus. How many hurt?"

"By some miracle, only Tim seriously hurt," Hazel said. "Poor kid. Rushed to the hospital in critical condition."

Susan rubbed the spot above her nose where pain was jabbing like a woodpecker. "Anything else?"

"A woman called saying she's been trying to reach her sister and the sister never answers her phone. She's left messages, but the sister hasn't returned any."

"Woman's name?"

"She wouldn't give a name." Hazel looked at her pad. "Sister's name is Kelby Oliver."

"She wouldn't give her name?" A woman calling to ask about her sister wouldn't give her name? How weird was that? With her head so muzzy, Susan couldn't track the thought any further. Family feud, maybe?

"I assume this Oliver woman is an adult, mentally competent, and can go and do what she wants, including not return the sister's calls, or go away on vacation, if she so chooses?"

"That would be my take on it," Hazel said. "And with this sister, I wouldn't return calls either. Talk about pushy."

"That it?"

"The day's still young."

"Right." Trying to swallow coffee with her raw throat turned out to be a bad idea. Susan set it aside and attacked the files on her desk. Shortly after six, just as she was piling a stack of work to take home, her phone buzzed.

"Yes, Hazel?"

"Osey called in and wanted to know if you could stick somebody else with Ida. She nearly got him killed."

"The first day?"

2

When Cary started having trouble seeing, she wondered if Mitch's hitting her or smacking her head against the wall caused it. Blackness nibbled at the edges of her vision until she saw through a narrow tunnel. Reading, her favorite thing in all the world, the thing that got her through the day, the thing she would absolutely die without, got more and more difficult. Book close to her face, she was forced to move it around to make out the words. When the tunnel started closing in, she decided to leave him, even though he'd told her he'd kill her if she ever tried.

The first time he hit her was about scrambled eggs. And not exactly a hit, just a slap really, inspired by Cary's inability to realize how grueling his job was—and how hard could it be to have breakfast made when he got off after working all night? He apologized with red roses and kisses, swore he loved her and promised it would never happen again. And it didn't.

For a whole month. The second slap occurred because she had the audacity to read the crisply folded newspaper before he got a chance to look at it.

But it wasn't until he switched to working days, and started having a few drinks after his shift, that she discovered there were worse things than getting slapped. On a filthy day, stormy and wild, downed power lines, flooded streets, and broken tree branches, she was out talking with their neighbor, Dave Cates, when Mitch got home. Dave was asking if she was all right, if she needed anything, and she waved at Mitch as he drove into the garage, told Dave everything was okay, and trotted home.

With the power out, it was pitch black inside the house. She rummaged for candles in a kitchen drawer and lit one. "Mitch?"

She found him sitting in his chair in the living room, still wearing his wet coat. "Mitch, honey? You okay?"

She stuck the candle in the holder on the mantle, knelt to untie one of his wet shoes and pull it off. He raised his other foot, put it on her bent head and sent her sprawling backward. She gasped for a breath, not understanding what happened. He kicked her in the side. Disbelief mixed with pain.

Grabbing her hair, he banged her head against the coffee table. "What's going on with you and Dave?"

"What?"

"Think I'm so stupid I don't know what you're up to?"

"Dave? I don't—"

He kicked her in the stomach, muttering she was a slut, and stomped off for the bedroom. Clenching her teeth against the pain, she dug her fingers into the gray carpet and stared at the underside of the coffee table, the first item of furniture they'd bought when they got the house. She'd laughed and asked him if he didn't think they needed a bed first. Remembering that carefree day made her feel sick. She rolled onto hands and knees and, in shaky fashion, got to her feet.

The slapping and hitting, the kicking, the slamming her head against the wall, were awful, really bad, but even more awful, more terrible, was the begging afterward. The pleading, the tenderness and the kisses, the saying he was sorry, it would never happen again, he loved her. But the worst, most awful, most terrible thing was that she believed him.

Tuesday evening she went to bed early, hoping to fend off a migraine. He sat up drinking and watching television. When he stumbled to bed, she pretended to be asleep.

"Hey, baby." He shook her and kissed her hard. "You've been reading too much. That's why you get these headaches all the time."

She lay like a dumb cow, waiting for whatever came next.

"You need to stop it."

Her heart jumped a beat and her breath caught.

"And stop going to that exercise place. That friend of yours? That Arlette bitch?"

Breathe. Pull air in, push air out. Don't say anything to set him off.

"You shouldn't see her any more. She puts ideas in your head." Hand on her throat, he squeezed. She couldn't breathe, started to panic. Just when a rushing sound began to fill her mind, he eased his grip.

"Okay?" He stroked her throat, barely touching with his fingertips.

She swallowed, swallowed again.

"Okay?" he repeated and squeezed gently.

The next day she ran into Arlette at Sylvia's. Mitch, furious when Cary's mother had given her a membership as a birthday present, told her she couldn't go. She'd pleaded and wheedled and emphasized it was only for women, no men allowed, pointed out he'd said she was getting fat and this would help her lose a few pounds.

"What's with you?" Arlette said. "Why are you hobbling around like an invalid?"

Cary tightened up her face in a rueful smile. "Just a little sore. I fell down the back steps running in to answer the phone. Two big bags of groceries. Everything all over the place."

A hot pit of shame formed in her stomach. Lying was foreign to her. She wasn't good at it and she hated the way the lie made her feel.

18

Sticky and slimy, like some nightmare creature wading through thick ooze.

Her whole life was a lie, and she piled lies on top of lies every time she deliberately tripped or bumped into a chair to prove how clumsy she was and give herself a reason for the bruises. How are you? How's Mitch? How's everything going? Good. Good. Good. Lies lies lies. And the fake smiles that went along with them.

Arlette shot her a sharp look. They were longtime friends and Cary worried about those looks. She was quick, Arlette, an attorney with the firm where Cary had been bookkeeper until Mitch convinced her to quit. Smart dresser, straight, sleek dark hair and brown eyes, Arlette was a take-charge kind of person. Unlike Cary.

She felt relief when Arlette glanced at her watch. "I've got to run. Got a client. Meet me at the Donut Shop at three-thirty."

"Oh gosh, I really can't. I have too much to do."

"One cup of coffee. Be there. Or I'll come and get you." Arlette strode off toward her car.

"I'm going to the library," Cary said.

"I'll pick you up. Look up books on battered women."

Cary looked around, horrified that someone might have heard, but no one was paying the slightest bit of attention.

Early on, Mitch tried to stop her from going to the library, but for the only time in their miserable marriage she'd stood up to him, told him she would go and he couldn't stop her. As soon as she got inside the building with all the books, she felt ease seep into her soul and smooth out the wrinkles. Glancing over the new fiction, she pulled out any that looked interesting, two biographies, a book on dogs and the phenomenal things they could be trained to do, then sat down at one of the tables to soak in an hour of peace.

Trying to read with her small circle of vision soon had her feeling the streaky beginnings of a migraine. Was his beating her causing the trouble? Detached retina? Did optic nerves get swollen, like everything else when they were smacked around?

Tears washed up and, before she could stop them, trickled down her face. She plunged through her bag until she found a tissue and mopped her face. Reading was something she'd always done excessively. If staying with Mitch would take that away, then she was ready to run. She wouldn't let him take away the books.

Carrying an armload, she stumbled fast down the stairs, staggered and fell. Books tumbled, her bag went flying, and the contents scattered.

"Cary? You okay?" Arlette crouched beside her, put a hand on her shoulder, and bent down to look directly into her face.

"Told you I was clumsy." Hands over her face, Cary started crying again, hard enough that people stared at her.

"Come on. My car's right here." Arm around her shoulder, Arlette nudged Cary toward the car and tossed the books in the rear.

Cary slid in, a puddle of embarrassment with tears running down her face. Arlette ripped tissues from a box on the console between the seats and offered her a handful. Cary pressed one against her eyes, then blew her nose.

"I don't know what's wrong with me." She crushed the soggy tissue in her fist.

"It's not hard to figure out, babe. Your husband beats the crap out of you. That's enough to make anybody cry." Arlette drove to the Donut Shop, parked in front, and herded Cary inside to a small, round table in the rear.

"Sit," Arlette said. "I'll get coffee."

She came back minutes later with two tall lattes, handed one to Cary, and sat down across from her. "You have to report him, Cary. If you don't he's going to seriously injure you."

"It gets harder and harder. He's taking that away, too. You're right, Arlette, he'll just keep beating me. I'm leaving him."

"Good. I'm glad. What gets harder and harder? The thought of leaving?"

Cary nodded, her head bobbing up and down like a tulip in a strong wind. "Worse." The word came out on a hiccup.

"What's worse?"

"Not being able to read." Even more horrible than her believing his lies about how he loved her and it would never happen again. "If I can't read I have nothing." Cary told Arlette about her sight and about wondering if Mitch had injured some nerves when he'd hit her in the face. "He hardly ever does, because bruises on my face would show, but sometimes he just gets so mad."

"Oh, Cary." Arlette took her hand. "Why didn't you tell me about this?"

"I just kept hoping it would get better."

"You have to get help. Call one of those numbers I gave you and get into a shelter."

"I can't."

"Yes, you can. I'll go with you if you like."

Cary looked at her. "Arlette . . . he's a cop. You think a cop can't get the address of shelters?"

"If you don't leave him, he'll end up killing you."

"He'll kill me if I leave."

Arlette took in a long breath, which meant she wanted to scream or shake Cary for being so stubborn, but Cary knew Mitch. He'd find some way to get the information he needed.

"I know I have to leave him," she whispered. Just saying the words out loud made her heart flutter like crazy. As though he were all-powerful and could hear any hint of defection.

Arlette took a sip of coffee, probably to cover her surprise that Cary was finally wising up. "You have to do it soon."

Cary looked down in her lap, at her fingers twisted together. That's the way they were, she and Mitch, twisted together somehow.

Arlette took in a long breath and let it out slowly. "All right, I know someone who might help. And you need to see an ophthalmologist.

Immediately. Maybe you should be taking antibiotics or eyedrops or something."

Arlette took her to the doctor's office and sat in the waiting room while she went in to see him. When Cary came out, she didn't say anything. Not while they walked to the parking garage, not when they got in the car, not when Arlette drove them to Hs Lordship's at the marina.

Not until they were seated at a booth and Cary was staring out at the bay did Arlette ask "What did the doctor say?"

"It's not Mitch's fault." She turned to look at Arlette.

"Well, what is it? What's the problem?"

"Retinitis pigmentosa."

"What's the treatment?"

"There is none. I'm going blind."

3

$\mathcal{N}$ervously waiting for Mitch to leave for work Monday morning, Cary gathered up the breakfast dishes and stacked them in the dishwasher, dampened a sponge, and wiped down the table. She tried not to make too much noise, tried not to exist too noticeably. A mouse, huddled and quivering.

When he finally left, she took in a deep gulp of air, sat down, and carefully sipped hot coffee through her swollen mouth. When the cup was empty, she put it, too, in the dishwasher. Nothing could be different about today, a cup on the table would be a beacon.

Kneeling on the bathroom floor, she reached behind the stack of towels for the box of Tampax, upended it, and shook. Twenty dollar bills spilled out along with the paper-wrapped cylinders. She counted the money she'd managed to squirrel away, sticking a twenty in the box whenever she could. Not all that many. Two hundred and eighty dollars that she had to lie and cheat to get. It wouldn't take her far. Maybe she should wait until she had more money. She ached to stay with a longing that had her bending over until her forehead touched the tile floor. She could save more, and then—

The garage door rattled open. Mitch! She jammed bills in the box, tossed it on the shelf and ran to the kitchen. Heart pounding so loud she feared he would hear it, she stood at the sink rerinsing breakfast dishes and tried not to flinch when he came up behind her, brushed aside the hair, and gently kissed the back of her neck.

"Just wanted to say I'm sorry."

She didn't say anything.

"You know I love you." His voice was gentle, coaxing, and he held her in the protective circle of his arms. Lips touching her temple, he murmured, "Don't cry, baby. Everything's going to be all right."

She leaned into his hard warm chest and nestled her forehead against his throat. It felt right, like she was where she belonged.

"I'm sorry, baby. Sometimes you just make me so mad and I lose it, you know? And then I feel like shit. I never mean to hurt you. I love you. You're everything to me."

She managed a nod and stiffened as he pulled her tighter against him. She could hear his heartbeat.

"What are you doing today?" he said.

No matter how much she wanted her voice to sound normal, it came out strained and false. Would he notice? "Groceries. We're out of a lot of things." He always wanted to know where she would be. If she didn't get home in the time he felt she needed for whatever errand she was doing, he got furious and pounded on her.

"I've been thinking." He put soft kisses in a semicircle at the top of her spine. Goose pimples broke out on her arms. "We need to get serious about starting a family. A kid or two will keep you busy." He turned her around to face him and looked straight into her eyes. "What do you think? Wouldn't that be nice?"

No. Oh God, no. That would be disaster.

"What else you up to today?"

"Library," she said. "I have books to go back." One of the few places she was allowed to go. Grocery store, library, and maintenance places when necessary, like the cleaners, the hardware store, the post office. She'd stopped going swimming. Too many bruises that couldn't be explained.

"You're spending a lot of time at the library." He kneaded the muscles in her shoulders.

"I like to read." He'd probably beat her to death if he knew she'd been reading about why women get locked into abusive relationships and why they can't get out.

Putting a hand on each side of her face, he lifted her chin and kissed her. "I'll try to be home early. Don't forget the papers."

She carted stacks of old newspapers out for recycling. Some were months old. She noticed a headline. JURY AGAINST DEATH PENALTY. Just below was a fuzzy picture of Lily Farmer's father: thin, agonized face, with features so angular he looked almost like a caricature of a fanatical Jesuit. During the trial he'd sat in the courtroom listening to the tortures done to his daughter. It was a long trial, recapped every day on the news. After the sentencing, Cary saw a clip of him, face twisted with grief and fury when the monster who killed his daughter didn't get the death penalty.

ONE JUROR HOLDOUT. WADE JEFFRIES TO GET LIFE. Lily Farmer's father wanted justice for his only child. "This isn't it," he'd yelled into the TV news cameras.

Cary dropped the last stack on the curb—the outer one showed another picture of Joseph Farmer, face twisted in fury—went back inside and turned on the shower. Just as she was stepping under the hot water, the doorbell rang. She ignored it. It rang again.

When the ringing continued, she grabbed her tatty terry cloth robe, wrapped it around herself, and went to the bedroom to look out the window. Arlette's Camry sat in the driveway. The bell rang again. In bare feet, Cary padded down to the living room and opened the door. Arlette swept in with a small plastic bag.

"What are you doing here?" Cary looked around nervously to see if any neighbors were watching, then quickly shut the door.

"I came to see if you were all right and to give you a couple things."

Cary's bare feet were freezing on the slate entryway. She kept standing on one, then the other. "What things?"

"Make me a cup of tea and I'll tell you."

Stepping back, she felt the welcome warmth of the gray carpeting, but her feet got icy again when she walked on the kitchen linoleum.

"Go get some slippers," Arlette said. "I'll fix it."

Cary went upstairs, scrounged her felt slippers from under the bed, and came back to find Arlette filling the tea kettle.

Arlette studied her. "Are you changing your mind?"

"Well, he's been different, and now that I know about the sight thing and it's not his fault and . . ." Cary shrugged.

"He beats you."

"He loses his temper. If I'd be more careful—"

"Bullshit. You're a battered wife."

"Why are you doing this, Arlette? Why are you here?"

The tea kettle shrieked. Arlette got up to turn off the burner and pour hot water into the tea pot. "I'm trying to get you to see the danger you're in."

"I love him." Cary felt like crying. "And he can be different. Sometimes he's sweet and kind and—"

"And other times he beats the shit out of you. He may not be causing your vision loss, but he'll either kill you or one night you will get his gun and blow a great big hole in his head.

"*Arlette!*" The horror was so great because the thought had come to mind more than once. "Don't say that," Cary said flatly.

Arlette nodded. "You have to get away." She poured tea into Cary's cup, pushed it across the table, and poured her own.

Cary pulled the cup closer and curled her arm around it like someone might snatch it away.

Arlette reached across the table and put a hand on her arm. "I have a friend. She said you could come and stay with her."

"Who is she?"

"Kelby Oliver. She was—" Arlette stopped.

What was it Arlette didn't want to tell her? "Why let me stay with her? If Mitch finds out, he—"

"He won't find out. She lives in Kansas."

"*Kansas?* That's as far away as the moon."

"The farther, the better." Arlette handed Cary the plastic bag.

Cary looked in, then pulled out a wig with short brown curls.

"And I want you to have this." Arlette held out a letter-sized envelope.

Reluctantly, Cary opened the flap, knowing what was inside. Twenty dollar bills. "I can't take this."

"Yes. You can. It's not all that much and you can pay me back."

"But . . ." Cary put the wig over her fist and stared at the brown curls.

"If you feel yourself backing out, remember the last time he beat you and yell at him." Arlette finished her tea and clattered the cup in the saucer. "Go to Kansas. Kelby's a good person, she'll help. And she has a suggestion about your vision."

"I don't even know where Kansas is," Cary said darkly.

"Look it up on a map." Arlette gave her a hug. "I have to get to work. You have to get out of here. And remember, do just what we talked about."

Cary didn't want to look Kansas up on a map. She looked around the bedroom she'd put in a lot of time making just the way she wanted. She'd refinished hardwood floors, painted walls a pale bluish green, Sea Mint, it was called. Finding the right bedspread with the swirls of blue and green. Making curtains that matched. She didn't want to leave. This was her home.

When she started crying again, she told herself to suck it up and get in the shower. With the hot water sluicing over her, she followed Arlette's advice and recalled the last time Mitch hit her. *You bastard!*

Cary screamed it over and over and let the words echo around the yellow-tiled bathroom. The yelling energized her. If she could get mad, she was still alive. Soap foamed over bruises on her arms that would never be there again.

No more beating me up! I will tell the truth. *I didn't fall down the stairs. He threw me.* She washed her hair. Long, because he liked it long. She turned off the water, grabbed a towel, and patted herself dry, then used the towel to swipe the steam from the mirror. Standing naked in front of the sink, she awkwardly cut off her hair, gathered all the strands and put them in a plastic bag.

No more! I'm through. I'm leaving. Free! I'm going to be free of you! She couldn't decide what to wear and finally dressed in pale denim jeans and a dark blue blouse. *Making me quit my job.* She blow-dried her jaggedly cut short hair and shook the curls loose on the brown wig Arlette had given her, then fitted it on her head. *Turning me into a liar. Telling my friends I had the flu when you beat me so badly I couldn't get out of bed.* Adding tinted glasses, she examined herself in the mirror. A stranger stared back, a skinny, owl-eyed stranger with a pale, frightened face.

With the money Arlette gave her and the money she'd managed to hide away tucked in her wallet and the wallet in her purse, she was ready. She couldn't take anything that didn't fit in the purse, and it wasn't very large, just a shoulder bag big enough for wallet, sunglasses, cell phone, Kleenex, the paperback book she always carried, and a change of underwear. She didn't dare pack a suitcase or take extra clothes. He'd know immediately that she'd run and would be after her like a cat on a mouse. *You won't catch me this time, you sick bastard!*

Using more makeup than she ever wore, she darkened the eyebrows of the stranger in the mirror, put blusher on her cheeks, mascara on her eyelashes and added bright red lipstick. She shrugged on her jacket, slipped the purse strap over her shoulder, and went to the kitchen. She couldn't take much or Mitch would notice, but she fixed two peanut butter sandwiches and put some instant coffee in a baggie.

You bastard! I loved you! She opened the door into the garage and stood there, unable to take a step.

After four deep breaths, she got in the Honda. With a shaky hand she stuck the key in the ignition. She was always afraid he'd do something so it wouldn't run, but it started right up. He'd been wanting to get rid of it, talking about how much a second car cost and they didn't really need it. She wouldn't have to worry about that anymore. Soon her dwindling vision wouldn't let her drive anyway.

At Albertson's in the El Cerrito Plaza, she pushed a cart up and down the aisles, thinking this was the last time she'd be in this store. Box of oatmeal, loaf of bread—white bread, the only kind Mitch liked—tomatoes, cucumber. She spent a few seconds selecting the best apples, toilet tissue, package of sliced cheese, pork chops, carton of milk, carton of ice cream. She wrote out a check. Number 4512, the last one she would write. As she was wheeling the cart to her car, a cop car drove into the lot.

Mitch! He'll kill me!

The black-and-white made a loop—the driver looked nothing like Mitch—and drove away. The panicky white fizz drained away, leaving her feeling weak. With pep talks to herself, she put the bags of groceries, one by one, on the back seat of the car, tossed her purse on the floor. She closed the door with a soft thunk and started to walk away without a backward glance, but when she got to the street, she turned and looked. There were so many black cars and so many of them were Hondas, she couldn't tell which was hers.

4

How long before the car was found, Cary wondered, as she crossed the street on the last Monday she'd ever be in El Cerrito, California. She hoped the milk would be sour and the ice cream melted all over the seat covers. Avoiding the tendency to slink and look over her shoulder, she raised her chin, strode into the BART station, and slid dollar bills in the machine. When her ticket popped out she snatched it, dropped her cell phone in the trash can, and trotted up the stairs.

Four people waited on the platform. She eyed each to make sure no one knew her. A man reading the *Chronicle*, a girl studying the colored map of destinations on the wall, two women standing near the edge chatting with each other. They all ignored the skinny woman with brown curly hair who got on the first train that came in and got off in Berkeley. Heart beating uncomfortably fast, she waited through minutes that dragged by before a San Francisco train came. She got on and stared out the window, not really seeing anything, not feeling nervous when the car went down into the tube under the bay, only feeling terrified when she got off at the Embarcadero station.

Mentally reviewing the street map she'd studied, telling herself she couldn't get lost in three blocks, she walked to Fremont Street, went inside the Greyhound bus depot. Using a big chunk of her money, she bought a ticket for far, far away. She waited, jittery, afraid anybody looking at her would know she was holding herself together by a few unraveling threads. When her bus lumbered in, she climbed aboard, sat in a window seat, and stared through the glass. A stout woman in her sixties sat down beside her, wiggled around to get comfortable and plopped a bulging tote bag at her feet.

"Hoo, it takes more and more energy to climb those steps." She smiled at Cary. "I've been visiting my new grandson."

She poked through the bag for a skein of yarn—fuzzy red, yellow, and orange colors that glowed like fire—then took out a pair of lethal-looking knitting needles. "Something to pass the time," she said. "I always have to be busy with something. You know what they say about idle hands." She rummaged in the bag again, produced a pair of glasses, and carefully hooked the ear pieces around her ears.

Cary watched the woman's hands flash like pale birds, as rows of bright red and orange stitches appeared on the needles.

"Are you married, dear?"

"Yes" was waiting in her mouth to slip out, but she caught it in time. "No," she said. Her reflection in the bus window watched her, a stranger with brown hair and the stranger's mouth moved to make a slight smile. She was unmarried, she was alive. Each breath brought air into her lungs and pumped blood through her veins.

The woman looked at her like she might be doubting what Cary had said, and the smile dried at the edges and the air stopped going in. When the woman went back to her knitting, the breathing started again.

"I was married once," the woman said. A keen glance came Cary's way.

Cary was startled at the sharp pointedness of it. Fear crept up to sit on her shoulder and whisper in her ear. *Don't take anything at face value.* Then the woman smiled. The sharpness melted and she was just a dithery, elderly lady again.

"I'm Amelia."

I'm missing.

Amelia waited for Cary to supply a name, but her mind blanked over. This woman was going to think she was defective, or mentally ill. "Kelby," Cary blurted the first name that came to her. She must make up a name for herself, one that sounded enough like her own so she would respond if anyone spoke to her. Her last name should be Fox. A hunted creature, running and hiding, always being chased, looking over its shoulder. Maybe she could be sly and cunning, darting into safe burrows as the hound sniffed her tracks. Cary Black, a.k.a. Something Fox. On the other hand, maybe it should be Something Chicken, that being more her nature.

Aware of her shoulders hunching, Cary deliberately took in a deep breath and forced them to relax. Mitch wasn't watching, there was no way he could know what she was doing, and it didn't matter anyway. He couldn't yell at her, question why she was talking to that woman, who was she, what did you say to her.

"A friend fell and broke her leg," Amelia said cheerfully. "I'm going to go take care of her until she can cope with things."

"A friend of mine was always having accidents." Out the window, the sun was shining.

Amelia peered over her glasses.

Cary rubbed her right wrist, the one he'd broken. It still ached sometimes, in painful memory. *I should have fought back, told him I wanted to keep my job, what does it matter if the laundry isn't done today, I'll do it tomorrow.* "And afterwards her husband was so sweet and brought flowers and candy."

"They're like that, these men, bring flowers, but useless in the sick room." Under Amelia's hands, the knitting grew as the bus rolled back the way Cary had come.

For the ten-minute wait in Oakland, Cary was terrified, frozen still, watching, waiting, expecting a cop to board the bus and haul her away. Relief when they were moving made her babble. "And she tried, my friend—well, she quit her job. And then she—" *I changed, I started to lie and say what I thought he wanted, to keep from being hit.*

Words spilled on and on, about her job and about her friend, sounding like she actually was talking about someone else, and making it seem like that other person was dead. She clenched her fist, digging her nails into her palms to make herself stop.

The needles made a soft clicking sound and Amelia looked at her with interest. Cary felt a jolt of fear. She was talking too much. Mitch always said she talked too much. *Be careful.* If Mitch found Amelia . . . If he questioned her . . . Her fingertips felt icy. From now on, no talking, not to anybody, and for God's sake, don't yak about a battered friend. Might as well wear a sign.

Amelia stopped knitting and peered closely at Cary's face. Cary shrank back, afraid Amelia was seeing the bruises under the makeup. "You seem nervous. You're too young to be so tense. How old are you, twenty-two or something?"

"More like thirty-two."

"So old as that." Amelia smiled, gathered up the skein of yarn and plopped it in Cary's lap. She handed her the needles with the long inches of knitting attached. "Here. It'll keep you relaxed. It works kind of like Prozac but doesn't cost as much."

"Oh no, no. Thank you, but I don't know how."

"I'll show you. There's nothing to it. Pick it up. Come on."

Cary did as she was told.

"Put the tip of the needle through the stitch and bring the yarn around and then slip the tip back. Good. Now again. Great. You're a natural. That's all there is to it."

Awkwardly holding the yarn close to her face and moving it around to find the best spot with her limited sight, Cary did a stitch, and then another. They looked sloppy and loose, not neat and tight as Amelia's, but she felt enormously proud of herself.

"What is this going to be?"

"A scarf. You just keep going until it's as long as you want it, and then cast off."

"I have no idea what that means, and no idea how to do it."

"That's all right. You ask somebody. If you can't find anybody to ask, go to a yarn shop and somebody there will show you."

Oh. Yes, of course. She could do that. In her amateurish way, she added several rows to the scarf. When her eyes got tired, she closed them.

When the bus slowed, she woke with a start and blinked at the darkness out the window. On the horizon, a pale moon was riding the top of a cloud. She wanted to laugh, she wanted to tell Amelia she was going someplace new, someplace she'd never been, someplace no one knew her, someplace she could hide.

"My stop." Amelia dug cookies and chips from her tote and stashed them in a plastic bag as the bus pulled into Reno, Nevada. She thrust the bag at Cary.

"But I can't—"

"Course you can. Take it." She patted Cary's arm and struggled from the seat. "Good luck, child. I hope you enjoy the place you're going."

With fifty minutes to kill, Cary shuffled after the rest of the departing passengers, and watched as Amelia hailed a young woman, engulfed her in a hug. Her watch said six-thirty-five. The bus left at seven-twenty-five. Panic trapped the air in her lungs.

I can't do this. I'll never see any of my friends again. Not Arlette or Georgia or Marsha whose husband left and who sometimes joined me and Arlette for coffee. I'll never go out for lunch or shopping or a movie with any of them.

And what was she going to do when her pitiful little pile of twenty-dollar bills was gone? No way to get a job. She couldn't use her Social Security number or her driver's license. How could she eat? Where would she live? She couldn't stay with Kelby Oliver forever.

She should just call Mitch. There was a pay phone right there. She could just walk over and pick it up. As though the phone pulled her like a magnet, she swayed toward it. Only about five hours had passed. He'd be off work. She pictured him coming home, finding no dinner on the table, and going through the empty house calling her name. Would he know immediately that she'd run?

Nausea tickled her throat with its furry fingers. She ran for the door and burst outside where she took deep gulps of air. It was getting dark, and the bus depot wasn't in the best area of town. Clutching her plastic bag of snacks, she walked up one block, turned, walked down the other side. She was afraid to go far, in case she got lost and couldn't find her way back. The shops were closed, many of them barred. She peered into darkened interiors with a light on here or there to discourage burglars.

A tree, stunted by exhaust fumes, struggled to grow in a small square of dirt in the midst of concrete and asphalt, the square was littered with fast-food wrappers, used condoms, and cigarette butts. In the gutter, a paper cup rolled a semicircle, moved by a tired breeze, and then rolled back in defeat, as though it realized the uselessness of the struggle.

She met him when she was riding her bicycle in Tilden Park. An elderly man driving a pickup clipped her rear wheel. She got tossed end over end and landed on her head. Mitch spoke softly and told her not to move, help was on the way, everything was going to be all right. He asked her name and she couldn't remember it. Frenzied panic scattered through her mind. Two weeks later he called, shy and hesitant. They went for coffee and little sparks sizzled around them like fireflies flashing in the dark. At the wedding, she floated on romance and happiness. They danced. He whispered in her ear that he loved her, would love her forever.

She looked down at the litter surrounding the sickly tree and imagined his arms around her, smelled the clean soap smell of him, felt his solid strength. At this very moment he waited at home, her home, the walls she'd painted, the sofa she'd picked out, her geraniums in the pretty blue pot. Close, it was all so close, just a bus ride

35

away and she could be home. Her throat tightened, she had difficulty swallowing.

Cars zipped past, buses pulled in and out, belched and groaned like tired old beasts. She crept up the block, moving in inches like a patient recently recovered from serious illness, and went back inside the depot. The bank of phones was right there. She lifted a receiver and fumbled coins from her purse. Mitch would pick up the phone in the living room, or maybe the kitchen. Maybe he was heating lasagna from the freezer. Taking the foil from the flat glass pan and sliding it in the oven. As the noodles warmed and the cheese melted, the kitchen would smell of rich, garlicky tomato sauce.

She hadn't put away her nightgown, it was hanging over the hook on the bathroom door. Would he hold it and smell the lingering scent of her perfume? Put his face in it and think he'd lost her? Would tears come to his eyes, those deep brown eyes that could look so warm? Coins were thumbed into the slot without conscious decision. The dial tone buzzed in her ear. She punched in the numbers for home. The impulses traveled through miles of wires and made the black phone on the kitchen cabinet ring.

He would snatch the receiver. He'd yell. Where the hell are you! Her hand squeezed the receiver. *He'd send somebody. Oh my God, he'd call the police department. Tell them to send a patrol car. Cops could be here in minutes.* She slammed the receiver back on the hook, fingered the coins from the little box. Her head ached as she walked away from the phone and over to the row of seats. A tired man looked at her and looked away.

She couldn't afford to buy anything to eat and she wanted to save her peanut butter sandwiches until she needed them more, but she did have Amelia's snacks. Isolating two chocolate-chip cookies, she nibbled off small bites and chewed slowly. With a deep intake of air, she pulled out the fiery red-and-orange yarn. Holding it close, with a fierce frown of concentration, she poked the tip of the needle through a loop of yarn.

After several rows she stretched it across her knee to examine it and was quite pleased with herself. As the minutes went by, sleep beckoned and she longed to close her eyes, stretch out on a bench like the nearby kid in ragged jeans and grimy denim shirt. She didn't dare even blink slowly, afraid she might miss the bus, or miss seeing a tall man in a uniform coming toward her. Raising her head to glance at the clock, she clamped her teeth against a gasp. Tall man in a uniform! Stupid, stupid, stupid to sit so far from the door. She'd never reach it before he caught her.

The man walked through the room, looking casually around. When he got closer, she saw no gun, just a radio and a cell phone. Then she saw the emblem on his shirt sleeve. Security. She nearly fainted with relief. Not a cop looking for her, simply a bus depot security man. For the rest of her wait, she stood by the door and watched the clock tick away the minutes, scrutinized the people who drifted in and out, watched a man sweep up discarded paper cups and empty French fry containers.

She longed for a cup of coffee, not only for the liquid that would coat her dry throat, but for the caffeine that might ease the headache scrabbling at her temples. What did it matter if she spent two dollars? Would two dollars keep her alive? Get her further away? She dug out a twenty and went to the snack bar. The wilted-looking sandwiches didn't even tempt her, though she was starving; she felt slightly sick. She asked for coffee, took the hot cup and added cream and sugar. Holding it with both hands, she sipped cautiously to keep from scalding her lips. Bitter coffee that had probably been simmering all day. She took another sip, bigger, and let the hot liquid burn her throat. The price of freedom.

When her bus departure was announced, she climbed aboard with stiff legs, found a seat midway back and dropped into it. A youngish man with brown hair plopped beside her and stowed a canvas bag under the seat. The bus rolled. The miles flattened out behind her, each one carried her farther and farther away. The band of fear clamped around her chest kept her awake for hour after hour, but finally she put her hands under her cheek and closed her eyes.

5

Running, running.

Joe had to wake up. The only way out was to wake up.

The ground was spongy, layers of rotted leaves. They slipped and slithered as he struggled to keep his balance. If he fell, he'd never make it. She would die.

The leaves had a sweet, sickly smell. He knew that smell, the smell of decay, of death.

It was waiting for him. Danger. He would die.

Lungs on fire, breath coming hard. His ankle twisted. He fell, rolled. The smell was stronger. Blood. He rolled in it. Palm prints, dripping blood appeared on his white shirt. The blood ran and swirled into letters, red dripping letters that spelled her name.

6
—

"Look, Mommy, the horsey's wearing shoes." Four-year-old Bethie, seated with her mommy at the square table for grownups, watched as the horsey with shoes was led past the window outside.

"Most horses wear shoes, Bethie, it protects their feet." Ignoring her daughter's hand tugging at her sleeve, Trudy studied the menu. Honestly, the child never shut up. From the moment she said her first da-da, she was off and running. Running off at the mouth, that is. Ha ha.

Trudy would never say a negative word about her child, never, but Bethie was just the teeniest bit chatty and her voice was a teeny bit high, and sometimes, like now after a long day, Trudy got the least bit—uh, weary. She touched fingertips to her temple. Her head was beginning to hurt, just a teeny bit. She'd thought taking Beth out for dinner would be something to occupy the child, but all she did was talk, and maybe it wasn't such a good idea.

"The horsey has shoes just like mine."

"No darling, horses wear shoes made of . . ." What the hell were horseshoes made of?

"Mommy! Mommy! Look! Look!"

Trudy lowered the menu just in time to see an irate manager rush over to a woman leading the tiniest pony she'd ever seen, with tiny white sneakers even smaller than Bethie's, into the restaurant.

As the clock ticked around past six, Susan shuffled papers from one side of her desk to the other. If she got out of here right now while everything was quiet, she might make an escape and be able to keep her dinner date with Fran. Yawning, she rolled her shoulders to work out the kinks. What she really wanted was a hot bath and to go to bed with a good book. Why was she so tired lately? Nothing more worrisome on the job than the usual. Being top cop meant there was always something to worry about.

Get on with it and slink out of here before a crisis arises. Susan signed on the appropriate line, tossed the pen on her still-cluttered desk, and pushed back her chair. Before she could propel herself upright, her phone rang. She eyed it balefully, got up, took in an irritated breath, and picked up the receiver.

"Hazel, I just left."

Hazel, the dispatcher and general all-around keeper of the flame, was laughing. "Well, I don't think this is anything that will bring you back. I just thought you might want to know that someone is trying to bring a pony into The Hyperbole."

"Pony," Susan said. The Hyperbole was new, and the place she was supposed to meet Fran. This being the third week of August, incoming college students should be busily concerned with classes. Adolescent pranks of this sort were usually the scene at Halloween. Cow in the bell tower. Eggs in a paper bag. Or dog shit. Place bag at front door, set fire to bag, ring doorbell and run. Homeowner stomps out flames. With a cop job, you always learned something new. Like a cow can be led up a flight of stairs, but it can't be led down.

"Just thought I'd let you know," Hazel said. "I sent Ida to deal with it."

"Right." She retrieved her bag from the bottom drawer and slung the strap over her shoulder. Ida nearly got Demarco killed by opening a gate and releasing a bull into the orchard where Demarco waited for the farmer to turn up and point out the damage kids had done to the trees by climbing up to steal apples. Being partnered with Osey hadn't gone any better. Patient, easygoing Osey could teach her a lot. Except Ida, impetuous, full of herself, thought she knew better than the old hand and had a tendency to leap right in. By disobeying a direct order, she nearly got Osey killed. Two out of two. Keep her on or let her go? Rookies who didn't follow orders were a menace. At the rate Ida was going, she had the potential to wipe out the whole department.

Susan waved a good-bye to Hazel on her way to the parking lot. Six-thirty and the temperature still hovered around ninety, with matching humidity. At the restaurant, she parked beside a van with LEADING THE WAY painted on the side and trudged through lethargy-producing heat. Opening the door released a blast of cold air and an outraged shout.

"Ponies are not allowed!" He sounded as though he'd shouted it many times.

"Miniature horse." The female voice was patient, as though she, too, had said it many times.

"Everybody relax." Ida, her brand-new rookie cop, trying to keep everything under control, sounded a little frayed.

"What's the problem?" Susan said.

"No problem. Everything's under control—" Ida turned impatiently and caught a better look as Susan came closer. "Oh. Chief. Ma'am."

The miniature horse was certainly miniature, about the size of a golden retriever, reddish brown in color, small white star on its forehead, paler mane and tail, interested brown eyes calmly taking in the excitement around it. It wore a beige-and-red blanket lettered with LEADING THE WAY, ASSISTANCE ANIMAL, DO NOT TOUCH.

"Ponies not allowed," the agitated manager said again.

41

"Horse," the woman snapped. "You have to let her in. It's the law."

"Uh, I think—," Ida began.

"Not sanitary. Smells." He threw back his head and pulled air into assaulted nostrils. "Offend guests."

"She does not smell. She's a darling, everybody loves her." She fondled the horse's muzzle. "Yes, baby, you're a sweetheart."

"Okay," Ida said. "Everybody just—"

Susan lightly touched Ida's shoulder and with a relieved breath Ida stepped aside.

"Just what kind of assistance does this—uh, animal do?" Susan said.

"Leading the way for the vision-impaired."

"Guide horse for the blind," Ida murmured clarification.

"Cannot come in," the manager stated.

"I'm afraid it can," Susan said.

"No."

"Yes."

"But—"

"The Americans with Disabilities Act requires businesses to admit service animals."

"Dogs, well behaved only, who wait under the table."

"There is no specifications as to species," Susan said. "Properly trained, no service animal of any kind can be banned unless it disrupts business or poses a threat to health or safety"

"Ginger is exceptionally well behaved." The woman stroked the horse's neck.

"It is impossible. Guests will flee in droves. What if she . . ." He held out a hand, palm up and bounced it up and down.

The horsewoman drew herself up in offense. "Ginger is house-trained."

The manager stepped back in defeat, muttering in some language Susan didn't recognize.

"I suppose you have something official that says this animal is more than someone's cute pet," Susan said.

A purse was unsnapped, a paper drawn out and handed to her. She read that Cinnamon Ginger, a miniature horse, had been trained as a guide for the visually impaired. She returned the paper and it was snapped once again into the purse. The woman and her friend walked into the dining room with Ginger, in her two pairs of tiny white sneakers, stepping smartly along beside them. Diners stopped eating to stare, but nobody fled, in a drove or otherwise. If anything they wanted a closer look. Susan told Ida to get back on patrol, and joined Fran at a booth in the far corner.

Fran was giggling so hard, tears glistened in her dark, exotic eyes. With her cloud of wild black hair, clothes of vivid primary colors and silver bangles, she always brought to mind gypsies. "I must say, Chief, you handled that well. Decisive. Informed. In—"

"Oh, shut up."

Fran tore off a chunk of bread. Silver bracelets jangled with every movement. "I wonder if the manager doesn't have a point. What if it . . ." Hand palm up, she mimicked his up-and-down motion.

"The horse is house-trained." Ginger, small enough to stand under the table where her owners sat, was waiting patiently.

"I didn't know you could do that with a horse."

"I didn't either."

"What's the difference between a horse and a pony?"

"God knows."

"A horse to lead the blind," Fran said in that flat voice of utter disbelief people use for the preposterous. She smeared butter on the bread. "Just what kind of con do you think these people are running?"

Yeah, Susan was wondering that, too.

Fran stuffed a chunk of bread in her mouth and studied Susan while she chewed. "You look like shit."

"Thanks. It's great to see you, too."

"Did you make an appointment with your doctor?"

"There's nothing wrong with me. I'm not sleeping well, that's all."

"It's not all, you're tired all the time and—"

The waiter sauntered up and rattled off specials. Susan ordered fettuccini and Fran asked for catfish. When the waiter left, Fran went on right where she left off: "—you droop around all the time. Go see the doctor. You might be anemic."

"Yes, Mom."

"Why aren't you sleeping?"

"I don't know." Susan moved around cutlery. "I have these weird dreams."

"Really?" Fran leaned closer. "What kind of weird? Erotic?"

"More like a sense of dread. I hear gunfire and I'm running around trying to prevent somebody from getting killed."

"Who?"

The waiter returned with Fran's wine. "Who?" Fran repeated when he left.

"I don't know, but it's vital that I prevent it."

Fran sat back, a fascinated look on her face. "You're having a premonition."

"Oh Lord, I hope not. That would probably mean Ida is going to shoot someone."

"I hope it's not you. Then I'd have absolutely nothing to do. The travel business is in the toilet. Nobody goes anywhere anymore. Airlines can't be counted on. Panic about smuggled weapons. Long lines while you're groped to make sure you don't have anything lethal. And everybody looks askance at everybody else, because who knows who has evil lurking in his heart. Don't you just love that word 'askance'?"

"It's always been one of my favorites."

The little horse was well behaved, better than the small child sitting with her just-about-had-it-looking mother. Patrons noticed the animal, were astonished, then sat down and ordered food.

As they lingered over coffee, inertia set in. Susan found it hard to force her spine to pull her upright. When Fran said maybe they should leave because the waiter was giving them dirty looks, Susan got herself to her feet.

Turning into her driveway, the headlights swept over a small form huddled on her back steps. She rolled into the garage, cut the motor, and went toward the house.

"Jen? What are you doing here? Is something wrong?"

"I didn't know you'd be so late. I brought you some dinner." Jen put an arm around the bowl on the step beside her.

"Oh, Jen, I'm so sorry. Did we have a date? I've been a little forgetful lately."

"No. I just thought I'd bring you something." Bringing something, because of Susan's lousy cooking, was the excuse Jen used to come by and hang a bit. She hadn't done that in a while, and Susan thought Jen was adjusting to her parents' divorce, her mom's new husband, and didn't need to clutch so tightly to Susan's offered hand of friendship.

Jen rose so slowly she might have frozen in a sitting position and was, muscle by muscle, joint by joint, ungluing herself.

"You all right, Jen?"

The harsh overhead light made the girl look almost frightened by the question. She nodded.

"Do you need some help with anything?" Sitting forlorn on Susan's back steps, she looked shaky, as if an inner storm was putting her in turmoil.

"What's the matter, Jen? Are you in trouble? Sick?"

"I'm fine."

"Unhappy? Is somebody hurting you? Your mother's . . ." An icy thought touched her mind. "Your new stepfather, how do you like him?"

"He's okay. I gotta go." She thrust the bowl at Susan.

Susan tucked it under one arm. "Well, is it all right if I walk with you?'

Jen shrugged. "I guess."

During the block-and-a-half walk, Susan felt as if she was mindlessly chattering with her questions of how was summer school, had

45

Jen made any new friends, did she like her teachers. Jen responded with grunts or one-syllable answers.

"I'm going to have this for dinner tomorrow." Susan patted the bowl. "Will you come and share it with me?"

Jen shrugged. "Maybe." She darted off to her house.

Worried, Susan watched Jen trudge up the steps, slouch across the porch, go inside, and close the door behind her.

7

—

$\mathcal{A}$ couple beers with the guys meant Mitch didn't get home early like he promised, but he stopped at See's and bought the dark chocolate–covered walnuts that Cary liked. He was sorry about last night. He shouldn't have hit her. She just got him so mad that sometimes he lost it. They needed a baby. That would keep her busy. She couldn't be reading all the time and traipsing off to the library, or going to that Sylvia's place. As he rolled into his driveway he hit the opener and the door rattled up on an empty garage. What the hell? Where was her car? She should have been home hours ago.

He pulled in, hit the remote to close the garage door, and went in the house. "Cary!" No food on the table, no smell of cooking. *What the fuck?*

A man worked all day, he should have a meal ready when he got home. Yanking open the refrigerator, he shoved stuff around until he found the last beer, pulled it out and popped the tab. He took a long swallow. He'd told her to pick up a couple six-packs. She was always doing shit like this and making him lose his temper.

"Cary!" He stomped up the stairs. Probably flaked out with one of her damn headaches. If she was asleep, he'd show her what happened to wives who didn't give a thought to their husband, tired after working the job and needing something to eat and a little peace and quiet when he got home.

The bedroom was empty. Spare room, too. It was going to make a great nursery. Where the hell was she? Car broke down? Ran out of gas? Visiting that bitch Arlette? Or forgetting everything and reading at the library. Always reading. You'd think she was going to school or something, the way she was always reading. He slammed open the bathroom door. Two long cracks ran down the center from when she'd tried to lock herself in and he'd smashed it with his fist. Need to get that fixed.

She's run. The thought hit him like a live wire. He shoved open the closet door in the bedroom and pawed through the hanging clothes. It didn't look like anything was gone, but she might have bought something new, or that bitch Arlette might have given her something. He went through her dresser. Panties, bras, socks. How the fuck could he be sure? It wasn't like he counted this stuff.

Suitcases! He went back to the spare room and yanked open the closet door. There they were, all the suitcases, on the floor just where they were kept. She wouldn't leave him. When she'd tried that trick before, he'd gone after her and brought her home where she belonged. Got herself all the way to San Diego. By God, she'd better not try it again. No matter where she went, he'd track her down. Wife of a law enforcement officer? Any police department in the country would help. "So you better not be stupid, baby. If you've taken off, you won't get far. And the farther I have to go to bring you back, the more it's going to cost you."

He hauled in a long breath. Maybe she got held up somewhere. What the hell did she say she was doing today? Picking up groceries? Yeah, that was probably it, she got held up at the grocery store. Stupid people, never thinking about anybody but themselves. Never thinking that when a man worked all day and came home hungry, he ought to find dinner on the table. Not this damn empty house!

He pounded his fist on the kitchen table.

Okay, he wasn't making anything better by getting so riled. Just take it easy and she'd be home any minute. Then he'd tell her how disappointed in her he was, how she should have had his dinner ready. Leaning both hands on the table, he sucked in another breath, then straightened and took a bottle of wine from the shelf. He uncorked it, poured a glass and went into the living room. He sipped. Yeah, just the thing. He'd sit here on the living room couch, have a glass of wine, relax, wait for her to get home.

Two hours later she still wasn't home. He found Arlette's number in her address book.

The bitch herself answered.

"It's Mitch," he said. "Let me talk to Cary."

"Good evening to you, too, Mitch. I hope you're enjoying this beautiful evening."

"Cut the crap. Let me talk to her."

"Who?"

He took a hard hold on his temper. Arlette always set him off, the stupid bitch. She knew it, too, did it deliberately. "I need to talk to her."

"Are you referring to Cary?"

"No other reason I'd call you."

"She isn't here. Why would you think she would be?"

He clenched a fist, swallowing all the words he wanted to yell. "Where is she?"

"What do you mean, where is she? What have you done to her? You sick bastard, if you've hurt her—"

He hung up before he ended up ripping out the phone, and flopped on the couch. Fumbling for the remote, he clicked on the television. When his glass was empty he opened another bottle of wine, and saw there was only one left. Couldn't even keep wine on the shelf. He had to do everything, earn all the money, make all the decisions, do all the work. What did she do? Nothing. Read all the time. Couldn't even buy a bottle of wine so he could have a relaxing drink when he got home. Well, he had ways of showing her he wasn't pleased. When she got back, he'd show her a few.

Like some clown in a sitcom, he turned his wrist to look at his watch and spilled wine on his pants. Goddamn it! Brushing at the wet spot, he grabbed her address book again, looking for her sister's number. What was it, an eight-hour drive to San Diego?

The sister's ten-year-old son answered. "Hey, buddy, how's it going?"

"Good."

"I need to talk to your Aunt Cary. Put her on, will you?"

"Aunt Cary? Is she coming to see us? Cool. She's fun."

In the background, he heart Sybil's voice calling, "Who is it, Bobby?"

"Uncle Mitch, he—"

Apparently Sybil snatched the phone from Bobby, because the next voice he heard was hers. "Mitch, what's wrong?"

"Put Cary on."

"She's not here. What's wrong? What happened?"

He told Sybil to have Cary call him when she heard from her and hung up. She had other friends. He should call and—

Bank.

Should have done this first. He went through all the shit of press here for this and press the fuck there for that and finally got the checking account balance. It matched the numbers in the checkbook. He had to do all the same nonsense for the savings account, expecting it to be seriously depleted. When he heard the figure, he rubbed the back of his neck. She didn't take any money. How far could she run with no money?

Idiot programs came and went on the television set, the news came and went. At midnight he thought he should do something. Stumbling on the stairs, he went up to the bathroom, took a swig of mouthwash and swished it around, spat it out. He tucked in his shirt, grabbed a jacket, and drove to the department.

"Hey, Mitch," Waters said, "you just come from a long party? You look like shit."

Mitch ignored the cretin and went in to the lieutenant.

"Evening, Mitch." Lieutenant Vargas leaned back in his swivel chair and tossed his pen on the cluttered desk. "Something I can do for you?"

"Talk to you for a minute?" Vargas always told the men they could come to him any time about anything, but he was an impatient kind of guy and didn't really like it when they took him up on it.

"Sure. Have a seat. Got a problem?"

"Yeah." Mitch parked his rear in a chair in front of the desk and rubbed an index finger over his jaw. Now that he was here, he didn't know how to get started. Gave him some idea of how it was to be on the other side of the desk. He didn't like it.

The lieutenant looked at him, waiting.

"It's Cary."

"What about her?"

"Something's wrong."

"You got a marital problem, take it up with a counselor or your priest."

"No, it's . . ." Mitch wished his head wasn't throbbing so much. He couldn't think straight. "She's missing."

Vargas let the chair tilt level. "Explain missing. You guys have a fight?"

"Nothing like that." Mitch took in a breath and spilled it. "She didn't come home tonight."

"You been drinking, Mitch?"

"Couple of beers is all."

"Uh-huh. Where'd she go?"

"I don't know. I expected her to be home when I got off work and she wasn't. So I figured she'd be there any minute, you know? But she wasn't, and I waited, thinking maybe car trouble or something and she'd call."

"You make a few calls, try to find her?"

"Called friends. Checked hospitals to see if an accident . . ." Mitch put his palms on the tops of his legs and rubbed up and down. "I gotta tell you, I'm worried."

"Could she have gone to visit a relative, a friend?"

"Not without telling me."

Vargas crossed his arms and looked at him, like the son of a bitch was doubting what he said. "Level with me, Mitch. You and Cary get into it and she took off?"

"Naw, nothing like that." Mitch didn't bother to mention she'd made him lose his temper last night and, before he realized what was happening, he popped her one. "She would call, Lieutenant."

Vargas studied him like he would a suspect he thought was lying, then yelled, "Manny!"

Sergeant Manfred stuck his head in the door. "You wanted me, Lieutenant?"

"Yeah. Mitch's wife is missing. Get started on it."

Manny looked at Mitch, then jerked his head toward the hallway and walked off. Mitch followed. Having to tell his coworkers his wife was gone. How did that look? Like he was some wimp who couldn't even keep track of his own wife.

Manny went behind his desk and sat down. Mitch hooked a foot around the chair leg and dragged it closer.

"You want to tell me what's going on?" Manny said.

"I'm worried sick, Manny." Mitch told him he expected Cary to be home at five.

Manny looked at his watch. "It's been seven hours. Why'd you wait so long? You guys have a fight?"

"No."

"Come on, Mitch, this is me. If she got mad and walked out, you need to tell me." Manny sat back, hands behind his head.

Mitch said nothing.

"Okay, I'm going to need it all. Start with her full name."

Cary Secunda Black. Five-three, blond, and blue. Last seen 6 A.M. Wearing old, white terry cloth bathrobe. Recent pictures. Make, model, and color of car. License plate number.

"Relatives?"

"Just the one sister in San Diego. I called her. Cary isn't there."

"I'll get this started," Manny said.

"Thanks." Mitch drove home and got to work on the last bottle of wine.

At three A.M. he stumbled up to bed. The whole place reeked of her perfume, the blankets, the pillows. Hell, the air in the room.

Raging thirst and a pounding head woke him. He'd forgotten to close the curtains and the sun streamed in, pooling on the carpet and catching dust motes dancing in the air. Cary ought to clean this place better. Stupid bitch can't do anything right.

Cary!

He rolled over and sat up too fast. Made his head swim. The sheets and blankets were tangled, the other side of the bed was empty.

Head pounding like a jackhammer, he found aspirin in the medicine cabinet, threw two into his mouth, and cupped his hand under the faucet for water to wash them down. He showered, shaved, got dressed, and drove to work.

It wasn't until the end of his shift that Manny contacted him to say no progress so far, but they would find her.

8

Ida ducked into the locker room to check her appearance in the mirror. Uniform pressed, shoes shined, belt, cuffs, extra clips, baton, gun. Hooking her thumbs over the belt, she gave it a tug of adjustment, brushed her hair, shook it loose, and concentrated on getting her breathing under control. For the second time in two days she was told to haul ass into the chief's office. Life can turn on you in the blink of an eye. Two weeks ago she'd been on top of the world, sitting on a cloud with a rosy glow. Now the cloud was a black thunderhead.

She'd messed up good. Almost got Osey killed. Damn it, how could she? Six months into a new job and she was making a mangle of everything. Her father always told her she'd never amount to anything. Well, Dad, right again. She could be flippant all she liked, but the bottom line was, she loved this job. She even loved this town and she wanted to do good on her first job as a cop. How likely was it she'd find a job with another department after getting fired from this one? Maybe she ought to take off running before she got the boot.

Okay now, let's not get any stupider. So I made a mistake. *Two, ac-*

tually. Okay, two. Two tiny mistakes won't get me axed, will it? Her mind, that mind that stood her in good stead when it came to tests but had some defects when it came to making judgment calls, pointed out that these mistakes weren't tiny. Both could have been fatal.

Ida pulled in a breath and marched into the chief's office. Chin up, back straight. Any man named Rather who called his only daughter Ida was setting her up to be a fighter. Ida started fighting in elementary school when her peers fell all over themselves laughing at such witty comments as Ida Rather be at the movies, Ida Rather sit with somebody else.

"You're running through partners like Ex-lax," Chief Wren said. "At this rate, they'll be nobody left." She sounded more weary than angry. "Tell me what happened."

"Right," Ida said. "We responded to a call with a hostage situation. All we knew was that this guy Simon—"

Oh Lord, Jen's grandfather was at it again. Something had to be done.

"—was barricaded in a house on Ivy Drive, shouting crazy stuff and popping at anything that moved.

A little girl, a three-year-old, was inside with him. Another kid, twelve-year-old boy, lay on the ground in the front yard. Hard to tell how badly he was hurt. Leaking blood, but yelling, so he was still alive. According to him, Lundstrom came hobbling along with a rifle, yelled 'There you are!' and shot him. Lundstrom snatched up the kid's little sister and carted her into the house."

"Who else was in the house?"

"Nobody. They were all next door. Kids playing outside, Mom's in the kitchen drinking coffee. Osey positioned me behind a tree and instructed me to keep the back door under surveillance." Actually he'd said to keep her eyes glued on it and holler if it opened. Then he proceeded to the front of the house. The kitchen window was open and she could hear the suspect inside, yelling and carrying on. " 'Rat going down a rat hole. That's what they do. Stinking rats down a rat hole.' I could hear the little girl crying and calling for her mommy. Then. . . ."

Boom!

The rifle shot shattered the hot air and had her ducking, even though she was on the other side of the house away from the action. She hoped Osey was okay. He didn't seem like he had the sense to step away from a speeding bullet. She listened, hoping she'd hear something that meant he wasn't dead on the ground. She eyeballed her surroundings and spotted another door in the side of the house.

They might have a seriously injured little girl inside. If she sneaked in that side door while the sniper's attention was fixed on the front . . .

She keyed her radio. "There's a side door. I'll see if it's unlocked."

"Ida, for God's sake—" Osey faded away in static.

She darted from behind her tree to the house, then plastered herself against the wall next to the door. She waited. Nothing happened. With a steady hand, she reached to the side for the doorknob and gave it a twist. It turned.

Before she could take a breath, or think a thought, the door snapped inward. The little girl screamed.

A wild-eyed man, breathing hard, pointed the shotgun at Ida's forehead. *Oh, shit, I'm dead.*

"Stinking Nazis! Never take me alive!" *Boom!*

Smoke and fire singed her cheek. The noise deafened her. Osey, blood streaming down his head, yelled.

The shooter racked another cartridge in the chamber. She went for her gun. He swung the barrel around, aimed at her face. She froze. Osey bowled into her knocking her off the step. *Boom!* They fell in a tangled heap. The shooter bolted.

Osey scrambled to his feet. "Simon! Simon!"

Simon hared off. Osey yelled and took off after him. He was covered in blood. She figured he'd drop down dead any second. She fumbled for her radio to call an ambulance and took off after Osey.

Raising her gun, she got a bead on Simon's back, took a breath and eased her finger around the trigger and—

"No!" Osey, turning back, snarled at her. "For God's sake, put it away! You're gonna get somebody killed!"

Simon cackled. "Fucking Nazis. Deserve to die!"

For an old guy he was pretty spry. He whirled and fired off another round.

"Private Lundstrom!" Osey yelled.

The old man faltered. "Who're you?"

"Corporal Picket. You saved us." Blood ran down Osey's face.

Simon looked confused. "I did?"

"Don't know what would have happened without you."

"Slippery bastards. One went in a rat hole. Got one."

"Need a medic." Osey went up to the old guy, put an arm across his shoulder, and sagged against him.

Simon staggered under Osey's weight, fumbled to get a grip on his injured comrade. Osey plucked the shotgun away and held it out behind him. Quick as a frog's tongue, Ida snatched it. Osey, moaning and carrying on, talked to Simon with lines straight out of a World War II movie.

Later at the hospital, when he was getting his head looked at, Osey told her the old guy had Alzheimer's and thought he was saving life and country from the Nazis. How he managed to get his hands on a shotgun was a mystery. It had been locked up in a cabinet, but somehow the old soldier managed to get a key and slide away from his caregiver. Fortunately, Osey hadn't been shot. A moment's thought had made that clear. If he had, half his head would have been blown away. Simon had nicked a corner of the porch and kicked off a chunk of wood that struck Osey's temple. Bled like a son of a bitch.

"Interviewing neighbors, we learned that Simon was first spotted near the cornfield on the east end of town. We went to question the homeowner, but no one was home." Ida stiffened her back, lest there be any weakening when the axe fell.

Silence stretched.

"If I keep you on, you think you can manage to stay out of trouble?"

Ida was so certain she'd be booted that it took a second or two before she heard the words and extracted the meaning. "Yes. Yes, ma'am." She clapped her mouth shut before more words could tumble out.

"Back to work." The chief sounded very tired. "And, for God's sake, listen to Osey."

"Yes, ma'am." Ida ducked out before the chief could get a glimmer of changing her mind.

Osey, white patch of gauze at his temple, was headed for the parking lot when she caught up with him. He slid under the steering wheel. She got in the passenger's side, snugged up her seat belt and stared out the windshield at the birds endlessly circling in the cloudless blue sky.

"How's your head?" she said.

"Feels like I been kicked by a mule."

Ida couldn't tell if he was still mad or not. "I'm really sorry."

"Yeah. You already said that."

"I know. Look, ever since I was a little girl I wanted to be a cop. You've never seen anybody so happy as when I graduated from the academy. I thought I made it, I'm really going to do this. And then out there . . ." She waved a hand. "I thought you were dead. It was my fault. I thought . . ." *That my father was right. I'm stupid, inadequate, useless, nothing but excess baggage.* "I was really scared. I'm glad you're okay."

"Hard head," Osey said. "Takes more than a mule kick to kill me. Just . . . would you believe I know a thing or two?"

She relaxed her shoulders. "Thanks."

Did he resent being partnered with her? Hard to tell with Osey. Unlike Demarco who radiated hostility, Osey seemed to deal amiably with whatever got thrown at him. Although he had gotten kind of tight-lipped when she rushed in where she shouldn't have. If he held it against her, he didn't show it. He looked slow and lazy, and had a lanky stride that gave the impression he was on the verge of collapse.

"Forget it." He braked suddenly to avoid a retarded squirrel who darted in front of the cruiser.

"Forget what?"

"Guilt about nearly getting my head blown off. Just don't do it again."

"Got it. Is he always like that? Simon, I mean. Lives in nineteen forty-two and runs around shooting people he thinks are Nazis?"

"The uniforms probably set him off. The thing about Simon is, he's clever about sneaking away from his caregiver. But if you just wait him out, he forgets where he is and what he's doing and you can just collect him and take him home."

"Right. Is he ever lucid?"

"Not really, I guess. Sometimes he recognizes his daughter, mostly he doesn't, thinks she's his sister." A second or two went by, then he looked at her and asked. "Why?"

"Just wondered." When she had—recklessly as it turned out—rushed into the house, Simon had shouted something about killing someone. But he hadn't actually, he'd only shot a boy in the leg. The kid was recovering quickly and was getting a lot of mileage out of it.

"When those blackbirds fly around like that, doesn't it mean they've found something dead?" she said.

"Probably. Why?"

"They're always flying around the cornfield?"

"So?"

She didn't want to sound like some stupid city chick who didn't know anything. And she didn't want to get in trouble again either. From now on she was going to follow orders, not take a step until she was told to. Well, maybe just one.

"You think Simon murdered somebody and slung the body in the cornfield?" A hint of amusement sneaked into Osey's voice.

"If something isn't dead out there, why are those birds constantly circling?" It spooked her, those big blackbirds flying their endless circles, like a shot from an old western.

"Farmers are into ecology. Nothing wasted. Cow drops a calf that doesn't make it, the calf gets spread out for the critters to feed on. Deer hit by a car maybe."

Dead calves thrown out on the hillside for other animals to eat kind of made her queasy.

Osey looked at her with a breath of inhaled patience. "What?"

"I'm leaving after work. Going home for my niece's birthday."

"I thought you were taking your car to the shop." Osey's father and brothers owned the garage where she took her car. "How you going to get there?"

"I'm taking the bus home."

"Aren't you working tomorrow?"

"Yeah, I'll only be gone a day. I get back around noon." She didn't have to report for duty until three.

"Want a ride from the bus station?"

"That'd be great."

They picked up Brett Foster at the swimming pool where he worked as a life-guard. Big football hero, he had to swagger to show his friends the tough don't worry about a thing. In the interview room, he slouched down in a chair. "What's the bandage for?" he said to Osey. "Keep your brains from falling out?"

"I've been hearing things about you, Brett." Osey sat across the table. "Things like you were involved in that accident yesterday."

"It's too late for the bandage. Your brains already fell out."

"I heard you were speeding. Racing one of your buddies."

"You heard wrong."

"I heard you caused the accident."

Osey questioned the kid quietly, patiently, relentlessly. Brett didn't look so tough when Osey pointed out what kind of trouble he was in, speeding, reckless driving, vehicular manslaughter if the injured kid died. This was the same easygoing, amiable Osey, except he never let up. Like

60

that Chinese water torture stuff, drip-drip-drip, never-ending. It was interesting to see Osey pin the kid down when he tried to squirm away.

Before she took her car in after her shift, she drove east to the huge cornfield. The house, probably a farmhouse in some distant past, was a two-story wood frame with a porch running across the front and along one side, turrets sprouted from the second story. It was not a house she would have chosen to live in, sitting across the road from endless rows of corn like it did, with the nearest neighbors nearly a block away. The birds were still there, doing their circle thing.

Leaving her car in the graveled drive, she tromped up on the porch and rang the bell. No answer. With the tight feeling of nerves, she crossed over to the field, determined to know what was dead in the middle. After only a few steps along a row between stalks, she felt claustrophobic. The huge stalks, at least seven feet tall, towered over her. Ears of corn surrounded her. The smell of heat and corn and dust was sickening. Even with the sun blazing down, it was dark inside. And hot. Horrendously hot. Her shoes left shallow impressions in the soft dirt and the wind kicked up a puff of dust with each step. A short distance in left her disoriented. Panic. The heart-hammering, fast-breathing kind that told her she'd never get out of here.

Carefully, she worked her way back to the road and breathed in a gulp of hot air. Shielding her eyes, she looked up at those damn birds. She either disturbed them or they were jeering at her, because now they weren't so much circling the cornfield as flying around the buildings behind the barn. Forget it, she had a bus to catch.

Ida occupied Susan's mind as she drove home around eight-thirty. Would she work out? Eager beaver, hot-headed, apt to use her own judgment rather than following orders. Late evening light filtered through the trees and dappled the sidewalk with shadow. When she spotted Jen walking slowly, backpack dangling from one arm, she pulled over and inched along. "Hey, Jen, like a ride?"

"No thanks."

"It's pretty hot for walking."

"That's okay. I got someplace to go."

A clear dismissal that Susan should mind her own business. "What is it, Jen? Tell me what's the matter?"

A long shuddering sigh. "There's nothing you can do."

"There sure won't be as long as you don't tell me what's wrong."

Jen gave her that look teenagers give adults when the adults are being particularly dense.

"Is it your grandfather?"

Shrug. "Yeah."

"Nobody was seriously hurt." But only by good fortune. Osey and Ida could both have been killed by a poor, befuddled old man who had been a prisoner during World War II and was probably exacting some revenge for the torture he suffered.

"I gotta go." Jen trudged off and turned the corner.

Susan watched, then took her foot from the brake and drove on, letting her mind drift back to problems less complicated than adolescence. Ida. Would she settle down and work out? Maybe, if she didn't leap into something beyond her ability to handle and get herself killed.

9

—

The bus rumbled its way across Nevada through towns many of which she'd never heard of. Cary dozed and stared out the window at alien landscape, mind disengaged by some numbing wonder at what she'd done. Each stop had her tense with worry, watchful. At Battle Mountain, the glimpse of a cop car jammed her throat with fear. The bus rolled, leaving the car behind. It had nothing to do with her.

A little after six Tuesday morning, the bus pulled into Salt Lake City. She was stiff and tired, sticky and grimy, head sweaty and itchy under the wig, teeth fuzzy. She needed a shower, toothpaste, mouthwash, deodorant, and clean clothes. What she got was her transfer point, with an hour-and-a-half wait. After splashing her face with cold water and washing her hands, she squandered some money on a cup of coffee. With it she ate her remaining peanut butter sandwich. The second bus took her across Utah, and when it reached Dinosaur, Colorado, she hit the twenty-four-hour mark.

Finally, finally, at eight-thirty Tuesday night, they got to Denver. After stiffly climbing from the bus, the first thing she did was find a bathroom and take off the hated wig. She stuffed it in the plastic bag with the knitting. Vigorously she scratched her scalp, digging in with her nails. Turning on the faucet, she stuck her head under the water, then blotted her hair with paper towels.

Tears of misery stung her eyes. She wanted to go home, she wanted California, she wanted Mitch to tell her he loved her. She wanted clean underwear! One foot in front of the other. Keep going. Think about all those steps you've already taken. Maybe Mitch found the car by now. He'd be furious. Minus the wig, her own blond hair still wet, Cary went up to the ticket counter.

"Help you?" The man behind the counter was middle-aged and tired and didn't have much patience. He had a look of either step away from the counter or pick a destination.

Ticket to oblivion.

Never again would she plant impatiens in the backyard, or smell the Cecil Bruner roses climbing along the fence. Never again would she watch the squirrels scamper through the oak tree, or watch the passion flowers bloom.

The people behind her in line shifted impatiently. "Where to, lady?" the man said.

Home. She swallowed and said softly "Hampstead, Kansas." She paid for her ticket with more of the twenties.

There was a two-hour wait for her bus. *Two hours.* Anything could happen in two hours. Mitch could have cops looking for her. Her picture could be out. *Missing person.* Her stomach rumbled and she bought a hamburger, then sat in a hard plastic chair next to three other tired, defeated-looking people.

The bus came, she got on, sat near a window, and felt herself getting farther and farther from home as it rolled across Colorado. Like she was disappearing, fading little by little. She closed her eyes. When she opened them she was in Limon, Colorado. Somewhere rain had started, and it fell like a heavy mist as far as she could see on the flat prairie. Miles and miles of emptiness, the gray sky like a dome closing down, landscape as bleak and desolate as she felt.

Maybe she'd gotten away from Mitch. Maybe. But she'd lost her sister, her niece and nephew. She dared not even contact them. If he got the idea that Sybil had helped her, he'd hurt Sybil, maybe even the kids. She would disappear from Sybil's life and Sybil would never know what happened to her.

Cary had only herself to rely on, and what a weak reed she was to cling to. No crying. A crying woman would attract attention. She mustn't attract attention. A ragged breath caught in her dry throat.

Head on the seat back, she looked out the rain-sluiced window. On the road, wind whirled up small funnels like miniature tornadoes. The bus interior reflected in the glass showed huddled figures trying to find a comfortable position in ungiving seats.

In the front, a young woman juggled a fretful baby while keeping an arm about a toddler asleep with its head on her knee. A teenage boy kept time to music coming through headphones. An older man, maybe a farmer, with leathery skin from constant exposure to weather, swayed, dozing in his seat. Overhead light shone on the book of a young teen sitting with her father. They all looked real and ordinary, like the rain and the wind, real and ordinary. Only Cary sat at odds in their ordinary world, unreal and unbelonging.

Wind blew a flurry of rain against her window. She focused on her image in the glass. Her stomach protested the length of time she'd gone without food. Why hadn't she brought more sandwiches, maybe an apple or two? Mitch might have noticed. She hadn't dared take anything that might suggest she was running. It had to seem as though she had simply disappeared.

A sob threatened to break through her clamped teeth and she pressed a fist against her mouth to hold it back. Once started, she feared she'd never stop. She was so scared. Totally alone, no one to offer her help, give her a ride, give her a bed, give her clothes, give her food. Through her small tunnel of vision, she watched the wet highway roll by, felt the turn as the bus arced in a curve, each mile taking her farther from everything familiar.

She dozed, woke when the bus stopped, dozed when it moved on, woke more completely at someplace called Colby, Kansas, where she looked at her watch. Three-forty Wednesday morning. She got off and stretched, got back on and dozed. In Salina, she bought cereal and coffee. At Topeka, a young woman got on and took the seat next to her. Barely twenty, Cary judged, with a curly cap of chestnut hair and four tiny turquoise earrings in her left ear. Her fingers were covered with turquoise rings.

"Hi." The young woman poked through her backpack and brought out two textbooks.

Cary brought up a smile. It had been so long since she'd talked easily to a stranger that she felt Mitch's shadow looming. He didn't like it when she talked to people. Males made him jealous, females made him suspicious. He questioned her later and questioned her until he found something that made him angry, then he'd hit. It was safer never to talk to anybody.

"My name's Ida." The young woman stuck out her hand.

Cary shook the offered hand and stifled the urge to say her name. She must not leave even the tiniest trace for Mitch to discover that a woman named Cary had been on this bus. She nodded at all the textbooks in the backpack. "Are you a student?"

Ida rolled her eyes. "Not full-time. Taking classes."

"What are you studying?"

"Classes to help me with my job. I missed a bunch today because Mom wanted me home. Family thing, you know? Niece's third birthday, but a buddy will give me notes."

Cary's niece would be seven in January. Cary would miss the party, and couldn't even send a card.

Ida dug through her backpack, brought out a bottle of water and took a slug. "Where you headed?"

"Hampstead."

"Me, too. You staying long?"

"I haven't decided yet." Cary tried a smile. "Till my friend gets tired of me."

To her relief, Ida didn't ask any more questions. When she mentioned she needed to study before her class tonight, Cary picked up her own book and stared at the pages as though she were actually making sense of the words, remembering to turn a page now and again. Nerves crawled up and down the back of her neck the closer the bus got to Hampstead.

What if Mitch had somehow managed to follow her? What if he was waiting? What if his face was the first thing she saw when she got off the bus? Maybe this was a huge mistake. Maybe she shouldn't have listened to Arlette. A heavy loneliness crept into her soul.

The bus trundled around a corner and pulled into Hampstead, Kansas, a little before noon. Ida gathered her things and swung out of the seat. Cary wished her good luck in her studies and slowly made her way to the exit, bobbing her head and peering through windows for a glimpse of Mitch. No sign of him, but that didn't ease her anxiety. That wouldn't be his way. He'd pounce when she let her guard down.

A boiling blast of heat smacked her as soon as she stepped off the air-conditioned bus. Inside the depot, she look around. Still no Mitch. "Call," Arlette had told her, "Kelby will pick you up." Cary fumbled coins in the slot. Receiver pressed against her ear, she turned and scanned the room. Weary travelers milled about.

Kelby's answering machine kicked in with instructions to leave a message. "Uh—this is . . ." For God's sake, idiot. Don't leave your name. "Uh—your guest. I'm at the bus station." She hung up.

Okay, now what? Think. Don't panic. She was never good at thinking on her feet. Sit, then. This is a bus station, people sit all the time. Maybe Kelby went out to lunch with a friend. Went to work. Stepped out to pick up the mail. Arlette never promised Kelby would be standing by the phone day and night just waiting for Cary's call. Maybe she went shopping.

A hand came down on her shoulder. Cary whirled.

"Are you all right?" It was Ida. "You look sort of pale."

Cary nearly dropped to a heap, her heart pounded in her throat, her mouth felt frozen in a startled O. "I always look that way." The lighthearted tone was stretched thin.

"Listen," Ida said, "why don't I give you a ride. If my friend remembers. He's not real happy with me at the moment, but—" Ida looked up. "Well, it's about time."

A thin, lanky young man with a white bandage on his temple ambled up, straw-colored hair and a strong resemblance to a scarecrow.

"Osey, mind if we give my friend a ride?"

"No problem." Osey picked up Ida's tote bag and backpack, held both in one hand and said to Cary, "Where's your bag?"

Cary dithered, like she always did when faced with the unanticipated. "I—it's coming later." What kind of idiot traveled with bags coming later? "Thanks anyway," she said, "but a friend's picking me up."

"Where does she live?" Osey said.

Ida jabbed him with her elbow. "Hey, you dope, maybe the friend's a he." She turned to Cary. "Osey knows everybody."

His lazy posture seemed to change, and when his gaze sharpened like a hunting lioness who spotted the weak antelope of the herd, Cary was startled by the glimpse of keen intelligence. "Nice meeting you." She excused herself and walked toward the restrooms, feeling two pairs of eyes watching as she pushed open the door.

After washing her hands, she splashed water on her face. The thought of a shower pulled at her like the Holy Grail. With one day, eighteen hours and fifty minutes of bus-riding, she felt ripe as a bag lady. She waited long enough for Ida and her friend to be gone, then went out and tried the phone again. Answering machine. She sat down, waited two hours, called again. The machine. She waited, tried once more. Same result.

Now what?

Sit here in the bus station until the janitor throws her out with

68

the rest of the trash, or spend some of her cash on a taxi? Cary went up to the man at the ticket counter and asked where she could get a taxi. He made a call on her behalf and she waited out front until a cab screeched up. Another thing to hope for, she thought as she climbed in, was that she remembered the address correctly.

Despite the shimmering heat, Hampstead was a pretty little town, from what Cary could see with her circle of sight. Wide, tree-lined streets, snug little houses swept up against small hills. Mixture of architecture, some old, some new. Inside one or two homes, she could see people sitting down to lunch. Were any of them wary of their husbands, tense, and putting out food with shaky hands, hoping he wouldn't find fault with something?

Sometimes when she'd called Mitch to a meal, he'd said, "Be right there." Then he'd finished reading the paper, come to the table, and slapped her across the face because the food was cold. She was such a fool. She should have picked up the food and dumped it in his lap. How could she have let that sort of thing go on all those years?

"This is the place." Past a section of older homes way on the edge of town, the cabbie pulled into the graveled drive of an old Victorian house, weathered white paint, with a porch running all the way across the front and along one side, turrets and a steep pitched roof. A thick row of trees grew behind it. Beyond the trees on the right was an uneven paving-stone path leading to an old stone barn and outbuildings. A dirt road ran past the barn; across the road was an endless field of corn.

This was a mistake. How could she just turn up on the doorstep of a total stranger like some stray cat? What if Arlette had steamrollered Kelby and she would be appalled to see her? What if Kelby had plans? Still wasn't home? Was in bed with someone? Oh, dear God, why didn't she just find a motel and think this through? Maybe she should go back to the bus station and take the next bus to California.

Forget it. She didn't have enough money for a bus ticket to anywhere. No credit cards, no checks, no ID. All left at home so she couldn't be identified. As she started toward the house, the wind swept in off the prairie with a hot edge of grit that sanded her face. At least in California the wind didn't push the words right down your throat.

"Thank you." She paid the driver and he squealed away. Corn stalks, stirred by the wind, whispered mockingly.

For a second or two she stood braced against the wind, then let it move her toward the house. With a little prayer to a God she no longer believed in, she went up the steps. Her heels made hollow clumping sounds.

Please be home. Please let me in. She pressed a thumb against the doorbell.

Her knock went unanswered. She peered in the window to the right of the door. Hardwood floors, Victorian sofa. In the corner where the porch turned and went along the left side was an old-fashioned swing, the kind mounted in a frame that rocked back and forth, sitting by the rail. She plopped herself down in it. A glance at her watch showed nearly five o'clock.

Surely Kelby would be back soon. Wouldn't she?

Cary took out her book. Her poor vision made reading a struggle. After two hours, daylight started to fade. She walked the length of the porch, peered in all the windows, stood at the east end, and stared out at the corn field. Something menacing about it. Like it was watching her. Despite the heat, she shivered. Anxiety had kept her awake the night before she left and she'd only been able to doze periodically on the bus. She felt near some zombie state. Sitting in the swing, she curled her feet under her and let her eyes close.

A bright light shone in her eyes.

Flashlight! Oh my God! Mitch!

She opened her eyes to darkness. Like a hunted animal, she made herself small and didn't move. It took seconds to figure out where she was. The light shining in her eyes was the moon riding in a black sky. She heard rustlings as small animals went about their business. How long had she been asleep? She squinted at her watch. Nine o'clock? Two hours.

She was so creaky and stiff, she felt permanently frozen in a curved position. With slow care she coaxed her spine into a more or less upright line, and was suddenly aware she had another problem. Urgent need of a bathroom. In frustration she tried the doorknob. It turned easily.

Surprised, she looked around. Nerves skittered across her scalp. Nothing behind her but black night. An owl called somewhere. Feeling like a thief, she pushed gently on the door. Silently, it eased open. She fumbled for a light switch in the entryway and squinted in the sudden glare.

Living room on her right. Easy chair at right angles to the fireplace, magazines on the hearth, flowered Victorian sofa under the wide window. On the left, dining room. Oval table, chairs, hutch with china. Windows looking out at the cornfield. Door to kitchen.

"Kelby?" she whispered. Stupid. Anybody inside couldn't hear a whisper.

If she didn't find a bathroom soon, she'd have to find a bush. She closed the door behind her. "Kelby?" Louder this time.

The clock on the mantle ticked. She tiptoed toward a hallway and with a sigh of relief spotted the bathroom at the end. She went in, closed the bathroom door, and unzipped. She slid down her pants and underwear and sat on the toilet. If Kelby came home this minute, Cary hoped she wouldn't be scared to death by the sounds of a burglar using the bathroom.

When she finished, she pulled up her pants, washed her hands, and went into the living room. She really ought to go back out and wait on the porch, but the thought of sitting in the dark was too depressing to contemplate. As she gingerly seated herself on the sofa, it occurred to her that she was making a lot of assumptions. Maybe Kelby would mind a lot that this stranger, sent by a friend, just walked in uninvited, used the bathroom, and plunked herself on the couch.

She tried to stay awake, but as the hours grew late, her need for sleep grew strong. Her head dipped, she dozed, caught herself and jerked awake. She nodded off again and again. Finally, she tucked her feet under her, folded the Afghan draped over the curved back for a pillow and let her eyes close. Just as she was drifting along in the current toward sleep, the thought occurred that maybe this was the wrong house.

1 0

Cary dreamed she was running through the cornfield. The stalks weaved and snapped as the dark man chased her, footsteps getting closer. Fear jolted her awake. She looked around in panic. Dark. Totally unfamiliar room. Confusion sparked through her mind. Then sleep-lagged brain cells kicked in. Bus ride. Kansas. Kelby Oliver.

Mouth dry, neck sore, back aching, she slowly straightened her legs, then sat up. Her left foot was completely numb and she clamped her teeth against the sizzle of returning life. Through the living room windows she could see a quarter moon and millions of bright glittery stars. The open curtains made her feel on display for all the world to watch.

Did Kelby like sitting on the edge of an endless cornfield? Did she look out there and see desolation and loneliness? Or promise and dreams and possibilities? Where was she? Had she come in when Cary was asleep and tiptoed past so as not to wake her? Was she upstairs in bed?

Cary felt trembly and slightly sick from hunger. She pushed the stem on her watch to light the dial, peered close, and turned her wrist back and forth to make out the time. Ten after four. Moving like someone suffering from a debilitating handicap, she got herself upright. She switched on the lamp on the end table and nearly yelped as the light stabbed into her retinas. Squinting, she found the cord for the curtains and yanked them closed, then stepped aside so her silhouette wouldn't be apparent to anyone outside watching. She stood perfectly still and listened.

No sound, except the creaks and groans of an old house talking to itself. At the bottom of the stairway, she looked up. All dark as far as she could tell. She flicked on the light. A chandelier on the landing dripped with tear-shaped crystals. Two bulbs were burned out. Hand on the banister, she went up the stairs and looked down the hallway. Three doors, no light in any. Polite houseguests don't go snooping around and waking their benefactors.

Shaky and slightly queasy, she went back down the stairs. Would Kelby mind if she found something to eat? A cracker, toast? Orange juice! Visions of orange juice danced in her head. In the kitchen, she flipped the wall switch, hesitated a moment, then opened the refrigerator door. Ah. A carton of orange juice. She picked it up and shook it, judging the amount. Almost full. She took down a glass and filled it.

The phone on the end of the cabinet rang, sending her shooting nearly three feet into the air and making her drop the glass. It shattered in the sink, orange juice flew everywhere. Shit! What a mess.

She stared at the phone. Who called anyone at four A.M.? Kelby wanting to explain where she was? A neighbor seeing the lights and phoning to see if Kelby was all right? Cops wondering what the hell Cary was doing there? The phone rang four times, then a woman's voice recited the number and told the caller to leave a message.

A voice whispered, "Did you have a nice day?" Male and threatening.

Mitch! Oh God, he found her already! Taking a breath, she tiptoed to the answering machine, studied it, then pressed play to listen again. "Did you have a nice day?" The menace in the tone made the hair stir on the back of her neck.

Not Mitch. Was it? Hard to tell from a harsh whisper, but she had

74

heard Mitch threaten in a low voice many times, and this didn't sound like him. He wasn't Superman. She'd only been gone three days. Since she was a cop's wife, they'd start searching immediately, instead of holding off the however many days it was for an ordinary person who disappeared, but even he couldn't have found her this fast.

How long before he told anybody she was gone? Monday night when she didn't come home? Or would he go to sleep and not realize she was gone until he woke up? By Tuesday morning, he'd start the whole missing persons thing, if he hadn't already. What day was this? She'd arrived on Wednesday, yesterday, so this was Thursday. Four A.M. Thursday, August twenty-first. Incipient hysteria bubbled up in her chest. Oh God, that was enough time. Maybe he had found her.

What about Kelby? Arlette said she'd be here, that Kelby would pick her up at the bus station. Had he done something to Kelby? Arlette knew something about the woman that she hadn't told Cary. What? Why hadn't Arlette told her? Something dangerous? Something Arlette didn't want her to know?

Okay, take a breath. Maybe the voice wasn't threatening at all, maybe it was a friend of Kelby's calling to wish her a nice day. Yeah? Then why whisper and why make it sound like a threat? Clean up the mess. Maybe it's your overwrought imagination. Yeah, right.

Tearing paper towels from the roll on the cabinet, she mopped up the juice and brushed the broken glass into a little pile. In a narrow cabinet next to the door leading to the rear porch, she found dust pan and broom, swept up the glass and dumped it in the trash under the sink. Using a spoonful of crystals from a jar of instant coffee, she made herself a cup, drank it slowly standing by the dining room window looking out at the endless starry sky. She was a city person. It made her uneasy.

A sour laugh almost strangled her. Everything made her uneasy. She was so timorous and shrinking it was disgusting. She hated herself. Why had she put up with all the abuse, beatings, threats, slamming against the wall, and throwing down the stairs? She pulled in a breath. Because he said he'd kill her if she tried to leave. She knew it was true. At this very moment he was looking for her, and when he found her he would kill her. Shoulders hunched, she huddled over the steaming cup.

Weak, cowardly, sniveling! When she could stand herself no longer, she tore off a paper towel and blotted her face. A shower would help. The thought of no clean underwear almost started her sobbing again. To come in and fall asleep on the couch was one thing, but to go using the bathroom, dirtying towels, went way beyond acceptable.

A shower pulled, irresistible. It turned out to be quick. The noise of the water drowned out—ha, joke—other sounds. She couldn't hear if anyone else was in the house, if the phone rang, or if Kelby woke, or burglars broke in. Using the towel on the towel bar, she rubbed herself dry, then felt her body cringe as she put back on her dirty, travel-weary clothes. At least she'd rinsed off some of the grime. She made another cup of instant coffee and sat on the sofa sipping it. Kelby didn't seem to be much of a reader, there were no books in the living room.

At first, she just sat, then she turned on the television set and watched an old movie, then early morning talk shows. The sky outside went through cobalt to deep purple to lavender to pale blue as day arrived. Still no sign of Kelby, no sound from upstairs. She picked up the *Hampstead Herald,* and peering close, struggled to read about the heat wave that was in day twenty, the church supper, the coming of the county fair, the band concert in the park. With no more words to read, she got out the knitting.

At six o'clock in the evening, when she'd been waiting over twenty-two hours and Kelby still hadn't called or returned, Cary knew something was wrong. First, go through the house and make sure Kelby wasn't here. Oh God, she should have done that sooner. What if Kelby had fallen and was unconscious upstairs? Stop imagining disaster. Look and see if there was anything to explain her absence.

Even with the icky feeling of wrongdoing, Cary went up the stairs. Stifling hot up here. Along the hallway. Office room, desk and computer, office supplies, printer, file cabinet, view of the small hills and vast sky outside. Dust behind the lounge chair. Paper, CDs, paper clips, envelopes in the closet. No books, only a dictionary and texts on insurance. How did anybody survive without books? A pair of binoculars sat on the small table next to the chair. She picked them up and looked out. Billions of miles of empty sky, a transparent wafer of moon, and endless horizon-to-horizon corn stalks.

Down the hallway. Spare bedroom. Nothing in the closet or under the bed. Across the hall, the door was closed. She tapped. Waited, tapped again. "Kelby?" No sound. Pulse jumping, she eased the door open. Master bedroom and second bathroom. Clothes in the closet and the chest. No books here either. A pink velour robe hung on a hook behind the bathroom door.

She retraced her steps, went to the kitchen, and opened the door leading to the basement. Wasn't it always in the basement that murderers dug up the concrete to bury the body? Searching fingers found the light switch and she clicked it on. Idiot. Just a basement. You're not going to find a bloody corpse on the floor with the axe lying nearby. Oh yeah?

She put a foot on the first wooden step. It creaked. The next and the next and the next until she reached the cement floor at the bottom. Thin murky light crept in through shallow windows. She groped for the dangling cord and pulled, turning on the bare bulb. Furnace, shelves with boxes and dusty mason jars, washing machine and dryer. No Kelby slumped in a corner. Blowing out a long breath of relief, Cary went back upstairs.

At eight she looked in the refrigerator and found a block of cheese. Crackers were in the cabinet. She took an apple from the bowl on the table, sat on the sofa and watched television again. She dug out old *Country Living* magazines from beneath the sofa and looked through those. Like an alcoholic without booze, she fidgeted and waited. She squeezed a dab of toothpaste on a fingertip and rubbed her teeth, then rinsed. She watched more television. She waited.

Around two A.M. she dozed and again woke with total confusion, but this time it didn't take long to realize where she was. Kelby Oliver's house, Hampstead, Kansas. She couldn't remember a time when she felt so rumpled and dirty. And bored. She ached for books to read. After eating another apple, she paced from living room to dining room to kitchen and back again. Like last night, she turned on the television, watched an old movie, and slept fitfully.

When the darkness outside faded to gray with the first of the morning light, she went up to Kelby's bedroom. Feeling like the worst kind of intrusive thief, she opened drawers and looked through everything. On top of the small chest under the window lay a set of car keys. A shelf in the closet held a beige leather purse; inside were Kelby's wallet with driver's license and credit cards. Cary studied the picture on the driver's license, holding it close to her face and moving it around to find her small circle of sight, looking from Kelby's picture to her reflection in the mirror. Kelby was thirty-eight, brown hair, five-two, weighed a hundred and thirty-five pounds. Eyes blue.

There was a superficial resemblance between Kelby and herself. Cary was thirty-four, also five-two and had blue eyes, but her hair was blond. She didn't know what she weighed. Since she'd lost so much, probably around a hundred pounds.

Where would Kelby have gone that she didn't take her purse with her? An awful uneasy prickliness took hold. Something was very wrong. How could she have been so stupid as to leave home and come all this way to stay with someone she didn't even know?

Why did Cary trust Arlette's word that Kelby could offer sanctuary from Mitch? Why let Arlette disclose those most private and shameful secrets to a perfect stranger? Who was Kelby? Why did she agree to let Cary come here?

Get a grip, she told herself. Do you think Kelby deliberately lured you here for some evil purpose? To carve you up for body parts and sell your kidneys and heart? A master criminal who needed a new identity, she planned to steal yours and bury your body in the basement? Cary took a shaky breath. She'd been reading too many mysteries.

What if this was some kind of trap Mitch set up? What if he was just trying to see if she'd jump at the chance to get away? What if he was even at this very moment waiting for her to step outside? Oh, for God's sake. Cary shook her head. Maybe she should take up writing thrillers.

Mitch didn't have that kind of imagination. He wasn't devious. He was dead-on direct. What you saw was what you got. He couldn't have arranged for her to come here. It was Arlette who knew Kelby and urged Cary to come.

Before her courage gave way entirely, she grabbed the keys, trotted down stairs and put on her shoes. When she walked into the screened porch, the air felt like warm soup. Five in the morning and the temperature must be close to eighty. A dry, dusty smell of corn hung over everything. She followed the flagstone path around to the left side of the house and stared at the cornfield.

"I'm as corny as Kansas in August." Tall rows of stalks, at least eight feet high, clusters of fat cobs. Hot wind caused stirrings and rustlings that sounded like malignant whispering. When the wind died, the stalks fell silent. The vast field seemed alive, like some dangerous predator she mustn't turn her back on.

Goosebumps popped up on her arms in the muggy air. Shivering in eighty-degree heat, she took the path to the barn and rolled open the large door. Pearly gray light seeped into the dim interior. A Honda, similar to the one she had owned, except this one was white, sat inside. Doors unlocked. Nothing in the glove box but a map of Kansas and a flashlight. She clicked it on. Batteries were working. Car was clean, like it had recently been washed and vacuumed inside

A strong smell of what she assumed was hay, grass of some kind anyway, made her sneeze. A small room just to her right. Officelike, old wooden desk, shelves with cardboard file boxes, pegs on one wall. Stalls on both sides of the center aisle. All empty, except one with straw on the floor. A ladder went to a loft above and she climbed just high enough to see what was up there. Stacks of hay, or maybe straw. A fit of sneezing attacked her and she backed down.

Okay, nothing for it now but the car trunk. Hadn't she read this scenario a million times? Idiot woman goes off to deserted place like old barn and finds body. She pressed a spot on the key and the trunk lid popped up an inch or two. Big intake of breath. She nudged it open. It contained nothing more sinister than old newspapers.

Cary slammed the trunk lid. She needed to talk with Arlette. Since she couldn't call from Kelby's house, she had to find a public phone. Where was the nearest? In town, of course, but she didn't know how far that was, or exactly how to get there. She couldn't walk to a neighbor and ask. That would be the same as wearing blinking neon lights in big letters saying "something not right here." A second thought had her opening the trunk again to retrieve the stack of local newspapers. At least they contained the printed word, and she needed something to read. She slammed the trunk lid again and stepped from the barn.

A high-pitched scream sliced through the predawn stillness.

11

$\mathcal{B}$y six o'clock, the pounding in Susan's head and the crackling in her ears had reached a point where she wanted to bang her head against the wall or soak it in a bucket of water. She shut down her computer and navigated the hallway, tacked a hard right and went into George Halpern's office.

When she came in, he dropped his pen on the desk and rose to his feet. Gray hair circled a tonsurelike bald spot, pale blue eyes, kind, sympathetic, always ready to help anyone in need. Even thirty-some years in law enforcement didn't shake his faith in the innate goodness of humankind. She'd lost that faith the second day on the job, when she arrested a woman who set her baby in the sink and poured boiling water over him.

"How's Tim?"

"Serious condition. Burns over thirty percent of his body." Susan lowered herself to a chair so he could sit back down.

"Poor boy." George shook his head.

George had grown up in Hampstead, lived here all his life and knew everything about everybody. Whenever she wanted information about a local, he was better than the computer for facts, gossip, and rumor. "You know anything about an outfit calling itself Leading the Way? Miniature horses to lead the blind."

He smiled. "I believe we call that 'vision-impaired.'" He leaned back in his chair and tented his fingertips over a flat stomach. "Veronica Wells. Parents were farmers here for years, then like so many others, they couldn't make it. Her father recently died and her mother went to live with her sister in Colorado. Ronny just moved back, bringing those horses. Always was a horse woman. Competition riding as a kid. Blue ribbons for cutting and roping, even jumping."

Opening her mouth slightly, Susan moved her jaw back and forth to make her ears pop, hoping she could hear better. It didn't help.

"Ronny always had horses, probably loves those four-legged beasts better than people. I went to see her when she got back, extend a welcome. We've been friends forever, since high school, me and my wife and Ronny and her husband."

"Horses to lead the blind," Susan said. The thing about George was, sometimes you got more information than you needed.

"Ronny told me the first mini was a gift. A friend gave it to her for her birthday. Then she thought the little guy needed a companion so she got a second one. And one thing led to another. The idea about a guide horse came when one mini paired up with a blind horse she owned and led the blind one around. Why are you asking?"

"Just checking that she's not running some kind of con game."

He shook his head. "Not Ronny. She's got a business going."

Because George thought most people were—deep down—good, Susan took that with a grain of skepticism and got directions to the Wells place. Letting Hazel know where she was headed, she went to the parking lot. The sun had bleached much of the blue from the sky, leaving it the color of dirty muslin. Heat from the pavement seeped up through her shoes.

Windows lowered, air-conditioning on, she waited the required minute or two for cool air to kick in. Directions on the passenger seat, she headed east of town, took a county road for a mile and a half, turned right at the crossroads and continued another mile, past pasture land, horses in some, cows in others. All very bucolic. When she came to the gate with an arched sign, LEADING THE WAY, she turned in.

After going up one hill and down another, she arrived at an old farmhouse recently painted white with deep blue shutters. The barn, red with white trim, sat behind. She pulled up near a corral where small horses walked around in a circle. A woman calling out commands noticed her, handed over a long whip to an assistant, and ducked under the rails. Susan climbed from the pickup. Heat slapped her in the face.

"Ronny Wells," the woman said. "I figured you'd be out sooner or later." Salt-and-pepper hair, tall and slender, wearing well-washed jeans and white T-shirt with sweat stains down the back and under the arms. "Let me show you around."

In the barn, a tiny horse stuck its nose over the stall door and whickered softly. Ronny opened the door and the horse trotted out, nuzzled Ronny's pockets. Ronny produced a carrot.

"This is Ginger," she said. "The one we took to the restaurant Tuesday evening. She's the smartest one we've ever had."

Ronny rubbed Ginger's neck. "This little girl is special, but she's very sensitive. She'll need to be with someone gentle, soft-spoken. If she gets yelled at, or anyone says a harsh word to her, her feelings get hurt. She gets depressed and withdraws in a sad huddle. Then she has to be played with, jollied back to a good mood. We're very serious about fitting the animal with the handler. Personalities are taken into account, as well as how their walk fits."

Ronny gave the horse a final pat and took Susan around to the corral where an assistant was putting four small horses—not ponies—through their paces. "These four are beginners. They're learning the basics."

Susan rested a hand on the railing and watched. "And these animals are safe to lead the blind?"

"Under all kinds of conditions. Horses are very good at it because they have a three-hundred-and-fifty-degree range of vision. They can see traffic in a flash, for instance, and they always look for the safest, most direct route to get from point A to point B. And they have fantastic memories."

"They can be housebroken?" Susan's voice was heavy with skepticism.

Ronny smiled, apostle to the unbeliever. "If they need to go out, they tap a hoof by the door. They're good for up to six hours."

Back in the sunshine, Ronny focused on the horses in the corral. One decided it had enough of this walking around getting nowhere and broke ranks. A command from the trainer brought it back in line.

"You worried a guide horse might spook and take its handler into traffic or let him fall in a lake?" Ronny said.

Actually, Susan wasn't. Mounted police have horses trained to be calm in all kinds of noisy, chaotic situations. Fireworks, gunfire, vehicles honking, motors revving, balloons bursting, umbrellas popping open in their faces. There is nothing like a thousand-pound animal backing into a person to keep him in place.

"These guys like people. They bond, horse and handler, just like a Seeing Eye dog does. We're careful to make the right pairing."

The sun was beginning to make Susan feel a bit light-headed. "They live in the house with the handler?"

Ronny shook her head. "No. They're horses after all. They need a barn or outside shed."

"Are blind people interested in a small horse as opposed to a trained dog?" What would it be like to trust your welfare to a horse?

"Some people like horses, they ride, or used to ride. If it were me, I'd chose a horse every time. There are advantages."

"And they are?"

"A dog has a working life of eight to ten years. Some blind people have had as many as three dogs. It's heartbreaking when a dog gets too old to do his job. A horse, especially these guys, can live thirty-five, forty years. They stand quietly in line, even take a nap, at the grocery store. Dogs have to sniff things. And for a bonus, horses keep your grass mowed. They have only one problem."

"Yes?"

"Just look at them. They're so damn cute everybody wants to pet them."

"Do you have many people wanting these animals?"

"Thirty on the waiting list. A woman here in Hampstead is interested."

"Who?"

"Woman named Kelby Oliver. She called to find out about the program. Said she was calling on behalf of a friend."

Kelby Oliver? For a second, Susan couldn't trace the name to a memory in her mushy mind. Ah, the woman who hadn't called her sister. Did Kelby have vision problems? If the sister called again, Susan would ask.

Ronny showed Susan the classrooms where handlers memorized basic commands, learned how to care for a horse. They went out to the pasture where beginners started training.

"We go to shopping malls with escalators and elevators, airports and get on planes, heavily trafficked areas. Set up situations where the horse has to lead his handler out of very tricky conditions, like roadwork with streets torn up or flooded areas with downed power lines."

Susan thanked her for the tour and went back to the pickup. She took her aching head and crackling ears home, swallowed two Excedrin, and went to bed. Los Angeles Guitar Quartet on the CD player, she thought about Tim Baker and kids driving too fast, and what she could do about it. Sleep overtook her before she got anywhere.

In the dream, she was running through a grove of trees, afraid she wouldn't get there in time. Wind whipped the branches overhead and they tore at her like beseeching hands. She heard gunfire.

"Hurry! Someone's been shot!"

"Who?" She pounded along tangled undergrowth, stumbled and—

She woke with a jerk, sticky with sweat, heart banging away at her ribs.

1 2

As he sped along I-80, Mitch's mind played out gruesome scenarios. He peeled off the freeway at Central Street and took direct aim toward the shopping center, slowed slightly as he skidded into the parking lot and pulled into a slot two rows beyond the recognizable PD cars and a detective's sedan.

Jerking open his door as he turned off the ignition, he loped across to the uniformed officer leaning against the squad car, arms crossed like he didn't give a shit what the commotion was all about. Yellow plastic crime scene tape was strung from the patrol car's side mirror across to a sign that read LEAVE CARTS HERE and around to an unmarked. Cary's Honda sat inside the tape. Sitting here for four days. If she was in the trunk . . . All Mitch could see as he jogged up were bags of groceries on the backseat.

The patrol cop, beefy, young like he didn't know his ass from his elbow, straightened as Mitch approached. Mitch didn't know him, he was El Cerrito PD. The nameplate said POST, and he stared at Mitch through mirrored sunglasses where Mitch could see twin images of himself.

"Black? I don't think you're supposed to be here, man."

Mitch wasn't surprised that Post knew him, probably every cop around knew his wife was missing. Most of them would be worried and sympathetic, but a few would be telling jokes and sending knowing looks at each other.

"Who's got this?"

Post shrugged. "Sergeant Fuller."

Mitch knew him slightly.

"You found the car?"

"Yeah." Post was proud of himself.

"You touch it?"

"The door handle. Opened it to see if she was scrunched down in back or something."

The *she* this clown was referring to was his wife. "Touch anything else?"

Post planted his feet wide, getting defensive. "Thought about popping the trunk lid. In case she was inside. Missing four days . . ."

Cary in the trunk for four days. Mitch didn't want the image that brought.

"Detectives came along and yelled at me."

"Should have done more than yell. I appreciate that you were checking this out, but you could have fucked up a crime scene. You understand that?"

Post tightened up. "If it was my wife, I'd want somebody to check the trunk on the chance she might be stuffed in there and still be alive."

"Next time don't touch anything. Report it, let the detectives do what they're trained for." He'd have done more than touch the trunk release, he'd have popped the fucking thing.

Ducking under the yellow tape, he walked toward Cary's car. Roy and Irving, the odd couple, were talking to the gawkers standing around. Irving was skinny as a wire and wrapped about as tight. Roy was squat and thick, built along the same lines as a Hummer. Crime scene guys were working the car.

"Mitch, what the hell you doing here?" Roy said.

"If it was your wife, where would you be?"

"Go home. We'll let you know what we find."

"What've you got?"

Roy took a stance and crossed his arms. "Look, Mitch, I know this is hard but—"

"Just tell me what the fuck you found! I know you found something. I can tell from the way you won't look at me. What? Blood? Ransom note? What?"

Roy squinted at him, then stuck his fingers in his back pockets. "We found her purse."

Relief caught up there somewhere high in Mitch's throat. He had to clear it before he could talk. "Empty?"

Roy shook his head. "Driver's license, credit cards, checkbook. Stuff women carry around with 'em."

Cary wouldn't walk off and leave her purse. "You check in the trunk?"

"Mitch, we have to do this right."

"Open the trunk, Roy."

"We're just about to do that." Roy put his hands on what would be his hips if he wasn't one solid block up and down, looked around at the crowd that had gathered to watch what was going on and back at Mitch. "You shouldn't even be here. If you give me trouble, I'll get somebody to cart you away. Swear to God. Cuff you and take you in, if I have to. Understand?"

Mitch wanted to squash his round, lumpy face.

"I'm cutting you some slack here," Roy said. "But you're using it up real fast. If something happened to your wife, we don't want to mess up evidence that tells us what went down here."

"Open the goddamn trunk, Roy, or I am personally going to shoot you in the nuts."

"That's it! You just ran out of slack! Get your stupid ass out of here and let me do my job!"

Maybe Mitch had a thing or two to learn in the charm department, but he was going to see if she was in that trunk, or he would kill every fucking person in this lot. "Come on, Roy. Have one of the techs check the fucking lever and pop the trunk!"

Roy stuck his face in Mitch's. "I know you're under some serious shit here, but there's a limit to my patience. Now get the hell out."

Mitch wanted to wring his thick neck. Except Roy's neck was big as a tree trunk and Mitch wasn't sure even both hands would fit around it. Reaching hard, Mitch pulled out a level voice. "Please, Roy, I'm beggin' you. Just open the trunk and I'm outta here. I have to know. Just do it. Please."

Roy took a breath of such magnitude most of the air in the parking lot got sucked in. Mitch thought it would be used to blast him, but Roy relented and nodded at the tech guy.

Mitch moved in close, stiffened himself, and locked his knees so hard a strong wind could have blown him over. The tech popped the trunk, the lid raised a few inches. Roy nudged it up.

No Cary. Spare tire, jack, old blanket, empty paper bags, flat of bottled water, first aid kit, sack of books.

Relief came crashing down with such a jolt that Mitch staggered to keep his balance. Then rage took over with equal force. How dare she put him through this?

"Okay," Roy said, voice flat, but Mitch could hear the relief under it. "Now get the hell out of my way."

Mitch didn't leave, but he did get out of the way.

A flatbed truck arrived, Cary's car was loaded and the truck drove away. That's when the car keys were found. They were laying on the ground, under the car. Like they'd been dropped and accidentally kicked.

Nothing to explain what happened. If some sicko grabbed her, the only sign of possible struggle were those keys on the ground.

13

Dreaming.

Running. Running.

The leaves smelled sickly sweet. Joe knew that smell. The smell of death, decay. Keep running. Don't wake up. Stay in the darkness.

The leaves turned slippery and black. He was running through a river. The water got thicker, turned red. Blood. It splashed when his foot hit down.

The body lay ahead. He ran. Turned the body over.

A battered, broken face grimaced with an empty smile.

Noooo!

14

───

Standing just inside the barn door, Cary listened. The smell of corn lay heavy in the hot air. No sound except the corn stalks sighing and whispering in the wind, murmuring spiteful and cancerous secrets that dropped to the soil where they decayed and disintegrated like dying leaves returning nutrients to the plants. She gathered newspapers from the car's trunk and closed the lid. Shoulders tight, papers clutched to her chest, she hurried to the house and dropped the papers on the kitchen table. After drinking a glass of water, she struck out for town.

Last night, she hadn't paid much attention, now she made note of landmarks so she could find her way back. Kelby lived on Wakarusa Road. She went north, turned right on the first wide-looking street, which was Hollis. Hampstead was a small town. How lost could she get? Ha. With *her* eyesight?

Sweat beaded her forehead and plastered the shirt to her back, her breathing came in a wheezy pull. Monterey Street made her think of California. She took another turn and found a small park. Berry Park. Trees, leaves changing to gold and red, lined a grassy bank. A clubhouse sat behind a play area with swings, slides, and jungle gym. The park was deserted, but there was a phone at the side of the building. If this were Berkeley, or even El Cerrito, the phone wouldn't be working. However, this was Hampstead and the phone appeared to be intact. Scooping a handful of dimes, nickels, and quarters from her pocket, she lifted the receiver, then hesitated. Surely there was no way this call could be traced. How could there be?

Mentally, she shook herself. Being careful was one thing, being paranoid was another. Why would anyone put a trace on a public phone in Hampstead, Kansas? Whoever heard of Hampstead? Or Kansas? More important, only Arlette knew she was here.

Her watch said seven-fifteen, two hours earlier in California. Arlette wasn't going to be happy about the phone ringing at five-fifteen A.M. After four rings, Arlette's recorded voice said she was busy and couldn't come to the phone right now, please leave a message. Cary hung up. Where was Arlette at five in the morning? Still asleep?

She thumbed coins in the slot and tried again. The answering machine responded. Stuffing the remaining coins back in her pocket, she trudged back to Kelby's. Oatmeal for her breakfast with milk that was just on the edge. As she sipped instant coffee, she thought with longing of a good cup of Peet's coffee. Nose almost against the page and maneuvering it to find her spot of sight, she read about the church rummage sale and the damages to crops and livestock caused by the heat wave.

After perusing the ads, she went up to Kelby's office, picked up the binoculars, and looked out at the wide-open spaces where the deer and the antelope roam. None were roaming at the moment, but in the distance blackbirds circled in the blue sky, just like they did in old westerns where the music grew ominous and the hero was about to die.

With the deck of cards from the desk, she went downstairs and played solitaire. In the middle of the afternoon, with the sun so hot on her shoulders she felt she might spontaneously combust, she made the trek back to Berry Park and called Arlette again. The answering machine kicked in. Nearly fainting from heat by the time she returned, she splashed her face with cold water and stretched out on the couch with the fan blowing over her. At nine in the evening, she tried calling a third time. Still no Arlette.

Maybe she didn't answer because she didn't recognize the number. Receiver in her hand, Cary dithered. She had to talk with Arlette.

"It's me," she said when the machine beeped at her. "You there? Pick up!" She waited, she waited, the machine beeped letting her know her time had run out. Damn it, where was Arlette? Another try got her the machine again, and Cary said, "Call."

Slapping at mosquitoes feasting on exposed flesh, she trudged through the summer night back to the house. The cornfield stirred in the wind. It was an unnerving presence and she felt it was watching her. The darkness was busy with rustling and scrabbling sounds. Small animals? She hoped they were small. Crickets chirruped, fireflies flickered, and somewhere in the distance a coyote yipped a forlorn cry. Maybe it had made the scream she'd heard when she was in the barn.

Lying on the living room sofa, she waited for Arlette's call. It got later and later. She dozed. Arlette didn't call. Daylight crept in before she fell asleep. When she woke, she knew where she was without that sickly period of confusion.

Bread and strawberry jam for breakfast with another cup of instant coffee. She showered and put back on the same clothes she'd worn when she left on Monday. She looked through the *People* magazine on the coffee table. Already she could tell her sight was slightly worse. As her field of vision closed, she felt this urgent compulsion to read. Read, read, read every moment while she still could. Did Hampstead have a library? Probably. So what? She didn't have a card, or any way to get one.

All morning she paced and watched snatches of television, fighting the pull of clean clothes. Midafternoon she gave in, went to Kelby's bedroom, and found underwear in the top drawer of the chest, a short-sleeved knit shirt and a pair of jeans in the closet. Feeling like the worse kind of scum, she showered—long, and using a lot of soap and shampoo. When she stepped out of the tub, she rubbed herself red drying off. Kelby's clothes, even too big, felt luxurious. She might be scum, but at least she was clean scum.

Gathering her smelly garments, she carried them to the basement. Nervous and halfway expecting something to jump out at her, she stuffed clothes in the washer, added soap from the box on the shelf above and spun the dial. While the washer took care of dirt, she paced the living room again and watched more television. She wanted books. She threw clothes in the dryer, wandered from living room to dining room to kitchen. Maybe Kelby had a library card. Surely, stealing a hostess's underwear was worse than borrowing her library card.

She raced upstairs and looked in Kelby's purse. No library card. Credit cards, driver's license, checkbook, money. Nine dollars and two cents. She took the driver's license and the money. Superficial likeness at best, but maybe okay, unless someone really looked carefully.

Using the keys in the purse, she locked the kitchen door behind her. Heat rose up like a blast from opening a furnace door. She struck out walking. In a town this small, if she couldn't find the library, she could ask. Someone would tell her. Kelby's house was so isolated it took a minute or two of walking before she came to the nearest neighbors. By that time she was dripping sweat and her spirits were flagging.

The homes were mixed, some large old farmhouses, some newer, wood frame or brick. Trees spread blazing red and gold colors against the vast sky. The sun burned against the back of her neck, but movement felt good, even with the hot wind blowing in her face. More houses, different neighborhoods, some beautiful old Victorians with gingerbread and fancy windows.

When she reached the business area, her feet hurt and she felt the pull of muscles in her calves which hadn't been used so much in days. Many of the commercial buildings were made of creamy stone, giving the place an old look, like it had been around a long time. *And so it probably had, dummy.*

The downtown area was only two blocks long, department store, bank, church, boutiquey places, hardware store, something called Feed and Grain, fabric shop, antique shop, and, to her joy, a bookstore. She would investigate that later. Outside the bank was a phone. Scooping coins from Kelby's purse, she lifted the receiver and thumbed in coins and punched the number. The phone rang four times and the answering machine kicked in. Damn it!

Cary looked at her watch. Idiot. It was only three-thirty Friday afternoon. Arlette was still at work. Call there? Cary punched the work number and was told Arlette wasn't in. She declined to leave a message. The urge to call Mitch came on strong, just dial the number because it was familiar and she was so scared, and so alone, and she didn't know what to do.

No!

She flipped pages in the phone book and found the library. Iowa Street. "Excuse me," she said to a woman coming from the bank stuffing money in her wallet. "Could you tell me where Iowa street is?"

"Sure." She pointed. "You go down that way. I think one block. Or two. Then left at the picture-framing shop and continue until you come to it. You can't miss it."

With her eyesight? She could miss a marching band if it weren't making any noise. Aiming herself in the direction the woman had indicated, Cary ran right into the police department. Or, at least, her path took her straight past. She kept going. Half a block farther, she stopped at the magazine shop and picked up the *San Francisco Chronicle*. And there was her picture. Right on the front page for all the world to see.

Her jaw clenched. She held it close to pick out the headline. WIFE OF BERKELEY POLICE OFFICER MISSING. Fear touched a cold finger to her spine. She glanced around, feeling instantly recognizable, like the whole world was watching, pointing, saying, "There, there, that's her, she's the one."

She threw money at the counter and fled. Outside a man came toward her and she quickly tucked the paper under her elbow and hurried in the other direction. Slow down! Nobody runs in this heat. Sure way to call attention to yourself.

She turned and asked if he knew where Iowa Street was. He gave her better directions. She thanked him, went two blocks, turned left and found the library, a surprisingly modern building, red brick with lots of glass. Just inside the door, she stopped and took a deep breath. The musty, dusty, slightly mildewy smell of books. The best smell in the world. It calmed her, raised her sagging spirits.

The librarian, soft brown hair held together at the nape of her neck with a butterfly clip, sat behind the checkout counter. A teenage girl slouched at one of the small tables that dotted the room, consulting a book and scribbling notes, an elderly man read a newspaper. Fear froze her throat. When she saw it was the local paper, she managed to swallow. At a far table, she spread out the *Chronicle* and stared at her picture. Taken at their wedding. Mitch looked handsome, dashing and just a little dangerous.

She'd aged since then. In body and spirit. The girl in the picture looked young and happy. Untested. Gazing out at a future with the joy and unawareness of youth. Bending close to the page, she read the article.

Wife of twelve-year police veteran Mitchell Black still missing after four days. The day she disappeared she planned to go grocery shopping at the El Cerrito Plaza. The distraught husband, greatly worried about his missing wife, asks anyone who saw her that day to please come forward.

Missing. She felt suddenly dizzy. The air got too thick, the room seemed to shift. The small print on the paper looked like lines of marching ants. Clenching her fists, she dug her fingernails into her palms and waited for the room to settle.

When she felt she could walk without collapsing, she went to the new book section, where she collected eight books without much looking at them. Had someone recognized her from the picture? Was at this very minute calling the police?

A reward. There was a reward out for her. Like she was a criminal. Would her photo be up in the post office? Would people study it? Memorize her face?

In a mad flurry of recklessness, she carried the books to the counter to see if she'd be recognized. She said she wanted a library card. A form was handed over. She dutifully filled it out, using Kelby's name and address.

"Have you anything with your address?"

Cary slapped Kelby's checkbook down and waited to be denounced as an imposter.

The librarian made out a card, used it to check out her books, then handed her a slip of paper with a list of the books and the date they were due. Cary grabbed her books and hustled out. She got as far as the entryway when her knees threatened to buckle. To give herself time to gather starch so she wouldn't melt in a heap on the floor, she stopped and looked at the notices pinned on a bulletin board. Lost dog. Car for sale. Cat needing new home. She could have a cat now, if she wanted. There was no one to tell her she couldn't. Piano lessons. Ballet lessons. Business cards pinned up by gardeners and people who did housecleaning.

Companion wanted, light cooking, cleaning. Call Stephanie Farley.

Could she get a job like that? Lord knows, she could cook and clean.

"She really needs somebody," the librarian said. "She's desperate. I can give her a call if you like."

Cary turned and found the librarian watching her. "Uh . . . thanks, that's okay—"

"Only take a second." The librarian punched in a number. "Hi, Steph. I've got somebody here who's just who you're looking for." She listened a moment, smiled at Cary, then said, "I'll send her right over. Her name's Kelby Oliver."

"Oh . . . uh no, it's . . ." Oh Lord, after using that name to get a library card, what would happen if she now said she wasn't Kelby?

Cary accepted the note with the address and asked for directions. Newspaper and books clutched to her chest, she trudged through the heat. She didn't have to go. She didn't know anything about being a companion, she didn't think she'd be good at it.

You need a job. Should she or shouldn't she went back and forth in her mind until she got to Carson Street.

The house, an old Victorian, sat on a slope, porch along the length of the front, door painted a bright yellow, half-circle of stained glass above. The second story had small arched windows with yellow trim. The grass needed mowing and weeds had sprung up in the flower beds. Next door two young children were squabbling about whose turn it was on the swing.

You need money.

Squaring her shoulders, Cary went up the porch steps and pushed the doorbell. Stephanie Farley opened the door, stepped back, and finished putting on earrings. Twenty maybe, Cary judged. Short chestnut hair, curling up around a blue hat, blue cotton pants, white blouse. Cary braced herself for an accusing finger and *You're not Kelby!*

"It's my grandmother," Stephanie said. "She had a stroke and I can't really leave her by herself. She can't get around, she..." Stephanie blinked back tears. "I need somebody to come in about this time every day and—well, you can see the place could do with some cleaning."

Cary looked around as Stephanie waved with a broad gesture.

"Not that I expect you to make the place spotless," she went on hurriedly, as though Cary might not take the job if spotless was expected. With her vision, the spot would have to be boulder-sized.

"Fix her lunch and feed her. I get home around six. Are you interested?"

"Yes."

"Have you ever done this kind of thing before?"

"No," Cary admitted. Now the young woman would ask for references and Cary would have to say she couldn't give her any. And

Stephanie would say, I'm sorry, but I can't hire a perfect stranger without references. Thank you for coming.

"You're hired anyway. Actually, you're the only one who's showed up and I've got to . . ." She stopped, took a breath, and started stuffing books in a backpack. "She's difficult. Her name is Elizabeth. Dr. Elizabeth Farley. Psychiatrist. Bigtime teacher at Emerson. Private patients. And she . . ."

She zipped the backpack and swung it around on her shoulder. "She's pissed. She's used to being in charge. She won't talk."

"The stroke?"

"Yeah, that's part of it. But she can talk some. Her speech is garbled and she has trouble retrieving words. If she can't get words to put with a thought, she loses the thread. It's really frustrating. She says 'shit' a lot."

Stephanie looked at her watch. "Oh, God, I'm going to be late again." She grabbed keys from the mantle. "Can you start tomorrow?"

"Uh—sure," Cary said.

On her way home, she stopped at Erle's Market and bought a can of ground coffee, two cans of tuna, some milk, two candy bars, and a toothbrush, then discovered she didn't have enough money to pay for them. She used one of Kelby's checks and signed Kelby's name. When she handed it to the clerk, she stiffened in anticipation of being denounced, a phone lifted, and a call made. Since the police department was just up the street, it wouldn't take them long.

Without even looking at the signature, the clerk gave her a smile and a receipt and wished her a nice day. Cary picked up her illegally obtained groceries and set off for home. She would explain to Kelby, promise to pay her back. She had a job.

Not bad for an almost-blind missing person, identity thief, and underwear-borrowing scum.

15

How much more of Kelby was she going to take? Her name, her money, her food, her house, her shower, her laundry, her clothes, and now her nightgown—and she hadn't even met the woman who'd offered her shelter. Pushing aside the phone, she plopped library books on the bedside table and crawled into bed. A stack of unread books made her feel rich, like having money in the bank. She adjusted the pillow, looked at titles, and selected the autobiography by Katharine Hepburn. Doing her book-to-the-nose, bobbing-her-head thing, she read until nearly midnight. A binge reader.

After she turned off the light, anxiety came to sit on her chest and ask what she thought she was doing taking care of a sick woman. She could do harm, or if not harm, then not do things right. Every creak and groan of the old house, the rustling of the wind in the trees outside, had her starting in panic. When she finally slipped over into sleep, she dreamed she was running in the cornfield, squeezing through one row into the next, and the next, and the next, but no matter where she went the big blackbirds were flying overhead like a pointer for her stalker.

The phone rang, pulling her awake with a hammering heart. Arlette! She reached for the phone, then raced down to the kitchen and listened as the machine kicked in.

"Kelby?" Woman's voice sounding irritated. "It's Faye. Your sister? Remember your sister? I've been worried sick. You give me a call! Immediately! If you don't I'm going to do something!"

Pick it up! Tell her Kelby isn't here. No. First she had to talk with Arlette. Why hadn't Arlette called? She'd leave another message after she got off work.

Work. For the first time in months, Cary had a purpose for the day. A small ray of light seeped into her soul, and she hummed "Amazing Grace" as she showered. She used more of Kelby's underwear and another pair of her pants, a light-weight tan cotton, and found a short-sleeved brown knit shirt. There was something satisfying about brushing her teeth with her own new toothbrush. Heat hit her as soon as she stepped outside, but since she knew the way, it didn't take as long this time to get there.

Stephanie, looking a little frantic, shoved books in a backpack and looked around as though making sure she wasn't forgetting anything. "See if you can get her out of bed. And encourage her to talk even if she doesn't want to."

"Okay." *How?* No background in caring for the sick, no knowledge of stroke victims, and God knew, she wasn't a forceful person, which this Dr. Farley probably was before the stroke. How was Cary going to get her to talk and eat and get out of bed?

"The washer and dryer are in there." Stephanie pointed to a door off the kitchen. "I just did a huge grocery shop yesterday." She opened the refrigerator on shelves of milk, eggs, cheese, fruit, and vegetables.

"You have to cut her food up real small. Most of the time she doesn't want it, but just keep trying. She's used to having lunch at twelve-thirty."

"Okay," Cary said.

Stephanie let out a breath with a nervous huff. "I guess we better tell her you're here."

In the bedroom at the back of the house, light filtered through sheer white panels on the windows, brass lamps gleamed on the bedside tables. Drapes and bedspread were a deep burgundy. Bookcases lined two walls, mostly, from what Cary could tell, professional texts dealing with physical and mental illness.

"Kelby is here," Stephanie said.

Dr. Farley, in a pink-flowered nightgown, had a string of drool clinging to her mouth. She stared at Cary with alert brown eyes, wary and angry. Her brown hair sprinkled with gray was matted and in need of brushing.

"Remember what I told you," Stephanie said in the singsing voice people use for small children and mental defectives. "She's going to come everyday and get your lunch and bath and, you know, clean a little and take care of things."

"No!" The word was a rusty croak of protest.

"You behave yourself. I'll be back around six." Stephanie kissed her grandmother's forehead and dashed off with all the grace and confidence of youth.

Cary moved a straight-backed chair closer to the bed and sat down. "What should I call you? Dr. Farley? Or Elizabeth?"

"Not . . ." The brown eyes, angry and frustrated, watched her closely. Early sixties, Cary guessed. Straight nose, high cheekbones, and firm chin. Except for the left side of the mouth where the stroke had pulled it down in a look of petulance, she was still an attractive woman and must have been pretty when she was young.

"I understand you'd rather not have anybody around. I feel that way sometimes, especially when I'm not my best. I'll call you Elizabeth. Is that all right?"

Cary took in a breath. As long as the woman couldn't speak, she couldn't fire her. "What would you like for breakfast? There's cheese and eggs in the refrigerator. An omelet?"

Stubbornly, Elizabeth clamped her mouth and refused to respond.

"An omelet it is. I'll see what else there is to put in it." She fled before Elizabeth could shake her head no, she didn't want an omelet.

In the kitchen, Cary set a skillet on the stove, chopped ham, tomatoes and green peppers, whipped eggs, mixed in the diced items and turned on the burner. When the skillet was hot, she poured the whole thing in, let it cook, then slid half on one plate and half on another. She cut an apple into nearly paper-thin slices, found towels and napkins in a drawer, and carried everything in on a tray.

"Let's give it a try." Cary spread a towel over Elizabeth's chest. "I know I won't be able to do this exactly the way you like it. Nobody can get it right for somebody else, but I'm going to try and I'll get better as we go along."

"Whooo . . . ?"

"Something to drink. What would you like? Milk? Orange juice? Coffee?"

Elizabeth nodded so quickly, Cary wondered if coffee was forbidden. She must ask Stephanie if there were any restrictions in the diet, like no caffeine.

"Okay. I'll get it started and be right back." Cary found grounds in the freezer, and the coffeemaker was enough like the one she had at home that she could figure it out. The smell of the coffee dripping into the carafe followed her into the bedroom.

"Do you use cream or sugar?"

Head shake no and no.

Cary forked up a tiny bit of the omelet and offered it to Elizabeth, who kept her teeth clamped. Cary calmly ate from her own plate until Elizabeth slapped the mattress, opened her mouth, and accepted food. Cary alternated bites of omelet with apples slices. The silence got heavy and eerie and finally Cary couldn't stand it. If she didn't say something to break the oppressive quiet, she would scream.

"I'm thirty-four years old," she blurted. "I have retinitis pigmentosa and can barely see. Soon I'll be stumbling around in the dark.

103

I'm not a criminal, or a bad person. I don't take drugs. I'm not a thief. And I won't hurt you in any way. Not deliberately, anyhow."

Apple, omelet, apple, omelet. "I'm from California, El Cerrito, California, which is near Berkeley."

Elizabeth suddenly got agitated, saying "naan, naan, naan" and clawing at her arm. "Whoo . . . where . . . ?"

"Kelby invited me to visit." That was more or less the truth.

Elizabeth leaned back against the pillows, looking puzzled.

"Even though my eyesight is poor, I still love to read." She thought she saw a sharpening of interest in Elizabeth's eyes. "Would you like me to read to you?"

The tiniest of nods.

"Sometimes I have to go slow to decipher words. I know there are books on tape. If my reading is too awful, I could look into getting those and we could listen to them."

"Nooot . . ."

"Not the same, I know. They don't go at the right pace, and I hate it when the reader changes his voice to make the characters sound different. Every female has a high breathy voice, the bad guy has a gravelly thug voice. Women readers make their voices deep to *sound like a man*. Bah! Why don't they just read."

Elizabeth was looking at her as though for the first time she'd said something intelligent. "I'll get the coffee. Do you mind if I have a cup with you?"

She poured coffee into two mugs, set them on the tray with cream and sugar, and carried everything into the bedroom. "I used mugs instead of china cups. I thought it would be easier, but if you'd rather have the china, I can change."

Cary sat down and offered Elizabeth a sip of coffee. It was awkward and coffee dripped down her chin. Cary wiped it off. "What we need here is a straw. I'll start making a list for Stephanie." Cary spooned coffee into Elizabeth's mouth. She had no idea how difficult it was to feed another individual. When Elizabeth indicated she'd had enough, Cary took all the dishes back to the kitchen and washed up, then she peeked in on Elizabeth and found her asleep.

At six Stephanie came dashing in with a stir of hot air, face rosy from the heat and the freedom to continue her life. "Did you manage to get any food down her?" Stephanie asked.

"Quite a lot." Cary listed what Elizabeth had eaten.

"Fantastic. She must like you. That's more than anybody else has gotten her to eat."

Cary wondered how to ask when she'd get paid.

"Since tomorrow's Saturday I don't have any classes, but I could use some time in the library. Could you possibly come back at nine?"

Cary nodded. The sun still blazed in a heat-scorched sky and she walked slowly. Her first full day of work left her exhausted. Partly the anxiety of not knowing if she was capable, and partly everything else—Arlette, Kelby, Mitch. Everything.

Detouring to the downtown area, she stopped at Weber's Department Store and bought six pair of underwear. Which was worse, wearing Kelby's underwear or using Kelby's money to buy her own? She must ask when she'd get paid. Tomorrow. She'd do it tomorrow.

At home she checked for messages first thing. Arlette hadn't called. Dinner could be whenever she liked, if she wanted to skip it altogether and have a late snack in bed, that was possible, too. The freedom was so heady she giggled out loud and thought she should write everything down. She'd never kept a diary, not since she was eleven and someone had given her one for her birthday, but she had the urge to write down all the dizzying feelings she was experiencing.

Just as quickly, her mood changed. With far less hesitation—she was getting quite used to snooping through Kelby's things—she went upstairs. In the office room, she opened the top file drawer and flipped through folders. Kelby'd had a house in Berkeley which she'd sold. Berkeley? Mitch worked in Berkeley. Did he know her?

Another folder had papers on the Hampstead house. Kelby had bought it six months ago. She'd lived here only six months? Why had she come?

Cary flipped through cancelled checks. Erle's Market, Weber's Department Store, Kansas Power and Light, Southwest Bell—

Elizabeth Farley, M.D.

Kelby had been a patient. Elizabeth Farley knew Kelby Oliver.

No wonder Elizabeth had croaked out such an emphatic "no" when Cary got introduced as Kelby. Elizabeth wasn't saying no, I don't want you to take care of me, she was saying no, you're not Kelby.

16

The twenty-second of August was notable for a thunderstorm, rain pissing down, hail bouncing, tempers flaring, residents huffy because Berkeley didn't get rain in the summer. Traffic was a bitch, fender benders and asshole drivers giving each other the finger. The only good thing was the bad guys stayed home. They hated to get wet just like everybody else. Hard on the homeless, though. They'd have another poor drone die of exposure if this kept up.

Shift over, Mitch drove home through all the shit, wipers clunking. Wind broadsided the car and it shuddered from the blow. Streets were full of water, gutters overflowed. He pulled into his garage and went in the kitchen door, shrugging off his jacket. Gone four days and the place smelled empty, like she'd taken its soul with her.

He flung his jacket over a chair and let it drip on the floor, then yanked open the fridge. He pulled out a beer, twisted off the cap and tossed it on the cabinet, and went to the bedroom. Shoving aside a stack of Cary's books, he set the bottle on the bedside table and flopped on the unmade bed. The place was a pig sty. Dirty clothes lay where he'd dropped them when he'd pulled them off. No clean jockeys to put on this morning. He could smell his own sweat.

Where the fuck was Cary? Jesus, there'd been no hint of her. Like she'd disappeared. Not even a puff of smoke, just poof, gone. He'd dreamed about her at night, saw her dragged from her car, thrown into the perv's, taken to the marina. Raped and murdered and thrown into the black, polluted water of the bay.

God, he missed her. He cleared his throat and swallowed. His temper got away from him too much. He really should try harder. Where the hell could she be? Her name and description had gone out to all law enforcement agencies. She hadn't used credit cards, hadn't cashed a check. She had to eat, have a place to stay. What was she using for money?

Stacks of her books sat in the corners, on the dresser, on the chest with his socks and underwear. He should gather all those books and dump them at a library sale. The day after she'd gone missing, he'd started going through them looking for a pointer, a hint, suggestion, anything to give him a direction to move in. Hell, he'd hoped for a phone number penciled in the margin, along with a name and address.

He'd found lots of crap. Scribbles in margins, underlined passages, stuff about abusive, controlling males. A loser of a wife who locked herself in the bathroom. Idiot husband would smashed the door in. Mitch sat up, took a glug of beer, and glanced at the bathroom door. He couldn't even remember what he'd been so mad about when he'd put a fist through the thin panel.

No point in sitting around here feeling sorry for himself. Tipping the bottle, he finished it off, tossed it in the trash, and rummaged through shelves in the garage for the large trash bags. Bag in hand, he went through the house gathering dirty clothes, threw the bag in the car, and headed for a laundry. After dropping them off, he went to a grocery store, the same one Cary had shopped at the day she disappeared.

People went in and out. Everywhere he looked he saw her. Slender women with long blond hair; some had a child with them and he'd feel a sharp stab of pain. Jesus, if they'd had a baby, he'd have something of her besides all those goddamn books! Wandering aimlessly up and down aisles, he picked up two apples, two oranges, bologna, bread, cheese, two cans of soup. That ought to hold him for a while. For good measure, he threw in a few frozen dinners.

Some broad seemed to be following him. Everywhere he turned, she'd be staring at him. Not bad-looking, thirties, brown hair, little on the hefty side. Just when he found the beer and got two six packs in the cart, she approached him.

"Excuse me," she said. "Aren't you Cary Percy's husband?"

"Mitch Black," he said.

"Oh, right. Black. I thought she said her name was Percy."

Maiden name. What the hell was she doing using the name Percy? People didn't sneak around saying their name was something it wasn't unless they were up to no good.

"You don't know me, but I'm Velma Dowler. I met Cary at Sylvia's. The exercise place? I saw you pick her up there once. She's such a nice person, always a smile. I'm just really sorry about . . . you know, her disappearing and all. Has there been any word?"

Mitch shook his head. He didn't want to talk about Cary with some nosey bitch looking for dirt, but he didn't want to blow her off, in case she knew something.

"It's just awful. First Kelby takes off for Kansas and then Cary disappears. It makes you wonder, doesn't it?"

"Kelby?"

Velma looked flustered. "Oh, well, you know, Arlette said that awful trial just took so much out of Kelby, all the gruesome details. And having to listen to that awful torture and all, but nobody's heard from her, and now Cary. Gone, just like that."

"Who's Kelby?" Cary met someone and ran off with him! He checked that Sylvia's place when Cary wanted to go and she hadn't lied to him, it was just for women. But women had friends and relatives. Acquaintances.

Velma gave him a fish-eyed look. "Arlette's friend, really."

He knew it. He knew that Arlette bitch was trouble. "What's Kelby's last name?"

"Oliver." She took a step back. He'd asked too strong.

Mitch told the Velma broad it was kind of her to be concerned, but he had every hope of finding Cary alive and well. And he was, damn well, going to make it his business to find out all there was to know about Kelby Oliver.

17

$\mathcal{S}$usan sent a baleful glance at her in basket, opened her mouth slightly, and moved her jaw back and forth in an attempt to make her ears pop. They did pop, and they crackled and they fuzzed over, but nothing made an ounce of difference on her hearing. *Fluid in your ears. It takes time for it to be absorbed.* Timing is all, and right now was the time to go home. A soggy mind does not clarity make. Just as she yanked open the bottom drawer for her shoulder bag, the phone rang. Damn. The phone seemed to have a malignant tracking device that sensed when she was about to defect. She sighed, punched a button, and picked up the receiver.

"It's her," Hazel said, "the one who called about her sister."

Susan searched through sludge in her brain, which took a while, but she finally got to the datum. A sister who didn't return calls. "What's the sister's name?"

"Kelby Oliver."

Oliver. Right. The woman who had inquired about a guiding miniature horse. Was she blind? "Put her through." Susan pressed the receiver against her ear and pushed up the volume.

"She still hasn't called me," the woman said in way of a hello.

"Your name, please?"

"Why do you people always ask for my name? It doesn't have anything to do with the fact that Kelby doesn't answer her phone or return calls. It's been nearly five days."

Five days? Who panics when a phone call isn't returned by five days? "Ma'am, unless you give me your name, I can't help you."

"What kind of stupidity is that?"

Susan pinched the bridge of her nose where her sinuses were beginning to throb. Something weird was going on here. If her brain didn't have fluid sloshing around in it, maybe she could figure it out. "Where are you calling from?"

Long silence. "I'm not supposed to be doing this."

Doing what? "You're not supposed to be calling the police?"

"No."

"Why is that, ma'am?"

Another long silence. "She's had some—difficulty lately and I'm worried."

"What kind of difficulty?" Mental? Physical?

"I'm not supposed to say."

What the hell? Susan tucked the phone between chin and shoulder. She didn't know if this woman actually was Oliver's sister. The only thing coming through clear was the caller's frantic need to talk with Oliver. Without identifying herself. Susan's headache was getting worse. "Does she have vision problems?"

"Vision prob—what is wrong with you people! She could be dead on the floor and you're talking about glasses?"

"Have you had an argument with your sister?"

"No!"

"Is there some reason she's avoiding you?"

Silence.

"Ma'am?"

"It's just that—look, I'm worried. Could you just please check and see she's all right."

"Yes, ma'am, but if you want me to get back to you with that information, you'll have to give me a number where I can reach you."

"Just find her and tell her to call." A click and then the dial tone.

Some kind of weird identity theft? Attempted scam of some kind? Complicated family situation? Families produced the most virulent, convoluted, and tangled emotions that were impossible to figure out unless you knew the history. Susan pressed a button for Hazel. "Have someone take a ride out and talk with this Kelby Oliver."

"You think she's dead on the kitchen floor?"

"I think she's ducking calls."

Hazel laughed. "It's what I'd do if I had a sister like that. I'll send Ida. And hope she doesn't get anybody killed."

Susan looked at her watch. "Where's Marilee? You're supposed to be gone."

"I'm out the door."

"Me, too." Susan put in three more hours of chipping away at the pile on her desk. Enough. Her head pounded like a jackhammer. Scooting back the chair, she picked up her empty mug and wandered along the hallway to the small kitchen behind and filled the mug, then she wandered farther along the hallway to Parkhurst's office and planted herself in the chair by his desk. "Hi, sailor. Got any nylons? Chocolate bars?"

He leaned back and raised an eyebrow. "You look terrible"

"Water on the brain."

He retrieved his gun in the shoulder rig from a desk drawer. "Let's go," he said as he slipped it on.

"Where?"

"I'm taking you away from all this."

"Oh, goody. Where you taking me?"

"For a drink."

"Forget it. In my condition, a drink would have me dead on the barroom floor, like what's his name in that poem."

"Play your cards right and I'll get you a giant box of chocolate."

"Oh. Well now." She trailed him to the parking lot, got in her pickup, and followed him to the Holiday Inn. Just what kind of drink did he have in mind? She parked beside his Bronco. They went in and walked through the lobby to the coffee shop. The waiter herded them into a round, padded booth in a corner and handed out menus.

"Hot tea," she told him when he asked if they wanted anything to drink. Parkhurst asked for iced tea.

When the tea came, she took a cautious sip that burned all the way down her raw throat. "Any reason why we're here?"

"Kelby Oliver. Of Berkeley, California."

A stab of homesickness caught her. Four years in Kansas, but still a misplaced San Francisco resident. *"I left my heart in . . ."*

"What do you know about her?"

"Not much," he said. "She stayed here one night. Checked in, checked out. June twenty-seventh."

"And you know this because—?"

"She used a fictitious name."

Susan looked at him. "How do you know that?"

"She had a credit card in the name of S. D. Turney. She was nervous enough that it made the receptionist suspicious. He went out and checked to see if the license number she'd given him was the number on her car."

"And was it?"

"Yeah. The kid wondered if maybe it was a stolen car, so he checked on that. Emerson student. I think maybe he's thinking of writing screenplays. The car was registered to a Kelby Oliver and it had not been reported stolen."

A waitress, another Emerson student, young, blond, tanned, with "Tami" stitched over the pocket of her shirt, came up. Parkhurst closed the menu he'd been perusing and placed it on the table. "What can you tell us about Kelby Oliver?"

Tami smiled. Perfect teeth. "I can tell you what she had for breakfast. Two eggs poached, whole wheat toast, and coffee."

"Was she alone?"

"Yes. Sat over there. All by herself, didn't talk to anybody."

"What can you tell us about her?" Susan said.

Tami tapped her perfect teeth with the eraser end of the pencil. "Umm. Tired. Worried. Nervous. Like she didn't get any sleep. Bags under her eyes. Slow about answering stuff like 'Would you care for some more coffee?'"

"Did she say anything about what she was doing here? Or where she was going?"

"I asked if she was staying long and she said no, she was just passing through. She had this kind of inward look, staring off into space and sort of having to pull herself back when I asked what she wanted. Something on her mind, probably a guy."

"Why a guy?"

Tami stuck the pencil behind her ear. "She'd look up real quick, like, if a man came in."

"Physical description?"

Tami rolled her eyes as an aid to thought. "Average, I guess. On the short side. Blond hair. Had this intense look. Like maybe she'd been sick."

"Sick," Susan repeated.

"Yeah. You know, thin, like she'd maybe lost weight, and kind of pasty-looking. Sort of haunted eyes."

When Tami left with their order, Parkhurst looked at Susan. "Haunted eyes?"

Susan wondered if Tami's major was English lit and she'd been reading the Brontes. Over dinner, frogs' legs for Parkhurst, grilled chicken breast for her, he told her how far he'd gotten tracking the speeding teenagers who'd caused the accident. Watching him eat the rear ends of frogs made her slightly queasy. She pushed her plate aside.

When she got home, the heat inside the house made her think of Death Valley. She turned on the window cooler. Getting out while the house cooled and the thought that exercise might help her sleep better moved her into a walk. Nearly eight-thirty, with warm breezes and mosquitoes. She slapped at the back of her neck and walked slowly, letting thoughts amble through her mind. Why had Kelby Oliver used a ficitious name? Why wouldn't she call her sister? Would Ida make a good cop?

Late evening light slanted through the maple leaves. Shouts and laughter from the young girls playing tennis floated on the humidity in the air. Through the fading light, Susan spotted Jen sitting alone on a bench, looking like a sprite that might flit away at any moment. Blue shorts, cheerful, red-striped tank top. Typical teenage garb, but her misery made it all seem wrong, pulled all the brightness from the autumn light and made the shirt seem dark. Her pain was so deep Susan could almost feel it in the air.

"Hey, Jen. Mind if I join you?" Could this child possibly be fourteen now? Time did those tricky things that made you unsure of when things occurred and ages got blurred.

Jen shrugged without looking up. "Sure."

A more unwelcoming invitation couldn't be imagined. Susan perched on the end of the bench. Jen, looking as forlorn and desolate as a lost kitten, had a book open on her lap, her backpack on the bench beside her. Her misery was so palpable Susan was pulled into it. Complete and utter absorption of despair that only an adolescent can fall into weighed over them both and squeezed the oxygen from the air.

Jen stared at a page, the very picture of being engrossed in the story and not wanting an interruption. Susan knew she wasn't reading, and also got the message. Go away and leave me alone. When did Jen turn in to such a teenager? "Why aren't you playing tennis, Jen? Aren't you feeling well?"

Jen shrugged. "I'm okay." She scrunched further in on herself and slapped the book shut, but not before Susan saw a spot that looked like a raindrop. Jen hooked a forefinger and rubbed it under the eye that betrayed her. Gaze averted, she poked around in the pockets of her backpack and found a tissue which she squeezed in her hand.

"What is it, Jen? Tell me what's the matter?"

A long shuddering sigh. "There's nothing you can do." The words were so soft Susan had to lean closer to hear.

Hot anger built in Susan's chest along with a fierce urge for revenge. Who hurt this child? Impotence followed, bringing a sinking feeling that this was one of those teenage things she couldn't do anything about. She was only Jen's friend, an adult friend at that, and only God and other teenagers had access to the teenage world. "Jen?" she whispered.

Jen looked up, eyes bright. "It's just this book." She flipped open the book and stabbed at a page. "I have to finish. It's due today."

She had much to contend with. Parents divorced a couple years ago. Grandfather's mind slipping away into Alzheimer's. Mother who didn't like conflict, dripped pretty pink paint over strife and pretended everything was rosy. She invested most of her time and energy in the new husband and Jen was left to fend for herself.

"What's the book about?"

"The railroad." She showed Susan the cover.

"Are you interested in the railroad?"

"I've been reading to Grandpa. Sometimes reading calms him down."

"Do you like reading to him?"

"Mostly he doesn't recognize me. Do you ever have nightmares?"

There was a wealth of meaning in the question Susan couldn't interpret. She wasn't good at this, she wished Hazel were here, or George or even Osey. "Sometimes. How about you? You ever have nightmares?"

"Grandpa does. He wakes up screaming."

"He had some horrible experiences—"

"He was tortured. Beat up, shocked on his—you know." Jen touched her lower abdomen. "Made him pee on himself. And forced to stand naked in the snow for hours."

"He talks about this to you?"

"All the time. Certain things really set him off. Like uniforms. And yellow. I don't know why it makes him rant. Something to do with armbands, I think. I never wear yellow when I go see him."

"Jews were forced to wear them."

"How did he survive that?"

"I don't know, Jen. He was very brave."

"What's it like to be brave?"

What the hell kind of question was this? What was going on in this kid's life? Susan leaned back, stretched out her legs, and hooked her elbows on the back of the bench. "I thought we were friends."

"So?"

"So friends talk to each other. Friends tell each other what's bothering them. Friends ask each other for help."

"You can't help."

"You never know." Susan stared at her ankles and wiggled the toes of her shoes. "Come on, Jen, let me try."

Jen shook her head, brown eyes apprehensive that Susan might blunder into whatever the problem was and make it worse. "I gotta go." Jen got up like a decrepit old person about to take her last breath, and slumped off, a picture of total dejection.

Susan crossed campus, went to Eleventh Street, then up Walnut and home. Despite the exercise, troubled sleep brought the usual dreams. This time Jen was in them. Gunfire. Somebody shot. She needed to find out who. Dear God, please not Jen.

There! Body face-down! Dead.

She knelt to turn the victim over. Before she could see who it was, she woke.

18

After five days with no sign of Cary, Mitch began to seriously believe she was dead. Her car parked at Albertson's was the last trace of her. The crime scene guys had gone all over the vehicle and come up empty. Traces of blood on the front seat, a smear on the steering wheel, but not enough to indicate serious injury. She simply disap peared. When he dealt with grieving parents whose daughters went missing, or boyfriends whose girlfriends disappeared, the first response was another female pissed off at parents or boyfriend and teaching them a lesson by taking off, sunning herself on the beaches in Baja to let them simmer, then coming home.

The whole department came through for him, piled everything they had in the search and there was not one trace of her. The rage that scared through him the first two days had pretty much burned itself out and now he missed her. He got mad all over again when he didn't have clean socks, or he had to get his own dinner, or there was no beer in the house, but mostly he just felt hollow inside.

The fog was depressing. Neon lights bled colors onto slick pavements. He watched for Cary wherever he went. His eyes automatically searched every face on the street. He called her former boss to ask if he'd heard from her, went back again and again to the library where she'd spent so much time.

He'd spot a blonde with long hair, curved mouth, and hurry up behind her only to see a stranger. Anywhere he went, he was always looking, always searching. At work, the guys eyed him, making sure he wasn't cracking up. When he wasn't on the job, he spent hours going through her books again, looking for a trace, a clue, a small arrow that pointed at somewhere she might go. Like any addict, she had stashed a hidden supply, under the bed, in closets, behind shoe boxes, in the suitcases. He would move a stack of towels and there'd be books. He even found the damn things behind the cereal boxes.

He went through every freakin' one more than once, hoping for a note in the margin, an underlined word, a receipt used as a bookmark. The hours spent looking got him nothing. A whole bunch were psychology books of one kind or another. Psycho-shit. If only they'd had a baby. That would have kept her from trotting off to the library all the time. He'd been suspicious of all those hours she'd spent there. Reading, she claimed. He'd followed her a few times, watched to see who went in behind her, who she talked to, who came out after her.

People had habits. If Tuesday was library day, they went on Tuesday. He ran a few license plates, but no likely males swam across his radar. Plenty of elderly or homeless. Not good candidates for running off with his wife. No matter how hard he worked at it, he couldn't find squat to tie anyone to Cary. Still, with all the fucking books she lugged home, why did she have to go to the library to read?

"The ones I'm reading can't be checked out," she told him when he complained about it.

"What ones?"

"Expensive art books."

Sounded like a stupid lie to him, but he'd gone in one time and asked to check out one and was told those didn't circulate. He tried to stop her buying any, explaining they couldn't afford it, but nothing did any good. She always had to have more.

He noticed the plants on the desk looked dry and wilted. Dying. Like Cary? Alone and dying? Or dead, rotting, and covered with maggots. His Cary with the soft blue eyes and compliant nature. Maybe he should water the plants, maybe that would prolong their lives, maybe they'd survive until she came home to take care of them.

Saturday had Mitch cursing under his breath and fuming with impatience through his shift. Why did he keep turning up on the job? Plodding through shit as though it made a damn bit of difference to Berkeley, or California, or the fucking world, if Mitchell Black turned up for work every day. When the light turned green, he tromped the accelerator and peeled away like better luck awaited him today.

Just as he'd been doing every day after shift since that broad approached him in Albertson's, he drove to the El Cerrito Plaza with a six-pack on the passenger seat, parked where he could watch the entrance, and waited. He popped a tab and took a long swallow. Should have gotten her last name and address, wouldn't be wasting time.

Cary ran off with some man. It was the only thing that made sense. Women talked with their friends. They probably giggled about him, Mitch the sucker, who didn't know what was going on under his own nose. Last night he'd dreamed about her. Her perfume drifted over to tickle his nose. When he reached for her, the dream turned dark, the perfume heavy and thick, choking, vile. He put his hands on her, but instead of his soft, eager-to-please wife, he touched something putrid and slimy, hair matted with mud from the grave. He'd make her pay for what she was doing to him. Sleepless nights, falling behind on the job, the guys looking at him with sympathy but not getting too close, like what he had might rub off.

Reassuringly, he patted the Glock on his hip. When the time

came, it would be there for him. Maybe he couldn't count on his wife, but, by God, he could always count on the Glock. People went in and out of Albertson's, but no sign of the broad he was looking for. He'd taken to sleeping with the television on, trying to ward off dreams of a bloated, stinking Cary in bed with him. Real horrors he'd actually been involved with at work folded down over the dreams, and he'd see Cary's face on a rotting corpse hauled from some stinking basement. Empty eye sockets would wink at him, skeletal fingers would reach for him. He'd rear up from sleep, heart pounding, dripping sweat, and hear some asshole on TV whining about his miserable life.

Made him wonder if he was losing it, if he'd had too much of the job and maybe should take some vacation time, maybe go somewhere . . . There! Wilma—Wanda—*Velma!* Yeah! Getting out of a green Lexus and stuffing keys in her purse. Jeans stretched over a broad butt, gray sweatshirt, New Balance running shoes. She hitched the purse strap higher on her shoulder and went inside the store. He waited.

And waited. Jesus, what was she doing in there? Buying food for an army? When she finally came out, she pushed a cart piled with grocery bags. No wonder it took her so long. She loaded the bags in the trunk. When she pulled out, he followed her, up the hills and along Arlington Avenue. Just past the huge rock in somebody's front yard, she took a right onto Rifle Range Road and signaled a left into the driveway of a two-story stucco, new and expensive. She hit a remote that opened the garage door. He parked on the opposite side of the street and jogged across. She'd popped the trunk and was bending over to retrieve grocery bags when he walked in the garage. She whirled.

"Sorry. Didn't mean to startle you. Mitch Black. You spoke to me a week or so ago. At Albertson's. About Cary. My wife."

"Oh, Mr. Black."

Officer, but he didn't throw that in.

She patted her chest, like he'd scared her heart into pumping. "Yes, of course, I remember. Is there any word?"

"No, not yet."

"I'm so sorry," she said.

"Let me help you with these." He started gathering up bags.

"Oh, well—that's not really—oh, thank you."

Arms loaded with grocery bags, he stood at her heels while she fumbled with the key, and stuck like glue as she headed through a sun porch, or some such room, and into the kitchen. All white and shiny modern, with stainless steel stove and refrigerator. This was some house. Probably worth upwards of a million and a half. "I know you've probably got things to do, but would you have time to go for a drink?" When he saw her tensing, he quickly added "or coffee, or something." He did the defeated, crushed, poor husband in agony, worried about his missing wife. "If you're too busy, I understand. I just wanted to ask you about her."

He plopped bags on the counter. The kitchen was huge with a stone fireplace taking up one wall. Another wall, almost all window, looked out on Wildcat Canyon. Messy housekeeper. Bag of disposable diapers on a chair, table littered with tiny, folded garments. Dishes in the sink, sticky stuff all over the floor. Sour smell, like she hadn't emptied the garbage in a while. He started rifling through groceries, pulling out perishable items, as an excuse to see what she bought. Nothing that told him anything, except she was one of those health nuts with organic this and tofu that.

"I already told the police everything I know. Nothing, really. We just had coffee once after exercising, you know? Cary and Arlette and me."

Mitch nodded and kept his face blank with effort. Cary never told him she sneaked off to have coffee with a group of ditzy broads. Why not? Because she had something to hide, that's why not.

"It would mean a lot to me." He put a hopeful look on his face.

"Well, I suppose, but—"

"That day you saw her. If you could just tell me what she said."

He could see Velma looking him over, trying to make up her mind. He didn't push it. Pushing would make her skittish and she'd show him the door. He simply stood there. If he had a hat, it'd be in his hand.

"Well . . ." She drew out the word, and he knew he had her. The old Black charm, worked every time. "I could make some coffee. But it can't be long. My neighbor watches the baby while I do the shopping. We trade off. It's a lot quicker and faster if you aren't dealing with a fussy little one. And you wouldn't believe the equipment you have to carry around. Diaper bag and extra pacifier, in case one gets lost, and diaper wipes, and plastic bags for dirty diapers, and . . ."

Jesus, that's more than he needed to know. "We were trying for a baby." He put a hint of sorrow in his voice.

She gave him a look of sympathy. "You'll have to excuse the place. I didn't know I'd have company." She took the items he handed her and shoved them in the refrigerator.

Divorced, he'd bet. She had the harried look of single parent.

"With the baby, I never seem to get on top of it." She hustled around picking up baby clothes and tossing them in the basket under the table.

"Are you a real coffee drinker? I mean, some people grind the beans fresh and only use Peet's and—"

He smiled. "Don't you watch television? I'm a cop. We drink roofing tar."

She smiled back and rummaged through cans and jars for coffee filters. If she had stuff organized, she wouldn't have to move everything to find what she wanted.

"Let me help you with that." He spooned in grounds and poured water in the top of the coffee maker. "What did Cary talk about?"

"Oh, just—you know, what we all talk about. What we had to do that day. Pick up prescriptions at the pharmacy, do the laundry, that kind of stuff. I always talked about the baby. And made them look at the latest pictures." She slid a box of crackers onto a cabinet shelf. "We just talked, you know? Nothing really."

"Other stuff, too, right? Women always do." He dredged up another smile. "Troubles, hopes. Ambitions."

Velma got out two cups. "Actually, I didn't know her that well. She was reading some book—"

"Yeah. She was a great reader, always had a book in her hands."

"A book about Kansas, I think."

"Kansas," he said, too sharp. She shot a look at him like he was a cat about to pounce and she was the mouse. "What was the name of the book?" He softened his tone and added that sad note.

"Oh, I don't remember, but she said she'd never been there before."

"Was she planning to go?"

"Well, not that I recall, she just had this stack of books Arlette said had belonged to Kelby and they were all about Kansas, and then somebody else said all she knew about Kansas was that it was flat. And Arlette said it went on forever if you were driving across it." Velma got up to get the pot and fill his cup. "Cream and sugar?"

"Black." He sipped. Lousy coffee. He'd have to pace himself, drinking this shit could put him off coffee completely. "What's the name of her friend in Kansas?"

"Friend?" She looked sideways at the door, like she was maybe thinking it hadn't been such a good idea to invite him in. Stupid bitch. Women who invited strange males into their homes deserved what they got. Not that he would hurt her, but he felt like squeezing her pudgy neck.

"Yeah. I know she had one, but—" Mitch rubbed his forehead, like he was tired, and God knew that was true, not sleeping and having nightmares of Cary rotting in bed beside him. "I've been forgetful. Worry has me not thinking real sharp."

Velma nodded sympathetically. "I'm so sorry, she didn't mention any friend."

"What about Kelby?" Tell me about this son of a bitch who went to Kansas.

"Oh, well, I promised not to talk about that."

Is that right. What if I slap you a time or two, would you talk then? "I understand. I wouldn't want you to betray a confidence, but I'm really worried about Cary. Anything you can tell me that might help find her—"

Tears welled up in her eyes. "I'm really sorry."

What did she have to cry about. He was the one with a missing wife. "Where in Kansas did Kelby go?"

"I don't know."

He looked at her.

"Really, I don't."

He thanked her for the coffee and fished a card from his wallet. "If you think of anything she said, anything at all, please call me."

She took the card and studied it like it came from a tarot deck. "Of course. I'm really so sorry, but there isn't anything I can tell you. I wish I could help, but she was just reading, you know, and . . ." A spark of intelligence came over her face.

"What? You remembered something."

"Well no, not really. I mean, nothing that could help, or anything, it's just—"

That slap or two was looking better and better. "What?"

"Oh, nothing. I just remembered that Kelby said the town was 'on the caw' and the house was in the middle of a cornfield."

"What is a 'caw'?"

Velma shook her head. "I have no idea."

Mitch figured he'd gotten about all this stupid cow could tell him, and he needed to get out of here and away from her lousy coffee before he smacked her stupid face. He gave her a thin smile and thanks for the coffee.

Velma threw him another one of those stupid sheep looks. "Arlette might know. Kelby was really her friend."

At home Mitch opened windows. The place smelled like nobody lived there. The dirty dishes in the sink didn't help either. What the fuck

126

was a caw? He pulled out the dictionary from the bookshelf in the living room and looked up "caw." *The harsh strident cry of a crow or raven.* What? Only the one definition. A code of some kind?

He tossed the book and yanked open the refrigerator door, snatched a beer and popped the tab. After a long swallow to wash away the taste of the vile coffee, he started throwing stuff from the refrigerator into the trash. Cheese with green mold, eggs past the pull date, bread that was hard, leftovers he couldn't identify. When he was done, he started on the cabinet shelves. He'd never paid much attention to what was on them. Cary did the shopping and put things away. If he needed anything, he just asked and she got it. Now he took down brown sugar and packages of spaghetti, boxes of cereal, boxes of crackers, a bag of flour.

The bag tore and flour scattered all over the floor. "God damn it!" He was headed for the garage and the broom when he noticed the small package that had spilled out with the flour. He picked it up. Birth control pills. Only two left. The bitch! She lied! All that time trying for a baby and her crying and saying how she wanted to be pregnant. He smashed a fist against a cabinet door. It splintered.

He stomped into the bedroom and threw himself on the bed. She lied about wanting a baby. What else did she lie about? Saying she was going to Sylvia's to exercise, lose weight. Monday, Wednesday, Friday. And the whole time she was having coffee with these broads. Lying and sneaking around. Meeting this Kelby. Kissing him. Sleeping with him. Going to Kansas.

He jumped up, retrieved his coat, and drove to the marina. In the bar at Hs Lordship's, he sat at a table by the window, sipped bourbon, and watched waves in the bay slap up against the rocks. He thought how the sound was the same as a palm striking a cheek. When they were first married, she liked to come out here. One time they'd come so he could apologize properly for hitting her. He'd given her roses and a black lacy thing, teddy or something.

One time he'd pushed her and she'd fallen down the stairs. Broke her wrist. She took off. He couldn't let her leave then and he wouldn't let her do it now. She belonged to him. He'd find out what caw meant, and he'd track her down. Tossing off the rest of the bourbon, he ordered another. How could she do this to him? Make him think she'd been abducted and murdered, or worse. Make him sob like a baby, mess up on the job. Waves rushed in to smash against the rocks, sending up a spume of spray, then receding, only to rush in again.

After another drink, he drove home and sprawled on the bed in the dark. Pictures drifted through his mind. Cary, smiling, radiant, in white lace at their wedding, smiling, confident and happy when they bought the house. Blank and shocked the first time he'd hit her. He couldn't remember why he'd lost his temper, she just would do stuff that pushed his buttons. Why wouldn't she learn not to do that? He shouldn't have hit her. He knew that. He was sorry. Didn't he tell her how sorry he was?

Sneaking behind his back. Telling him she was exercising and crawling into bed with somebody else. Laughing at him. All those months, he thought they were trying for a baby and she was using pills. Reading books, planning on running away. Making him think she was dead. Letting him sit in this empty house and look at her dead plants and smell her perfume on the clothes in the closet.

He took off his gun and put it on the lamp table. Countrywide bulletins had gone out on her. Calls had been made to hospitals, service stations. Triple A put a flag on her card. Highway patrols were alerted. He'd nudged traffic division himself. Airlines checked, car rental agencies contacted, credit card traces run. Bank records looked into. No trace of her. She had no money. Money in checking and savings hadn't been touched. Somebody had to pay for essentials like food and shelter. Some man was picking up the bills. Even if she had gotten too skinny, she was still pretty enough to look slant-eyed at a man and let him know she was hot. They were laughing at him while they lived it up.

Kansas. Halfway across the country from California, the last place that clown Mitch Black would think of looking. A town on the caw. He sat on the side of the bed. Their bed, where they made love and she told him how great it was, where they slept, side by side, where they tried for a baby. He pounded the mattress with his fist. Where she lied! Saying how much she wanted his baby and all the while taking the damn pills.

He picked up the Glock from the bedside table. Familiar and perfect in his hand. She was missing, maybe kidnapped, maybe murdered by some psycho like that creep who picked up Lily Farmer. You couldn't kill a dead woman. Find her, kill her, get rid of the body. The distraught husband couldn't be blamed. He was home grieving over her disappearance. Like two lovebirds, they were, he loved her so much. He'd kill the man, too. The son of a bitch she went away with.

First, he had to talk with Arlette.

19

On Sunday Cary woke early, bunched the pillow under her head, and rolled onto her back. Wind brushed the maple trees outside and leaves did a shadow dance across the ceiling in the translucent light of dawn. Except, with her eyesight, it was always the edge of midnight.

Why didn't Arlette call? All those things Cary kept telling herself—that Kelby went to see a friend, visit a sick relative, was seized by a sudden need for a vacation—were no longer possible to believe. If Kelby was simply away, why hadn't she called her sister? Unless she was totally irresponsible. Arlette wasn't the type to have an irresponsible friend.

Deep in her heart, Cary knew something bad had happened. Maybe an accident, maybe Kelby had gone somewhere and was taken ill, got hit by a bus, had emergency surgery. Amnesia. Ha, sure. How long before someone who knew Kelby would come by looking for her? Cary curled into a ball, arms hugging her knees. Could Mitch have known what she was planning? Know where she was going? Gotten here ahead of her? Could he have done something to Kelby?

Birds twittered outside with all the noise and busyness of starting a new day. She opened the curtain and sunlight slanted in. Grabbing Kelby's robe, she went to the kitchen and spooned grounds in the coffee maker, poured in water, and waited, watching the coffee drip through. If she told the police who she really was, and that Kelby was missing, she'd just have to face the consequences. But if Mitch found her . . . She felt like shrieking. Would there ever be a time when she could be herself? When she would be safe? Not a quivering bundle of fear?

With shaky hands she filled a mug with coffee and took it out on the screened porch. She could almost taste the heat and corn and dust. A cat ran along the fence, a small rodent dangling from its mouth. The hunter going home with the kill. Mitch was patient, like the cat, hunting, ready to grab her by the neck and shake her until it broke.

She took a sip of hot coffee. He'd never give up his search. Only upon looking back did she realize how much she had endured. How could she have just stayed, getting beaten, trembling like a scared rabbit? She peered closely at her watch. Still early, not yet six. Eight in California. She'd call again. Arlette had to be home at eight A.M. on Sunday morning.

After a shower, she dressed in blue pants and a white shirt. She was getting used to walking, it wasn't taking her as long or making her as tired, but people were beginning to recognize her. She could feel them watching. If they smiled or waved, it was lost in the dark around her tunnel of sight. At the public phone outside of Erle's Market, she thumbed in coins, pleading, *be there, be there, be there.* The phone rang four times and the answering machine clicked in. No! Damn it! Arlette, where are you?

"Got your paper ready," the elderly man who ran the magazine store called to her from his doorway.

Startled, she turned with the guilty feeling of having been caught at something. "Oh great," she said trying to sound like she hadn't been scared out of what few wits she possessed. "Thank you. And the *Hampstead Herald*, too, please."

131

"Hot enough for you?" He picked up the second paper and slipped both in a bag.

"I could do with a little less." She paid him with Kelby's money and took the bag without even looking at headlines. Holding the page at the end of her nose and shifting it around to read was embarrassing. She didn't want the world to know her weakness.

"Yep. What we need is rain. Break this hot spell."

She agreed. She must get a tote bag to carry stuff. When would Stephanie pay her? Tomorrow was Monday, maybe that would be payday. On the way back, she stopped at Clancy's Bakery and bought two glazed doughnuts. By the time she got home, the sun was burning through the blouse on her back and she realized why iced tea seemed such a good idea. Never mind, she wanted coffee. The screened porch off the kitchen was not yet unbearable. With coffee and doughnuts on the small table, she settled in the wicker chair and plumped a cushion behind her back.

With a snap, she unfolded the *Chronicle*, held it close to her face, and made out the headlines. She sipped and nibbled, brushing at glazed sugar that fell in her lap. She wasn't the lead headline, but there was an article about her disappearance. After six days with no word or indication what had happened, foul play was suspected. Suspected? The foul play happened long before she left, when Mitch was beating on her.

She folded the page and on the bottom half read BERKELEY WOMAN BEATEN TO DEATH. She brought the paper closer and peered at the small print. Local attorney Arlette—

Mouth open, she tried to draw in air. No. It couldn't be Arlette. Not Arlette. Oh God, no, please, no. Local attorney Arlette Coleridge . . . No mistake. Her hands tightened into fists, crumpling the paper. Arlette was dead, beaten to death.

When Arlette hadn't turned up for work for three days, a coworker went to check on her and found the body. Because there was no evidence the house had been broken into, police speculated she had let her attacker in. Whoever it was had beaten her severely. She died from the injuries. Mouth filling up with saliva, Cary dashed to the bathroom, crouched over the toilet, and vomited a vile brown mix of grief and fear. When her stomach stopped heaving, she leaned against the tub, weak and sweaty.

Staggering to the bedroom, she fell on the bed and wrapped herself in the sheets. She wept, bitter guilty tears. Arlette—smart, brave, funny Arlette, who made her laugh, and made her see truths, and helped her escape. Arlette was dead. Not possible. How could somebody with so much energy and intelligence and beauty be dead? Gone.

No. No. No. Oh God, not Arlette. Cary cried and yelled and beat on the pillow. Morning turned into afternoon and afternoon into evening and she lay in the sheets, shivering in ninety-degree heat. Why? Why was Arlette killed? Why beaten? Because whoever killed her wanted something? Like the whereabouts of Cary Black? Was Arlette beaten and beaten until she gave him that information?

It wasn't some stranger who just happened along. It was someone she knew, someone she let into her house. Cary had warned her that Mitch was dangerous.

The crying continued late into the night. When Cary finally slept she dreamed, terrifying nightmares of Mitch chasing Arlette through the cornfield with an upraised ax. He hacked off a hand, then an arm at the elbow, then the upper part of the arm. She woke up screaming. Monday morning, she moved like a zombie, showered, dressed, and walked to work. Stephanie was, as usual, in a hurry, but she paused long enough to throw a questioning glance at Cary.

Cary knew she looked terrible, dark circles under red-rimmed eyes. She bathed Elizabeth, fed her, turned her, rubbed lotion on her back, and read to her, all the while preoccupied and wondering what to do.

When she lost her place in the book the second time, Elizabeth grabbed her wrist and shook it. "Haay."

Cary watched her struggle to retrieve a word buried somewhere behind the stroke-injured brain.

Elizabeth hit the mattress with her fist. "Shit!"

Cary stroked the back of Elizabeth's hand. "It'll come. You just have to keep trying."

"Sss—sssaa—ssad?"

Cary nodded. "Yes. Not very good company today. Sorry."

Elizabeth shook her head. "Wh-wh . . . ?"

"Why? A friend died."

"Kkkk—"

"Kelby? No, not Kelby."

By the time Stephanie breezed back, bringing in a swirl of hot air, Cary had made up her mind. Instead of going home, she went to the bus station and bought a ticket to Topeka. On the bus, she sat with a damp tissue in hand, thinking about Arlette. In Topeka she left the depot, climbed on a city bus and rode until she spotted a phone booth next to a drugstore. She got off, fumbled coins from her pocket, and punched in a number.

"Berkeley Police Department."

She knew the call was being recorded. The shorter, the better. "Ask Officer Mitch Black about Arlette Coleridge's murder."

"Ma'am, what's your name?"

She hung up. They would know the call came from Topeka, and could probably find the phone if they wanted, but they couldn't know who made the call.

Ducking her head, Cary walked under a low branch that brushed her temple as she went past. A memory hit her like a slap, the strong odor of beer, the smell of it on his breath, the taste of it on his mouth. His gun against her temple when she talked of leaving. Gripped by cold terror, she stood behind a tree looking at the house. He was inside, waiting for her.

Stop! You're making up nonsense and scaring yourself. She forced herself to walk to the house, up the steps, inside the porch, open the front door. She peered into the living room. Empty. Kitchen empty. She didn't want to open the basement door. She could see him hiding back in the dim recesses under the house. Pushing herself, she started down the stairs. Her knees threatened to give way and dump her on the cement floor. The basement was empty.

Upstairs? The old house creaked and groaned. Nerves skittered along the back of her neck. She climbed the stairs, expecting a bullet to pierce her back, her blood to splatter all over Kelby's white walls. She eased into the little room that was used as an office. Empty. No one was in Kelby's bedroom. The bedroom Cary was using, also empty. Shaky, she smoothed the sheets and pulled up the bedspread.

What about Elizabeth? Had Cary put her in danger? Helpless, lying in bed, unable to talk, unable to walk. And Stephanie? Was she in danger? For helping, giving Cary a job? Leave. Take Kelby's car and all the money you can get your hands on and run. Oh yeah, that's smart. With her eyesight? Get in an accident and kill somebody. That'll help.

She could feel him out there somewhere. He would watch, from the cornfield, from the barn, from one of the other outbuildings. She was alone, with no way to get help.

20

At ten Cary turned on the television to watch the news, hoping for mention of Arlette's murder. An ad informing her she could get everything she needed for her party at their store reminded her of a party Arlette had.

Mitch drank too much and she drove home, only because Arlette had managed to get the keys and give them to her. It was raining hard, and when he got out of the car he stumbled and fell in a puddle. She tried to help him up, but he swore at her and pushed her away. In the house, she took his coat and hung it over the shower rod. When she left the bathroom, he was waiting. Tangling his fist in her hair, he smashed her head against the wall. She fought for breath as her mind struggled with how she could be lying on her back staring at the ceiling. Both hands at the neck of her dress, he ripped it, tearing off buttons. "Looking sexy, flirting with that jerk. You think I'm blind?"

"No. Mitch—"

"Don't play dumb with me. You think I didn't see what you were up to?" He kicked her in the ribs and the temple, and then stomped out.

Pain seized her chest, so severe she couldn't breathe, couldn't move. For twenty minutes or more, she lay on the gray carpet without moving. She rolled onto her side, brought her knees up and wrapped her arms around them. Mouth open like a fish out of water, she stared at the footstool her in-laws had given her. It matched the chair, covered in dark burgundy plush, the legs were dark wood and curved out.

The following day, when she'd gone to Sylvia's, Arlette zeroed in on her. "You're moving like the walking wounded. Mitch hit you again?"

Walking wounded, that's what she was. "You know me. Clumsy. I was taking laundry down to the basement and fell. All the way down."

Arlette just shook her head. "When are you going to leave that son of a bitch?"

"I'm all right, really, just a little sore." The heat of shame flashed over her.

"He's never going to stop until he kills you."

Cary hadn't quite figured out the pattern, but she could count on Mitch for at least one vicious rage per month. She learned to tiptoe around, make herself scarce, swallow fast when he hit her to stop nausea from flooding her throat, pretend she was asleep so he'd roll over and leave her alone, and worst of all, she learned to pretend she didn't hate the man she'd promised to love, honor, and cherish.

When her neighbor Peg had mentioned her husband got so mad he said he'd kill her, Cary had looked at Peg with horror and a shameful worm of happiness. She wasn't alone. Then Peg had gone on to say it was before the election and she had threatened if he didn't stop telling some silly joke, she'd go out and vote for Arnold Schwarzenegger. He'd said if she did that, he'd not only divorce her, he'd have to kill her. Cary hated herself for the disappointment that came over her. A threat of being killed was very real to her, only a joke for Peg.

Mitch was clever about hitting and damaging only parts of her anatomy covered by clothing. She wove a cloak of shame wrapped so tightly around her she couldn't get it off, and, she finally realized, no one else could get past it. Her life wasn't so bad, really, she'd told herself. Most of the time it was okay. She had only to read the paper to know a lot of people in the world were far less fortunate than she was. She didn't have to sleep on the street, she didn't have to beg for food, she didn't have to wear filthy, smelly rags. She just had to understand Mitch better, find a way to deal with him.

He wanted her to have a baby. Terror of getting pregnant had started small acts of rebellion. What he was doing to her, he could do to a baby, a tiny, helpless baby that she'd brought into the world. She told him she'd stopped taking birth control pills, she didn't know why she didn't get pregnant, but secretly she still took them faithfully.

She bought books. Mitch didn't like her to read. If he found her relaxed on the couch with a book in her hands, he'd yell. "Lying around all day reading while I'm out in the trenches." She learned to read when he was gone, after she'd made the house spotless, done the grocery shopping and laundry, and planned the meals. Most of her books were from the library, but she had taken to easing out small amounts from the money he gave her for household expenses. With glee she'd sneak into the house, clutching a book to her chest, and hide it under the bed. She read at night when he was sleeping, while she folded laundry, waited for water to boil, chopped onions.

Mitch hated food with onions. When she left out onions, he complained the food was tasteless. He always criticized whatever she cooked. Too hot, not hot enough. Too cold, not cold enough. Not enough salt, too many onions. She tried different things, got cookbooks and used new recipes, but he didn't like anything. Occasionally she would chop an onion very fine and throw it into whatever she was making.

There was no mention of Arlette on the news. Tears ran down Cary's face. Arlette beaten to death. Mitch? To make her tell him where Cary was? Arlette must have suffered so much pain. All because she helped Cary get away.

Had Arlette told him what he wanted? If she had, Mitch would be coming for her.

21

$\mathcal{L}$ou Armada, scribbling notes at his desk, looked up when Mitch walked in.

"You wanted to see me, Lou?" He was the only detective Mitch knew with a neat desk. No crumpled fast-food wrappers, messy case files spilling over, empty coffee cups, or any of the general junk cops have on their desks.

"Yeah, have a seat."

Mitch dropped into the chair by the desk. His heart banged along in his chest like he'd just run a marathon. *Cary.* Something turned up. About time. God, how long has it been? The days all blended together and he'd lost track of how many.

Lou leaned back in his chair, giving Mitch the once-over like he was a suspect. What the fuck? She was dead! Murdered. He stiffened, clenched his hands. He couldn't say he was completely smoked. He'd been preparing himself for this.

"Who do you know in Topeka?" Lou said.

"Topeka?" That threw him for a spin. "Kansas?"

"Only one I'm aware of. Who do you know there?"

"What the hell you talking about?"

"Just answer the question."

"Not a goddamn soul. Why?"

"We got a tip."

"About Cary?" Why was Lou being so cagey? What the fuck was going on?

"We found fingerprints in her car."

"Whose?"

"Yours." Lou looked at him like this was some big discovery.

"Sure, my prints are there. I own the car, for God's sake. Anybody else's?"

"Your wife's . . . ," Lou paused.

Well, that was no kick in the nuts.

"Some as yet unidentified." Another pause, like he was getting ready for a big announcement. "And prints belonging to Arlette Coleridge."

That was suppose to be a big whoop? Arlette was Cary's friend. Mitch wasn't liking where this was going. Hang on, he told himself, wait and see. He'd questioned enough losers to know silence came down hard, but, unlike those cretins, he knew enough to keep his mouth shut. While he waited Lou out, he made a conscious effort to relax his fists. Without taking his eyes off Lou, Mitch loosened each finger and moved his arms until his hands rested lightly on his knees.

"What do you know about the Coleridge woman?" Lou said.

"Not much. Attorney. Friend of Cary's."

"Yeah? What about her murder?"

"Beaten to death." Mitch leaned forward. "What's going on here, Lou?"

"Your fingerprints were in her apartment."

Keep it short, Mitch told himself. Respond to the accusation, don't elaborate. "Like I said, she was Cary's friend. I was there once or twice." And he'd told the bitch to stay away from his wife.

"This tip we got came from someone in Topeka, person said to look at you for the murder of Arlette Coleridge."

"You think I killed the woman? Come on, Lou, that's crazy. Why would I?"

"I don't know. Maybe to get information."

"Information about what?"

Lou opened his notebook and scanned stuff he'd written there. Mitch thought he wasn't really reading, just making it look like he was searching for something important that would throw a noose around Mitch's neck.

"You want to know my theory, Mitch? My theory is whoever killed the woman, didn't go there to kill her, he—I say 'he' because it probably was a man, women don't usually beat somebody to death—wanted information. And this Coleridge broad didn't want to give it to him. He started pounding on her. And he kept pounding."

"You think he got what he wanted?"

"Could be. Could be she died without saying a word. Gutsy lady, I'm told. You ever been known to hit a woman, Mitch?"

Mitch pulled in air that tasted like stale beer. "Should I be getting a lawyer here, Lou?"

"You think you need one?"

Mitch could feel the hold on his temper getting slippery. "I need you to stop whatever shit game you're playing and tell me straight what's going down."

Lou tapped a pencil against his neat desktop. "Like I said, we got this tip."

"Who called it in?"

"Anonymous."

"Oh, right, anonymous. And on the strength of this tip from somebody who wouldn't even leave a name, you're pulling me in like I'm a suspect."

"Just talking to you."

"Man or woman?"

"Tipster? Whisperer, like he or she was trying to disguise the voice. The tech guy said a woman."

Cary! Holy shit! Cary was in Topeka. How big was the place?

"Let's try that question one more time," Lou said.

"What question?"

"Who do you know in Topeka?"

"Not a soul. Not a goddamn soul." Except one. His lawfully wedded wife who had run away from him and was causing all this trouble. He would make her pay. "Keep me in the loop on this one, will you? She was Cary's friend. I'd just like to know." Mitch stretched his legs and crossed them at the ankles. "Ask you something?"

"Yeah."

"What does 'caw' mean to you?"

"Caw? You mean a bird sound?"

"Never mind." Mitch stood up. "Any suspects in the Coleridge homicide?"

Lou rested his elbows on the desk, picked up a pencil, and held it between two upraised forefingers. "Some reason you want to know?"

"Yeah, like I told you. Because I knew the woman." Not because I iced her.

"Beaten to death, that's about all I can tell you. We're looking into her cases. See if clients felt she didn't do right by them, handled the case wrong, charged them too much. Hell, you know, whatever it is that gets people mad at their attorneys. ADA told me she was a tough opponent. Fights for her clients."

"Maybe she got some bastard acquitted and the family, loved ones of the victim, whatever didn't appreciate it."

Lou leaned back and looked at him. "I've done this sort of thing before, you know."

"Yeah. I'm just, like I said, wanting to know, because she was Cary's friend."

"You talked to her when Cary . . . disappeared?"

"She was the first one I talked to." Careful, you're getting into deep shit here. "I heard she was friends with Kelby Oliver."

"Who told you that?"

143

Damn it, just shut up. You're making Lou suspicious. "Cary."

Lou cleared his throat. "We're putting in hours on this. Nothing about her whereabouts yet."

Mitch snatched a pen from the bunch in the cup and rolled it through his fingers. Lou looked pained, like he wanted to grab the pen and put it back. Most obsessive-compulsive type Mitch ever knew.

"Who's Kelby Oliver?"

"No idea. Just that Arlette knew a Kelby Oliver. Oliver left town and Arlette is killed." And my wife is missing. Three people who knew each other, two missing, one murdered.

"Where can I find this Oliver guy?"

"Don't know." On his way to his desk, he saw Paula hauling in a burglary suspect. Didn't he have a drink with her once and she told him she was from Kansas?

"Hey, Paula, got a minute?"

She looked up. "Sure. If you can wait till I take care of this jerk."

"Yeah." He poured himself a cup of coffee, sat at his desk and waited.

It was nearly twenty minutes before Paula came in. "What's up?"

"Aren't you from Kansas?"

"Yeah," she said warily. "Why?"

"What does 'caw' mean? And I'm not talking about birds."

"Caw?" She looked puzzled. "I don't have the slightest idea. Why?"

"Nothing. Forget it."

She started to leave, then turned back. "Are you talking about the Kaw?"

"What's that?"

She smiled. "It's a river. The Kansas actually. Locals call it the Kaw. I have no idea why, they just do."

"Thanks."

A small town near the Kaw river. What he needed was a map. On his way home, he stopped at the Triple A office on University Avenue and got a map of Kansas. When he got home, he shoved aside dirty dishes with the remains of fast food and spread the map across the kitchen table. He popped a beer tab and took a swallow. Cary was a wiz with maps. She loved them. Everywhere she went she had to have a map first to see what the place was all about. Then she got books and read about it.

He peered at the goddamn map, looked it up in the little squares with the numbers and letters and still he couldn't find it. Wait. There it was. Kansas River. Shit! It went for miles. Dozens of towns. How was he going to figure out which one? He leaned back, drained the beer, and opened a second. The anonymous tip came from Topeka, so it made sense that Cary was in some little town near Topeka. He studied the map again. How the hell was he going to find the right place? He couldn't spend the rest of his life driving from one small town to another along the Kansas River.

The Velma broad. Talk to her again? Get more information? He didn't think she had any more. When he got up to get another beer, a lightbulb went off in his head. A grin pulled tight across his teeth.

If you want to disappear, you don't ever go anyplace you went before you dropped off the world. You don't take anything with you, and whatever you liked to do in your previous life, you never do again. You like the beach? You never again set a foot on the sand. You like horse racing? You don't go within fifty miles of a track. You like sailing? You never get near the water. All your old footprints have to get washed away like tide swept over the sand.

Tilting his head, he guzzled beer, set down the can and rummaged around in the drawer under the phone for a pad and pencil. He made a list of towns, plunked the phone on the table, and started calling libraries. Cary could no more stay away from libraries than she could stop breathing.

He identified himself as a Berkeley, California, police officer and asked if a Cary Black had a card at that library. When the answer was no, he asked if a Kelby Oliver had a card. He checked off each town on his list. It took forever, and around four o'clock he started getting a recording reciting the hours the place was open. He wondered why they all closed up so early until he remembered the time change. It was two hours later there.

As soon as he got home the next afternoon, he started in. Nobody ever asked why he wanted to know. If anybody had, he'd have just said he was working a case and tracking down a lead. Glancing at his watch, he saw it was five minutes to four. Shit, this was going to take forever. Didn't matter, he had patience. He told himself one more call, then he'd order Chinese. He dialed Hampstead and went into his song and dance. Bingo! No Cary, but they did have a Kelby Oliver.

After shift the following day, he went in to see the lieutenant and asked for some time off. Request granted without hesitation. He was headed for Hampstead, Kansas, where he would question this Kelby creep and see what he could learn about Cary.

22

Dreaming.

Help me! Please help me!

Running. Running.

Her voice grew fainter.

Faster, or he'd be too late. The ground got spongy. Rotted leaves slipped and slithered as Joe struggled to keep on his feet. If he fell, he'd never make it.

Wake up. It's the only way out.

It hurts! Please make him stop.

A sickly, sweet smell rose from the leaves. He knew that smell. Death, decay.

Phone ringing. Wake up. Answer.

No. Don't answer. If you answer, you'll die. Only safe as long as you don't pick up the phone. She was safe.

Help! Please!

Danger. Waiting for him up there. Stay in the darkness. Phone ringing. Wouldn't stop. If the noise didn't go away, it would pull him up. He'd be in such danger, he'd die.

Why didn't she answer the phone?

Help. Why won't you help me?

Losing ground. Needed cleated shoes. Her voice was moving away, he could barely hear her now.

"I'm coming."

His lungs were on fire, his breath coming hard. When his ankle twisted, he fell and rolled through rotted vegetation. Rolled through mud, getting it on his hands. He rubbed them against his white shirt. Bloody palm prints appeared. The blood ran and swirled and dripped red letters spelling her name.

No!

Ripping off the shirt, he flung it away and scrambled to his feet. The smell was getting worse.

Rotten leaves. That's all it was, just rotten leaves.

The ringing was pushing against the misty darkness in his mind. Soon it would push through and there'd be no hope.

Answer the goddamn phone!

She couldn't. Gone. Everything gone. He had nothing. Except one last thing he had to do.

The leaves got slippery, turned into black liquid. It got thicker, turned into blood. The body was just ahead.

Breath whistling in his ears, heart banging in his chest, he ran. Crouching beside the body, he turned it over. A battered and broken face grimaced with an empty smile.

The ringing shattered the dream. He groped for the phone. Receiver against his ear, he muttered, "Yes."

"Good morning," a voice said. "It's seven o'clock."

"Thanks."

Joe hung up and scrubbed hands over the stubble on his face as he looked around and tried to remember where he was. Motel room somewhere. Motel rooms were all alike and blended together once left behind. Gray light filtered through the curtains. He was covered in sweat and knew he'd dreamed again. The same dream, over and over, tortured him every time he slept. It got so he hated to close his eyes, which left him averaging around three hours a night. He needed more, so he could function, think clearly.

Pain gripped his stomach and he folded his arms over the rage. His life was over. He was just moving an empty shell around until he could kill her. No decision yet on how he would kill her, he'd decide when he looked the place over. See how things went, figure the best way. Swinging his legs around, he planted his bare feet on the brown carpet and waited for his brain to realize his torso was upright, then stood and rummaged through his bag for a pair of jockeys. He found the Aleve bottle and shook two tablets into his palm, plodded to the bathroom, ran water in a glass, and swallowed them. He turned hot water on and stepped in the shower, washed away sweat, dirt, and fatigue.

He pulled out a clean shirt and put it on with the jeans he'd worn yesterday, then shaved, staring at a face that was familiar, yet the face of a stranger. The person behind the face he'd known all these years wouldn't be planning the torture of another human being.

23

Cary got very little sleep Monday night. She curled in on herself and berated herself for getting Arlette killed. Beautiful, quick, smart, brave, sure-of-herself Arlette, who stood right up there and looked people in the eye. If she hadn't been Cary's friend, she might still be alive. "I'm sorry," Cary whispered. "I'm so sorry."

At six on Tuesday morning, she got up, showered, and dressed. Standing at the mirror to comb her hair, she looked at her image and saw dark circles under bloodshot eyes, a face blotchy and red from crying. She thought about using some of Kelby's makeup, but decided it was too much trouble.

Another scorcher of a day. The thermometer on the porch had the temperature reaching for eighty, and it wasn't yet seven.

Stephanie, stuffing texts and spiral notebooks in her backpack, gave Cary a glance. "She's cranky now. I hope you can cope. I'll be home a little later today. Study group after class. I hope that's okay." Stephanie swung the backpack across her shoulder and trotted out.

Cary walked into the bedroom and said good morning to Elizabeth. Elizabeth glared at her and grunted. "Sss?" Peering like there was a sign painted on Cary's forehead, Elizabeth licked her lips. "Sad," she blurted, and she awkwardly patted Cary's hand.

"Breakfast, then a bath." Cary escaped to the kitchen before Elizabeth's attempt at comfort had her collapsing into tears.

She started coffee. While it was dripping through she scrambled eggs and made toast, then peeled an orange, arranged slices on a plate, and put everything on a tray. She laid a towel across Elizabeth's chest and offered a forkful of egg. Feeding another person was awkward and messy, but with a straw, at least coffee didn't dribble down her face.

When the food was gone, dishes washed, and Elizabeth bathed and dressed in a clean nightgown, Cary picked up the biography of Katharine Hepburn and read to her. The struggle with words was worse than usual. Cary's vision was blurred this morning, probably because of all the crying. Or her tunnel of sight had shrunk.

"Nooo." Elizabeth shook her head.

"You want me to read something else?"

Elizabeth pointed to the bookcase against the wall opposite the foot of the bed.

"You want something from the bookcase?"

"Bbboot—tt . . ."

"Bottom shelf?" Cary crouched and started reading titles.

Elizabeth made exasperated, impatient noises. "Wh-wh . . . horse!"

"A book about horses?" Cary didn't see a book about horses. All the agitation Elizabeth was showing made Cary uneasy. With no training taking care of the sick, would she recognize symptoms that needed immediate medical attention?

Getting more and more frustrated, Elizabeth made stuttering noises Cary couldn't interpret. "Book book book!"

"Yes, book, I'm looking." Cary worried that Elizabeth might have another stroke.

"Lit-el lit-el."

"Lit-el," Cary repeated.

With a doubled fist, Elizabeth hit the mattress at her side. "Lit el!"
Understanding dawned. "Little. A little book."

Elizabeth nodded and said "lit-el" again, as though anybody with
half a brain would have known.

"Smaller than little." Paperback maybe? Cary ran a glance over
the shelved books and saw a stack of pamphlets. She pointed. Elizabeth nodded. Cary pulled out the whole stack and carried it to the
bed. She went through them one by one, showing each to Elizabeth.
When she came to a pamphlet titled "Leading the Way," Elizabeth
jabbed at it with her clawed hand.

Cary read it from beginning to end, three pages. Miniature
horses trained to lead the blind. Why did Elizabeth want her to read
this? Trying to say she was so blind she needed a horse to lead her
around? If she couldn't even read, what good was she? Take your blind
eyes and go away, with or without a horse? Was she going to get
Stephanie to find someone else? Someone who could read smoothly?

No, please no. Cary couldn't lose this job. Where would she get
another one? She was keeping an accurate account of money she spent
that belonged to Kelby. As soon as possible, she'd pay it back, every
penny. How could she do that without a job?

With sounds and gestures, Elizabeth made known that she wanted
to hear about Cary's friend. Cary hesitated. Because she had no one
else and because she needed to talk about Arlette, Cary complied. Elizabeth couldn't speak beyond a struggling word or two. Putting together
an understandable sentence was beyond her. Maybe her speech would
return—it was getting better all the time—and maybe talking about
Arlette wasn't smart, but Cary thought it should be okay, as long as
Arlette's name wasn't mentioned.

When Elizabeth had dozed off, Cary poured herself another cup
of coffee, took it to the living room, and sat on the couch reading a
book of clinical psychology. Later, she fixed Elizabeth's supper, then
got her settled for the night and put a movie in the VCR. When the
film was ending, Stephanie arrived and Cary told Elizabeth she'd see

her in the morning. Elizabeth jabbed a finger toward the bookshelf where the guide horse pamphlet was. Not knowing what that meant, Cary nodded and left for home.

Walking through the clinging heat, she thought about how she'd slid into Kelby's life and taken over everything. Name, money, clothes, even thought of Kelby's house as home. Identity theft. How much longer was she going to let this go on? Standing under one of the large trees, she watched the house. Whenever she returned, she had this clutch of fear that Mitch had found her, was inside hiding, waiting for her like a large, patient cat.

Shoulders hunched, she went up the steps to the rear porch, squinted closely at the piece of paper she'd slid between the door and frame to make sure it was still there, that no one had gone in while she was gone. She unlocked the kitchen door and went inside. She waited, listening. Heart beating fast, she went around checking each little piece of paper she'd placed at all the strategic points. All were just as she'd left them.

She kicked off her shoes, turned on the fan, and sat in the easy chair with a library book. Tucking her feet up, she tried to read, but her mind always found itself with Arlette. When the phone rang, she jumped. The answering machine kicked in and a woman said, "This is Faye. Your sister? Remember me? Call!"

Was it her fault, whatever happened to Kelby? Like Typhoid Mary, did she spread death wherever she went? How long was she going to let this go on? Call the police! She dug fingers into her hair. And say what, when they asked who she was, and why she was using Kelby's name and taking her money and living in her house? She bent over, hands clutching her shoulders. If Kelby hadn't agreed to help her, would she be here in her own living room sitting on her own couch?

Car coming up the driveway! Run! Before she could get herself into motion, a knock sounded on the door. With her heart tripping away like crazy, she crept into the entry way. "Who is it?"

"Ida. Talk to you a minute?"

Ida, the young woman she'd met on the bus. She opened the door and saw a police officer. Oh, God, Ida was a police officer! What had she said to this young woman? The dark blue of the uniform got blurry and Ida's words fuzzed over.

Ida, thinking "Kelby" was going to keel over in a dead faint, stepped in to catch her, but she scuttled away like Ida had the plague or something. "Ms Oliver? Kelby? Are you all right?"

Cary sucked in a breath. "Yes, yes. I'm sorry. I got up too quickly and felt a little light-headed."

Ida eyed her. Right. The woman was terrified. What was she hiding? Drug deals? Something else illegal? Ambling into the living room, Ida looked around. Nothing unusual in sight. Pile of books on the coffee table. "You have a sister?"

Again, this Kelby got a ghastly look, like Ida had come to haul her off to jail. Was she sick? Had a mental problem? The only people Ida knew with that kind of reaction to a cop were criminals. Okay, be careful here. The chief was not apt to give her any more chances. Mess up one more time and she was history. "Your sister—what's her name?"

Cary started to say something, caught herself, and said, "Faye. Her name is Faye."

"She's worried about you. She called the department and asked us to check on you, make sure you're okay. Maybe you could call her. Let her know you're all right."

"Yes. Okay. I will do that."

Ida wanted to march this woman right over to the phone and have her call the sister now. Let's see what happened then, but that might be one of those impulsive acts the chief wanted her to stop doing. "Well, thank you for your time. You let me know, now, if you need anything." She took one last look around the room and took herself out. It ruffled her feathers to just walk away, but beating up a citizen to get her to spill her trouble was probably another one of those things the chief had warned her about.

From the front window, Cary watched Ida get in her car. What an idiot, nearly dropping in a faint and stammering like a retard. What does this cop think? Obviously, she noticed something was wrong. Cary paced to the dining room, looked out at the corn-field whispering in the wind like a malignant presence, sat herself on the couch, and tried to read. At ten Cary turned on the news to see if there was any mention of Arlette's murder. Nothing in the national or local news. Earthquake near Los Angeles. Nobody hurt. California. The thought of home pulled at her. She shivered.

The beatings, the bruises and broken bones, thinking it was her fault. Arlette had made her see how sick that was, made her realize they had made a pact, she and Mitch. The first time he'd hit her and she didn't jump up and down and yell and scream and walk out, she and Mitch had decided that it was okay for him to beat her up. It wasn't okay any more. Only, he didn't know that.

Susan glanced at her watch. Nine o'clock. Time to pack it in. She shut down her computer and tried to think what work she needed to take home. Ida tapped on the open door. Oh Lord, what now? Had her rookie nearly gotten somebody else killed? Motioning with her fingers to come in, Susan told Ida to have a seat.

"I went to see Kelby Oliver." Ida perched on the chair. "There's something wrong there."

"Wrong how?"

Ida gave a quick shake of her head, like a dog bothered by a fly. "She nearly fainted when she saw me. And she wasn't scared of me when I first met her."

Ida explained that she'd taken her car in to get the brakes fixed and took the bus to see her parents. On the way back, she'd met Kelby Oliver. "We talked a bit. She didn't say much, but she just seemed quiet, like she didn't want to call attention to herself. Today she was white with fear."

Susan wondered if Ida had come storming in like a tornado. "Did you ask her what she was afraid of?"

"Yes. And I didn't do anything that might be scary. Honest." Ida nodded to underscore the word. "She nearly dropped to the floor before I opened my mouth."

Fatigue and a long day had Susan wanting to get home, take off her shoes, and stretch out on the couch with Bach in the CD player. Was this something she should look into, or was it simply a civilian opening the door and seeing a cop on the doorstep? First response, something happened to a loved one. "What did you say to her?"

"That her sister was worried and Kelby should call."

A better approach would have been to ask about the sister first, before explaining why the visit.

"She said she would, but I got the feeling she only said that to get rid of me." With one hand, Ida flipped hair up from her forehead. "Don't you think only a criminal would react like that?"

"Is that what you think?"

Ida took a breath. "She's afraid of something. And somehow cops play in."

Susan told her to write up a report. When Ida left, Susan grabbed her shoulder bag, retrieved her keys, and headed out. A few hours' sleep unmarred by dreams and she'd be a hundred percent. Before she could escape, the phone buzzed. She snatched it. "Yes, Hazel."

"Bad news. The hospital just called. Tim Baker, the boy in Monday's accident, died six minutes ago."

24

God, it was hot. How did people live here? The heat must fry their brains. Leaning forward against the steering wheel, Mitch pulled the handkerchief from his rear pocket and swiped at his forehead, then stuffed the handkerchief back. He'd checked the phone book before leaving the motel. No listing for Kelby Oliver. Information told him the number was unlisted. What the hell kind of name was Kelby anyway? He drove around getting a feel for the place. This was some nowhere town. Main Street with a business section three blocks long, two blocks wide. The PD was one block over. He considered dropping in and telling them he was on their turf looking for this Oliver jerk-off in connection with a homicide back home. Might get him an unlisted number and an address. Naw. Too complicated. They'd want to accompany him, and that wouldn't fly. They might even check with Manny in Berkeley, or some shit like that.

He drove past a big-ass church made from some kind of sandstone. Churches could be good sources to look for a missing person. Depending. Not Cary, though. Her religion was worshipped in libraries. Books books books. All the time reading books. He should have dumped the piles at home before he left. Bring her back to the house with all her books gone. He grinned at the thought.

The library turned out to be new-looking, red brick and glass. He angled into a parking slot and went inside. Tables with old farts reading newspapers, kids—probably students—studying. At the checkout counter, he smiled at the frumpy broad who asked if she could help him. He went into a song and dance about looking for Kelby Oliver, old friend, lost the address, just passing through, wanted to say hello. The bitch gave him the fish eye and told him they weren't allowed to give out addresses or phone numbers.

This would be a lot easier if he could slap his ID in her face and demand answers, but he just nodded and got out of there. Even so, she'd remember him. That was the trouble with small towns, strangers stuck out. After the air-conditioning, the heat slapped him like a blast from hell. He rolled through town, up one block and down another, consulted the map, and took a drive down to the river, where he got out and stood on the sandy bank under some tall trees. Water moved along to wherever the hell water went. He didn't get this nature shit. Seen one river, you've seen them all. He got back in his car and meandered through the campus. Spotting a BBQ place, he stopped for lunch.

A waitress slipped him a menu and he asked for coffee. She brought a mug and a coffeepot, plunked down the mug, and filled it from the pot, then set down a saucer with little containers of cream. He pushed that aside and took a sip from the mug.

"Haven't seen you before. Here on business?"

"You could say that. What's good to eat?" With a badge he could just ask questions. Without it, the only way to go was play games and ease out answers.

"Can't go wrong with a burger."

He nodded and told her to put cheese and bacon on it and add a side of fries.

She wrote on her pad. "You staying long?"

"Just going from here to there." He put his arm along the back of

158

the booth. "Being so close, I thought I'd stop and see a friend. Name's Kelby Oliver."

She thought a moment. "Don't know anybody by that name. Don't you have an address?"

"Sure do." He smiled with the old Black charm. "At home in my address book."

She smiled back. "Don't you hate it when that happens?"

"The only thing I remember is it's right by a big old cornfield."

"I can help you there. East End. Just take Ninth Street. The one out front? Turn right and all the way to the end. Cornfield's right there. You can't miss it."

He eyeballed the other diners while he waited for his lunch. Mostly blue-collar working stiffs, just like he was. For all he knew, the waitress could be lying and one of them could be this Kelby guy. When his burger and fries came, he ate, and left a generous tip, figuring he might want to come back with more questions. He headed to the east side of town, food heavy on his stomach, and the heat making him slightly sick.

And then he saw it. By God! The cornfield! Jesus, it was a big sucker. He smacked the steering wheel. Was he smart, or what? A road bordered the field and he followed it until he came to a dirt road that right-angled into the cornfield. He turned. Car wheels kicked up a cloud of dust. Miles of corn stalks higher than the car started to creep him out. No way to turn around. Two choices, keep going, or back all the way out.

Christ, was there no end to this corn shit? He'd never suffered from claustrophobia, but he sure felt weird when he couldn't see anything but corn stalks. Eventually he came to an intersecting road and he gave that a try. After following it for miles, he started to think he'd been kidnapped by aliens and dropped in a maze for use as a lab rat. Finally he came once again to the real world. Not sure where he was, he had to drive around some to orient himself. He had the guy now, the bastard who was sleeping with his wife. It was only a matter of narrowing in, knocking on a few doors.

159

It was taking longer than he thought. All afternoon he asked questions, going house to house, getting damn sick of it.

The next house on his route was in need of a good coat of paint. A dog, tongue lolling, came loping up, barking enough to raise the dead. Which was what this Kelby guy would be as soon as Mitch found the bastard. A rangy woman in jeans and man's white shirt, tails flapping in the wind, came out to the porch and stared at him. He started to get out of the car and the dog snarled. He wanted to get out of this damn heat and he wanted a beer. Maybe he'd just kick the damn dog's head in.

"Help you?" she asked.

He rolled down the window. "I'm looking for a friend who lives around here."

"What address?"

"That's my problem. I left the address and phone number at home."

"Friend got a name?"

"Kelby Oliver." What happened to all that Midwestern hospitality people talked about? Weren't these people supposed to be friendly? This was the most unfriendly bitch he'd run into yet.

"Never heard the name. Sorry, can't help you." She snapped her fingers at the dog and he went running. The two of them stood on the porch and waited until he left.

Long way between houses out here. God, you couldn't even hear your neighbors if they shouted for help. The next house was in better shape, fresh paint, flowers and shit in the front. No dog either. He went up on the porch and rang the bell.

"Good afternoon." A woman opened the door and smiled at him. Her teeth were too big, but at least she didn't look at him like he was a murdering rapist.

He smiled back, the smile that got them every time, and went into the song and dance about forgetting the address.

"Kelby? Sure I know that name. Moved into the old Applegate place." She gave him an address and directions to get there. He repeated them to make sure he got it right, then thanked her.

He started up his car and drove back the way he'd come. After one wrong turn he found the place. A long gravel driveway led to an old farmhouse, looked a million years old. Two-story wood frame, big old porch on two sides. Stone barn and other outbuildings behind. Nobody came out on the porch. No dog sounded the alert. As soon as he got out of the car he knew why those fucking birds were circling. Something was very dead out there somewhere, and the smell came riding in on the wind. He went up the porch steps and pounded on the door. No response.

A scrap of paper was caught between the door and the jamb. He yanked on it and tore off a corner. Piece of newsprint. He pounded again. Nothing. He hesitated, wanting to kick in the door. Or break a window. Maybe just wait right here. He looked up at the birds, big suckers flying around the barn. What was in there? He clattered down the porch steps, followed the stone path, and rolled the door open.

The stone barn would probably last forever. The house was going to crumble into dust one day. Showed what kind of priorities whoever built them had. The best for the cows, the rest for the people. Probably had a wife who was unfaithful. He stepped into the dim interior. Dust floated in the sunlight that slanted in. A car sat inside, California license plate. He pounded a fist on the hood. Kelby's! The son of a bitch who talked his wife into going away with him. Just the thought of what he'd do to the fucker made his heart pick up a beat. Car door unlocked. Maps in the glove box.

He clambered up the ladder to the loft, stared at a bunch of hay bales stacked in the corner, then climbed down and went back out in the sunshine. Behind the barn, a flagstone path took him toward a tall octagonal building. Jesus, must be forty feet high. He craned his neck looking up. Made of wood, crumbling with wear and neglect. He was headed down a slope toward trickling water when the heat got to him. Dragging in air that felt too wet to breathe, he went back to his car before he died of a goddamn heart attack. What he needed was to get out of this fucking heat and around a cold beer.

Now that he knew where she was, there was no hurry.

25

Cary felt eyes watching her all the time. Whenever she left the house, she had the sensation someone was following her. Never anyone she could spot. Ha. With her vision, she'd miss anyone who wasn't wearing flashing neon antlers, but the creepy feeling of eyes staring at her back went with every step. Returning after being out brought panic that Mitch had found her, was waiting inside. Even once she was in and had checked all the little slips of paper placed at doors and windows, she didn't feel safe.

She dreamed Mitch was chasing her through the cornfield. The wind slapped the blades in her face as she tried to escape. Thursday night she didn't fall asleep until around four, then slept so hard she had trouble pulling herself from bed in the morning. She showered and dressed like the natives, in shorts, T-shirt, and sandals. Stuffing two library books in a tote bag, she went out to the screened porch and looked around before descending the steps. Just that small exertion had her sweating and the T-shirt clinging to her back.

She wanted to go home. She wanted Arlette. Swallowing hard, she blinked rapidly. Tears wouldn't bring Arlette back. An awful smell blew in on the hot wind. For several days she'd been getting that smell. Deep in her heart, she knew what it was, but wouldn't allow her mind to accept. Today the smell was so strong she couldn't pretend. It was the smell of decay, death.

Slowly, she crossed the dirt road and approached the cornfield. Wind tossed the stalks and they rattled menacingly. Heart picking up speed, she took a step into the field. Strong smell. Not of decay, of corn and dust. Stalks rose three feet above her head, shutting out the light. She took small steps, squeezed around a plant and into the next row. With her poor vision all she saw was tossing blades leaden with fat ears of corn. After weaving through two more rows, she realized they didn't run in a straight line and she didn't know how to get out. Panic seized her. She ran. Dust rose with every footfall.

She stumbled and fell, breathing in fast gulps of dusty air. Stop, she told herself, just stop. Don't move, breathe in, breathe out. The sun, where is the sun? The house is east. Even though she'd only ventured a short distance, it took an hour, luck, and a strong sense of direction to find her way out. She needed another shower before she went to work. Because she was in a hurry, she dropped the shampoo bottle. It hit the floor, the top rolled off, and shampoo spread everywhere. After she cleaned that up, she couldn't find her shoes, then she did her thing of placing slips of paper in strategic places.

The sky was a cloudless blue that stretched forever, and the temperature was around ninety-five. People said this heat was unusual, that it got hot in August but not this hot. They also said September was usually worse. Stephanie, moving even faster than usual because Cary was late, gathered an armload of books, kissed her grandmother, said her last class had been cancelled and she'd be home early, then dashed off.

Elizabeth restlessly plucked at her nightgown. Probably felt as sticky and hot as Cary did. Cary gave her a sponge bath, and the entire time Elizabeth kept trying to say something. Occasionally her words were understandable, which was a good thing, and Cary encouraged her, but nagging worry pointed out that, if she could talk, she could tell the world about Cary's lies.

When Elizabeth made motions like she was writing, Cary found a pad and pencil. Pencil clutched awkwardly in a fist, Elizabeth drew a C and then an A. Fear squeezed into Cary's throat. Somehow Elizabeth had found her out, and was writing her name to let her know. Suddenly, the effort seemed too much and Elizabeth tossed the pencil. She slapped the pad with her palm. "Ca-ca . . ."

Cary simply stood there like a dummy. Elizabeth put a hand near her ear, thumb and little finger extended.

"Call?" Cary said. "You want to phone someone?"

Elizabeth stabbed a finger at Cary.

"You want me to call someone?"

Elizabeth nodded.

"Who do you want me to call?"

Elizabeth pointed to the bedside table and kept pointing until Cary brought out the pamphlet about the miniature horse. "You want me to call about this?" Cary said.

"Ca-Ca . . ." Elizabeth held a hand near her face, as though talking on the telephone. "Ca! Call!"

"Yes, okay, I will."

"Now!" Elizabeth clawed at Cary's hand and pointed to the telephone.

"I'll do it later. From home."

"Now!"

Cary didn't want to call about a horse that led around the blind. She didn't want the world to know she was blind. For some idiotic reason, she was ashamed. Which was stupid. It wasn't a punishment, she hadn't chosen to be blind. Given a choice, she'd ask for her sight back in a flash. A Seeing Eye dog was one thing. Noticeable maybe, but not bizarre. A horse? She'd attract attention. She didn't want people looking at her.

165

Elizabeth got so agitated, Cary punched in the number simply to quiet her. "Ronny Wells," a woman answered.

Cary said she was interested in the Leading the Way program. When asked her name, Cary hesitated, then said "Kelby Oliver." More lies. She'd run from Mitch and all the lies, and here she was still lying.

"Oh, right. You called a while back. You were inquiring for a friend?"

"Uh—no, actually . . ." How well did this woman know Kelby?

"I know you're taking care of Dr. Farley. When are you free to leave?" Then, like a snowball gathering speed as it rolled downhill, Ronny was saying she'd come by, pick her up, and bring her out to show her around.

When Cary hung up, Elizabeth gave her a nod of approval. Bath, hair brushed, fresh nightgown. Breakfast, coffee midmorning. While Elizabeth napped, Cary did laundry and worried what would happen when Ronny Wells got a look at her. Elizabeth woke restless again, and kept trying to say something.

"K-k-k-ke?" She clutched at Cary's arm with more strength than Cary thought possible.

"Kitchen? You hungry?"

Head shake. "K-k-k-k . . ."

"Cold? You want a blanket?" Trying to figure out what Elizabeth wanted to say was like playing charades.

Head shake. "K-k-k-ke—"

"Kind? Kitten?"

"K-ke-kel—"

"Kelby?" Tell her Kelby was missing, had disappeared and left behind her car, driver's license, and credit cards? Lie? Say Kelby had gone to visit a friend?

Suspicious brown eyes glared at her. "Wh-ere?"

"I don't know where she is."

Alarm flared in Elizabeth's face. "In t-t-tr-dan-g . . ."

While Cary was trying to figure that out, Stephanie came home and Ronny Wells drove up in a van with LEADING THE WAY painted on the sides.

"Hi. I'm Ronny Wells. Veronica, if you want to be formal." She was maybe sixty, trim, athletic-looking, with short salt-and-pepper hair and a nice smile.

"Kelby." Cary slipped into the passenger seat and waited to be called a liar.

"You know anything about horses?"

They have four legs and a tail? "Not a thing."

Ronny laughed. "Did Dr. Farley bully you into this? I've heard she has the force of a tornado."

Ronny had a bit of tornado force herself. Getting blind was one thing, stumbling around in the dark with a white cane, maybe even getting a dog, but Cary didn't want anything to do with horses.

East of town, Ronny turned onto a gravel road that led to a gateway with a large arched sign, LEADING THE WAY. Pastureland stretched away into the distance, with horses of all sizes, heads down, munching grass.

"They don't cost much to feed. About twenty dollars a year in grain and they mow your lawn to boot." Ronny drove up to a red barn with white trim, just like a magazine picture. She got out of the van, motioned for Cary to come with her, and slid open the large barn door. A small horse trotted up to greet her.

"This is Cinnamon Ginger." The horse was about two feet tall at the shoulder. Ronny patted its neck. "Her favorite snack is popcorn. Her favorite activity is watching television while she's eating it."

Cautiously Cary reached out, halfway expecting the animal to bite her. It looked up at her with the sweetest brown eyes and stretched its nose to touch her hand. She had never felt anything so velvety soft as this small horse's muzzle. Every negative thought she'd had got erased when she knelt to stroke the animal and it kissed her cheek. Her heart went all gooey. When she learned she had to be evaluated before she was accepted into the program, she was, suddenly and with great regret, sure she'd be rejected.

"First you get to walk around with an old hand at this guide business named Janus. She's led many candidates."

Ronny took her out to a corral where a small, black horse was tied to a rail, and told her to take the reins and harness. "Phase I, candidate evaluation."

Nervousness, stumbling, and saying left when she meant right, had Cary limp with worry and certain she'd failed miserably. Finally, just when Cary was so frazzled she was ready to give up, Ronny said, "Congratulations, you've passed the orientation and mobility skills. You now advance to Phase II, introductory training."

Cary hadn't been this relieved and proud when she completed her master's. Phase II would be spent in classrooms learning all about the care of horses. Feeding, grooming, and proper facilities for housing. She would learn voice commands and get tested to determine if she understood how signals were communicated though the harness and reins.

With her poor vision, Cary tried to take notes and wished she had a tape recorder. If she passed Phase II, she would become an apprentice handler. One of Ronny's assistants drove her home. Exhausted and exhilarated, Cary sat in the van, running through the voice commands. When she was dropped off at home, she checked the slip of paper in the doorway. It was torn. Had she done it? In her hurry, because she was late, had she accidently torn the scrap and not noticed?

26

Around seven Susan split for home, collected the newspaper from the front step, and glanced at the headlines. HEAT WAVE CONTINUES. NO END IN SIGHT. Tossing the paper on the living room couch, she turned on the window cooler. The temperature approached that of a tin hut in the desert. Her fever hovered about the same mark, her head pounded, she still couldn't hear out of her right ear, and she had a dinner date with Fran in an hour. Cool air rattled out in a steady stream and she let it blow against her sweaty face.

The record heat was taking its toll on everybody. Drivers were spilling out road rage at the stupidity of the other people behind the wheel, fights were taking place on school grounds, and stray burglars were finding easy access because home owners were leaving windows open at night in the hope of catching a stray breeze.

Priorities: first, kick off shoes; second, fill cat bowl; third, find Excedrin; fourth, fix tall Coke with lots of ice. She carried the glass to her office off the living room. The desk had piles nearly as high and just as untidy as her desk at work. That probably said something deeply psychological about her. She picked up a folder and waited for the necessary oomph to open it. The hour before she was to meet Fran at the Broken Cactus was slipping by. Fran thought they had Mexican food there. Ha!

Okay, this is ridiculous. Call and cancel, then go to bed. Before she could find the number, the phone rang. She glared at it. Any messenger with news that would drag her back to work was dead meat. When it rang again, she picked it up.

"You have to eat. It's too hot to cook. We'll eat fast," Fran said. "Those are all the replies to all the reasons why you can't join me for dinner."

"I feel lousy and I—"

"You have to eat."

"All I want to do is—"

"It's too hot to cook."

"I was going to say, all I want to do is go to bed."

"By yourself?"

"I thought I'd take Bach."

Fran gave a theatrical sigh. "That's another thing we have to talk about. Stand up this minute and walk out the door. I'll meet you there."

"No."

"It will be cool."

This was true. She wiped the sweat from her face, shut off the window cooler, and grabbed her shoulder bag.

Fran, seated in a corner booth, was right about one thing. It was wonderfully cool inside. Susan slid onto the bench across from her. Western-style gear decorated the walls, hats and spurs and boots and coiled riatas. A saddle, with a brightly colored blanket draped over it, rested on a window seat. A candle flickering in a brass holder was reflected in Fran's eyes. Leaning forward, Susan raised the candle and held it close to Fran. "You dyed your hair."

Instead of the normal glossy chestnut, her shoulder-length hair was now a silver blond. "New man in your life?" Every time Fran met somebody new she dyed her hair a different color.

"What about Osey?" The last Susan knew, Fran had cast a spell over him and turned his mind from police work to love. "If you broke his heart, or did anything that'll make him less efficient at work, I'll have to shoot you."

Fran smiled slyly. "He's very sweet, but very young. I've decided to return him to the wild." She hummed a phrase of "Born Free." "He is now a wiser and more skilled male."

"Do I have to spend the entire meal listening to you extol the virtues of this new man?"

"You do."

The waiter, dressed in tight black pants, with a white shirt half buttoned, and a red sash around his waist, came for their order. When he left Susan picked up her water glass and held it against her forehead.

Fran studied her. "You look like you haven't slept in weeks."

"That's about right."

"Why aren't you sleeping?"

"I keep having these dreams. Weird dreams."

"Tell me about them."

"What are you, my psychiatrist?"

"Aha! Juicy dreams. Tell all."

"Not juicy." Susan breathed out a long sigh. "Variations of the same theme. I'm walking somewhere isolated and I get this feeling of dread, something really bad is going to happen. Then I hear gunfire."

"Wow. You get shot?"

"I wake up before I find out what happens."

"Maybe you should see a therapist," Fran said softly. "It's probably unresolved issues from Dan's death."

It was four years since her husband had died. Sometimes she dreamed about him and struggled to remember his face clearly. "More likely fever." Susan took a sip of water, swallowing made her ears crackle. "So, tell me about this new man."

Fran had met Barry at her high school reunion. A physicist now. She vaguely remembered him and hadn't given him a glance, back then anyway. "He was kind of nerdy and I was more into flash."

"So, having matured, you can see the goodness in nerdy."

"Correct."

Fran talked, Susan listened. The attractions of the new man were many, but Susan heard very little of them. Clogged ears, clink of silverware, hum of conversation.

". . . witness protection . . ."

"What?" Susan looked up.

Fran grinned. "I thought that might get your attention."

"You had my attention."

"Yeah, right. I saw your eyes glaze over."

"That was fever. What's this about witness protection?"

"I asked if the Witness Protection Program set somebody up here."

"Why did you ask that?"

Fran's eyes widened. "So it's true? What is she hiding from? Mafia?"

"Have you been watching television again?"

"What else do I have to do? With everybody booking flights and making hotel reservations on their computers, or worried about terrorists, who needs a travel agent? I'm thinking of opening a soup-and-sandwich place. And don't think you're leading me away from the topic. Where did she come from, and why does she need protections?"

"Fran, I don't have the slightest idea what you're talking about."

Fran tore off a chunk of bread, put a minuscule dab of butter on it, and bit off one end. "Come on, you can tell me."

Susan sighed. Her headache was getting worse and, dearly as she loved Fran, right now all she wanted was to go home and lie down. The noise in the restaurant was acting like a hammer against her temples.

"First, the idea of witness protection is to *protect the witness*.

Nobody except those directly involved know anything about anything. Nobody else knows anything. That translates to nobody knows anything. So, if there were such a thing as a person dropped here with a new identity, nobody would be told about it. Not even me, the chief of police of this town."

"Wow, I've never heard you so muddled. You must really be sick."

"I told you I was. Why are you talking about witness protection?"

"Debbie at the library. She told me someone named Kelby Oliver moved in practically in the middle of the night. Who does that, unless they have something to hide? She rarely left the house. Hardly anybody ever saw her. She could have been murdered in her bed for all anybody knew. Neighbors came by to drop off their cakes and casseroles like they do. Have you noticed they always do that when somebody new moves in or somebody dies? Arrivals and departures."

"Fran, what are you talking about?"

The waiter came up with a basket of hush puppies. When he left, Fran said, "I'm telling you it's weird. Here's this woman who barely left the house. Then all of a sudden, she's out walking around, she went in one day and got a library card, and not only that, but she got a job."

"A job." Eyes at half-mast, Susan stared at her friend. "From this you come up with witness protection?"

"She was hiding, Susan. She had everything delivered, made the delivery folks just leave stuff on the porch, and wouldn't open the door until they left. And now she's out prancing around. It's like she's a totally different person."

"Maybe she's shy."

Fran snorted. "Nobody's that shy."

"Busy moving in. Unpacking."

"Oh, right. And she didn't want the neighbors to see her empty boxes."

The waiter brought salads and Fran picked up her fork and stabbed a lettuce leaf. "Debbie also said she has checked out a lot of books."

"She checked out books from the library," Susan said. "That *is* weird."

"A whole bunch of books, and Debbie said she can barely see." Fran sat back as though she'd just presented the closing argument.

The food arrived, but Susan could barely taste it, and swallowing hurt her throat. Fran took pity on her, told her to go home, they'd have dinner again another time.

At just after nine, temperature still blisteringly hot, Susan got in the pickup. At home, she spotted a forlorn figure trudging up the street. She pulled into her driveway.

"Hey, Jen, where you headed?"

"Home."

"Want to come in for a minute?"

Jen shook her head.

"You got me worried, kiddo. What's it going to take to get you to talk? I'm ready for bribery here. I'm willing to go all the way to . . . six dollars?"

Jen gave her a withering look. "I'm okay."

"I'm glad to hear it. Tell me what's been bothering you. Are your classes difficult?" That earned Susan another withering glance. She couldn't imagine the classes would be more than Jen could handle. Jen liked school, she was smart.

"Would you shoot somebody for me?"

Susan slid from the pickup. "That bad, huh?" she said softly.

"I hate school. I want to transfer to somewhere else."

"Why? School has barely started. All your friends go—"

"I don't have any friends."

"What about Sheila?"

"We were friends when I was helping her with her math. Now all she does is whisper about me and send e-mail." Jen picked at a mosquito bite on her arm.

"What is she whispering?"

"How ugly I am and stuck-up, and think I'm so smart and always dress like a dork, and I'm crazy like Grandpa. They pretend they have a rifle and yell stuff like 'shoot those Nazis.' He can't help it. He's sick. Mom says because he was tortured during the war. And they say my daddy was forced to leave because he—did things to me, and . . ."

She choked and swallowed hard. "And he didn't—he never— Mom just wanted—they just got a divorce and . . ."

Susan sat on the porch steps and patted the spot beside her. Somewhat to her surprise, Jen flopped down on the step below.

"Sheila took a picture of me when I was changing for gym class, only she put my face on this gross fat body and sent it to everybody, and now nobody will talk to me. And she says I smell bad because I never take a bath, and it's not true—I take a bath every day—and they throw things at me in the restrooms, and—"

"Throw things? Who? What things?" Now that, Susan thought, she could do something about.

"Paper towels and used tampons and stuff."

"I'll stop it."

"*No!*" Jen took a breath and blew her nose. "You'll only make it worse."

"But Jen—"

"I just want to go away. Another school, someplace where she won't be."

"We can't let her get away with what she's doing." Susan didn't know exactly how she could stop these kids, but she was so angry she wanted to march into the school, haul the girl out of class, shake her, and yell in her face. "Where would you go?"

Jen shrugged. "Mom says I can't transfer. She can't afford it and . . ." Her voice trailed off into hopelessness.

Susan didn't think much of Jen's mom, but she didn't ever want to say anything negative about her. "Why is Sheila doing this?"

"They just hate me. They talk about me and laugh and bump into me in the halls and drop disgusting stuff on my lunch and shove me and won't let me out of the bathroom . . . And I thought Sheila was my friend and she—" Jen fiercely blew her nose.

"I'll talk to them. I'll—"

"You'll only make it worse. There's nothing anybody can do." Abruptly, she popped up. "I gotta go."

Watching Jen sling her backpack over her shoulder, Susan thought of those children who collect weapons and climb up the water tower. She ached for someone to talk to, someone all wise, all knowing, who could tell her what to do about Jen.

When Susan woke up in the morning, her throat was so scratchy it hurt to drink coffee. Instead of heading straight to work, she took a detour to the Barrington Medical Building and went up to Dr. Eckhard's office. She told the receptionist she would appreciate it if the doctor could see her for a few minutes. The receptionist slipped her in ahead of the first patient.

"Back so soon?" China said. "I figured I wouldn't see you again until Christmas. Ear still bothering you?"

"Yes, but that's not why I came."

Between and around the doctor looking in her ears and checking her throat and making her say "ah," Susan told her about Jen.

"I'm not a psychiatrist," China said. "It's a volatile situation and, unfortunately, it happens often. Some schools are trying sensitivity training, but I don't know that it's effective."

"What can I do to help this child?"

China smiled. "What? You want to march in there and smack a few kids?"

"Oh yeah."

She sighed. "The child is right. There's not much you can do. These kids are deliberately doing this. That kind of behavior is almost impossible to change. If it were just bigotry or thoughtlessly sexist, then maybe educating the kid might help. But with this situation, the kids know what they're doing. They get off on tormenting and seeing just how miserable they can make the life of the victim."

"I vaguely know the child who apparently started this whole thing, and she seems like just another sweet kid. She's attractive, has friends, doesn't knock off convenience stores on weekends."

"There you are. This is a girl who takes deliberate steps to cause pain. And trying to intervene will more than likely make it worse."

"Jen wants to transfer to another school."

"Much as I hate to say it, from the little I know, she's right. It goes against the grain. It's wrong, morally, ethically, and satisfactorily, but simply removing her from the situation is the way to go."

"Why is the other girl doing this?"

China sighed. "Who knows? Maybe something as trivial as a boy she likes gave Jen a smile. A boy in the same situation would go over and beat up on the smile recipient; girls are taught not to fight. They have to achieve results in other ways. This is one that works. And very effectively, too."

"Like the Amish and their shunning? Once you've become an object of shunning, you're an outcast forever?"

"Exactly." China wrote a prescription for newer and stronger and, no doubt, more expensive antibiotics.

Susan stuck the prescription in her shoulder bag. "What do I do to help?"

"Be ready to pick up the pieces."

27

Help! Help me!

Joe rolled out of bed and hit the floor ready to run.

Sleep-fogged, he looked around, then scrubbed his hands over his face. Motel room, like all the others, only this one was special. This was in the town he'd traveled so far to reach. The red digits on the clock read two minutes past four.

Easing aside the curtain, he looked out at the parking lot and then up at the stars glittering in the night sky. In the bathroom, he plugged in the pot to heat water and dunked in a coffee bag. He sat in the easy chair and sipped bitter black coffee.

She would suffer for what she did.

28

$\mathcal{S}$usan squinted bleary-eyed at the reports she needed to read and initial. The stack was so high it teetered. Her ears throbbed, her head pounded. All she wanted to do was rest her head on the desk and go to sleep. Screw it. She pushed herself back, grabbed her shoulder bag from the bottom desk drawer, fumbled for the keys, and told Marilee she'd see her tomorrow.

When Susan got home, she fed Perissa the cat and put a Vivaldi concerti on the CD player. That activity so exhausted her she pushed the window air conditioner up to high, stretched out on the couch, and let the music ripple over her like soft river water. Sleep took her to a wide, deserted beach, a place she'd been many times before, a gray world of gray sand, gray clouds, and a gray ocean. Footprints, deep, planted by a large man, led a trail along the edge of the water. She followed them. Her sunglasses were so dark she could barely see. Dread clutched at her throat.

"Susan."

At the sound of her name she tried to turn, but her feet were tangled in fish-net. By twisting her neck, she saw a black silhouette standing against the sun. The voice was not one she recognized. "Do you know me?"

"I've always known you."

"What do you want?"

"You're going the wrong way."

She changed direction and was walking through a forest, dread so thick it choked her. Ahead, a hunter raised an axe and brought it down against a fallen log. *Thud.* Axe sounded dull, it needed to be sharpened.

Thud. She ran toward him and saw it was a woman on the ground. "What happened?"

"She's been shot."

"How bad?"

The hunter just looked at her. She knelt and turned the woman and stared at her own face, her body lying on leaves soaked in blood.

"Susan?" With heart-pounding confusion, she woke and tried to make sense of continuing thuds. Someone knocking. She dragged herself to the kitchen and opened the door.

Jen stood there, looking miserable. "Can I come in?"

"Sure, Jen. You want something to drink? A Coke, or some tea?"

"No, thanks."

Susan poured a glass of orange juice and they went to the living room. She turned off Vivaldi, dropped to the couch and took a swallow of juice. Jen sat on the hearth.

"Are you hungry?" Susan asked. Her throat hurt, and every time she swallowed her ears made crackling noises.

Jen grinned. It lifted Susan's heart to see it, that cocky grin that said we both know you're a lousy cook.

"I could order a pizza," Susan said.

Jen shook her head. "Would you do something for me?"

"Of course, Jen."

"Would you talk to my mother?"

Oh dear. Jen's mother didn't like Susan and wouldn't welcome a chat about the weather, let alone anything to do with her daughter. "What do you want me to talk to her about?"

Jen took in a chestful of air. "Tell her I need to change schools."

The care and feeding of adolescents was way beyond Susan's ability. "Well, Jen, this is probably something you should discuss with her. I'm not sure—"

"You said you'd help me." Eyes accusing.

"Yes, but I'm not sure—"

"You already said that." Jen scratched at a hole in the knee of her jeans. "I hate school. I hate the teachers. I hate Sheila and Debby and Tiffany and everybody!" Her voice rose on each name. "They're stupid and hateful and nothing but bullies!"

"Oh, Jen. Nobody has a right to bully you. They—"

"They don't need the right, they just do it."

"I can do something about it. I can—"

Jen was shaking her head. "You'll just make it worse." Tears spilled over and trickled down her face.

Susan got up and gathered Jen in her arms. She spoke soft murmured words of sympathy. The noisy sobs grew quieter and quieter, then stopped on a short, fast breath. With a forefinger, Susan tipped up Jen's chin and looked into her miserable face. "Why do you want me to talk to your mom?"

"You can make her understand. She says it's just stupid kid stuff and it'll blow over. But it won't!" Jen clenched a fist. "It's never going to stop."

"I'll send an officer to the school. I'll—"

"No! That'll just make it worse. They'll call me an informant and say I'm a rat for squealing. No!"

"Okay. Calm down. I won't."

"I want you to talk to my mom."

Oh, Jen, I'm afraid, your mom won't listen to me. "Sure," she said. "I'll do that."

"Promise?"

"I promise."

On Friday Susan didn't feel any better, headache, scratchy throat, clogged ears. It all seemed a reason to stay in bed. Perissa the cat pounced on her feet. When that got no action, she leaped to the top of the tall chest and started knocking off items, a small marble seal, a framed snapshot of her dead husband, her watch. Susan hauled ass out of bed and shook dried food in the cat's bowl. She showered, dressed, skipped breakfast, and went straight to the coffeepot when she got to the department. The hot liquid hit her sore throat with teeth. She persevered.

At eleven she told Hazel she was taking an early lunch and drove to Walnut Street to talk with Jen's mom. Terry was not glad to see her, but she did open the door and murmur an invitation to come in.

"Is it about Dad? He hasn't sneaked away again, has he?" Terry was a woman who spent a lot of time on her appearance. Her light brown hair had been given warm, blondish highlights, her makeup was carefully applied. Even in the heat, when most people were wearing shorts and T-shirts, she had on a pair of pale green tailored pants with a white blouse.

"No." Animosity toward Susan was always present. Terry resented the friendship with Jen. With Terry's remarriage, her attitude had softened, but Susan was under no illusion that the woman would welcome any suggestions about her daughter.

"Would you like some coffee? It's already made."

Susan hesitated, then said she'd love some. The offer maybe meant Terry felt slightly less hostile and there maybe was a small chance she'd listen. She led the way to a newly remodeled kitchen, cabinets shiny-new, countertops black-and-brown-speckled granite with sparkly flecks.

"You've done a lot of work," Susan said.

Terry beamed. "Isn't it great?" She prattled on about the plans she had for the family room, and when that was finished the plans for the Jen's room.

"I know something's bothering her right now." Terry got out two china cups and saucers, set them on the table, and poured coffee. She handed a cup to Susan, sat down across the table, and picked up the other cup, holding it between the fingers of both hands.

"She's not happy." Susan didn't know how to proceed here. If she pushed, Terry would probably get stubbornly resistant.

"Yeah. She's in a squabble with some friends. You know how kids are."

"I think it's more than a squabble. She's being picked on at school. From what I can gather, it's gotten pretty bad."

"They'll work it out."

"I'm not sure that's true." Susan wondered if statistics would sway her, the appalling number of teenage suicides, children who had been in the situation Jen was in and didn't survive. "Jen is unhappy where she is. A change in schools would—"

"They're kids," Terry said. "Kids get in fights. I can't go running down to school every time Jennifer has a spat with a friend. She has to learn how to handle her own problems. It's part of growing up."

"She's very unhappy," Susan repeated. "Her schoolwork is suffering. She hates to go to school because she—"

Terry threw up her hands. "Well, what does she expect me to do? Trot down there and threaten to tell their parents?"

"That's probably the last thing she'd like you to do. She wants to transfer to a different school."

"It's out of the question. She can't be allowed to run from a fight. If she doesn't learn to stand up for herself now, she never will, and she'll be running away all her life."

"These kids are making her life miserable. It would—" Susan caught herself and substituted, "*might* be a good idea to let her transfer and—"

"That would be letting them win."

"It's not a question of winning, it's a question of what's best for Jen. If—"

"I know what's best for my daughter," Terry snapped.

Right. This was more or less what Susan expected. Drop it for now. Dig up more info on what's happening at school. Maybe do something.

"Besides," Terry said, "we can't afford a private school."

But they could afford to remodel the house. Some things were more important than others. Susan thanked Terry for the coffee and took herself out before she said something nasty to the mother of the girl she was trying to help.

29

While Ida was patrolling the east end of town, she made a swing out to Kelby Oliver's house. Creepy, the house, sitting across the road from the cornfield like it did, the birds weren't flying. Why not? They'd eaten everything? Somebody removed the body? Leaving her car on the gravel driveway, she trudged across the dirt road to the edge of the field, determined to go in and see what was there. After only a few steps of squeezing along between stalks, her resolve weakened. The huge stalks towered over her. The smell of corn, the dust kicked up by her footsteps, and the heat were stifling.

When she'd first come here, she'd read an article in the local paper about cornfields made into mazes. Apparently, they were intricate and beautiful, but what was the point? Only someone in a low-flying plane could see them. Parties were held where people could go in and try to find their way out. Mostly, guides had to round them up and bring them out. How embarrassing would that be? She could see the headline: HAMPSTEAD'S NEWEST COP LOST IN ALIEN CORN. Under the pervasive scent of corn lay a heavy smell of decay. She looked up at the endless blue sky. Something somewhere inside the field had drawn the carrion birds, but she wasn't going to find out anything standing here.

Fighting her way past the leaves or fronds or whatever they were called, she got back to the dirt road and immediately felt that itchy feeling between her shoulder blades of being watched. Looking around, she realized how isolated this house was. Trees—she had no idea what kind—grew across the rear. The grass had died from the heat. She wiped the sweat off her face with a handkerchief and stuck it in her pocket.

Shielding her eyes, she looked at the buildings behind the barn. She went to the house, climbed the porch steps, and rapped on the door. No answer. Kelby wasn't home, or wasn't coming to the door. The edginess of wanting to help somebody who doesn't want your help left Ida frustrated. She walked to the back and looked in the screen porch. Two wicker chairs, a small table, and an old wooden rocker. The screen door was unlatched.

Taking in a breath of hot sticky air, she followed the flagstone path to the barn. A glance over her shoulder, and she rolled the big door open. Dust suspended in the air. A car. Honda, newish. Smiley face drawn in the dust on the rear window. She memorized the license plate number. The air smelled musty, like old hay. Not that she knew what old hay smelled like. The loft held bales of it. Who owned this place before Kelby moved in? She'd ask Osey.

Outside, she squinted in the bright sunshine, and followed the path past a tractor shed, chicken coop, another small shed, and came to an octagonal silo—crumbling wood and maybe forty feet high. Sometimes, according to Osey, when farmers sold out, they simply left the grain inside. She wondered if grain left in this one had drawn the big blackbirds. He also told her rats got in to eat the grain and snakes got in to eat the rats. She decided to leave the snakes and rats and grain to their own business and get back to hers.

A smell of decay was everywhere, elusive. The wind, blowing strong, scattered the scent to the corners of everywhere, and made getting a fix on it impossible. On the far side of the silo, she found it, the source of the smell. Animal carcass, probably a calf from the size, covered with squirming maggots. The path continued to a grove of trees. It angled down the slope to a creek with an old wooden bridge. Trickling water, one of those sounds that erased words from your mind, flowed under the bridge. She made her way down the bank and squatted on a large boulder.

The sound of a car broke the spell. Jumping up, she clambered up the bank and ran along the path. Just as she rounded the corner toward the front of the house, she saw the car disappear down the drive and turn right onto the road. She sprinted toward the road, but she was too late to get more than a glimpse of the driver. Male, dark hair. The car was black, Honda or Camry maybe. How long had she sat by the creek soothing her spirit?

When she went back to the patrol car, she spotted the bouquet on the porch and trotted up the steps. A dozen red roses in a vase with a big, red bow. Boyfriend? Kelby's problem? The reason she was so terrified? A small white envelope was stuck in the bow. Open the card and see who sent the flowers. What could it hurt? Nobody would know. Her evil twin urged her to see what the card said. She looked at it, sighed, and rose to her feet. Okay, she was going to leave it alone, but she had noticed the name of the florist. No harm in finding out who bought the roses.

She parked at Angelo's Newspapers and Magazines and went in to get something cold to drink. From the refrigerated case, she pulled a Coke and took it to the counter.

"Miss Ida. Sweet as apple cida." Angelo, midsixties with cropped gray hair, came from the back.

"If you don't stop calling me that I might have to arrest you."

"For you it is free."

Ida dropped a five on the counter. "Forget it. You think I want to go through life beholden to the likes of you?"

"Aw, if only . . ." He placed his hand on his heart, took the bill, dropped it in the cash drawer, and handed her the change. "So, what's up, Miss Ida?"

"Just thirsty." She popped the tab and took a sip.

"Naw. I know you, you got questions on your mind. What is it this time?"

Actually, she had come in just for a Coke, but as long as he expected questions. "You know Kelby Oliver? She's not been here long."

"Sure I know her. She was just here. Stopped in on her way home from work. Nice lady."

"You say that about all the ladies."

"And why not?" He smiled. "It's true." He gave Ida a shrewd look. "And why are you asking about her? Is she in trouble?"

Ida shrugged. "She's new in town. Just wondered about her. Cops, you know. Always wondering."

"Oh, sure, of course. Yeah, you wonder." He made a soft snort. "I used to deliver her newspapers when she first moved here. *San Francisco Chronicle* and *Oakland Tribune*. Told us to just leave them on her porch. Wouldn't even open the door. Thought that was kind of strange, but people have their ways."

"You ever see anybody with her?"

"Nope. Never even saw her till she started working over there for Dr. Farley. She's started stopping in and buying the papers now. She in any trouble?"

"Not that I know of. Why?"

"You're not the first person to ask about her."

"Who else was asking?"

"Some man. Wanted to know her name, where she lived."

"You tell him?"

"Why would I talk about my customers?"

"What'd he look like?" *I knew it*, Ida thought. Kelby is in some kind of trouble. This man is trying to find her. The description was so vague it could have been any male. Late forties, thin, tired.

188

Ida wanted to call Kelby's sister and see what the sister knew. What could it hurt to just call and talk? Maybe ask why Kelby didn't wear glasses when she obviously had a vision problem, find out why she was so terrified.

30

*H*ouse key in hand, Cary turned a complete circle in small increments, dipping and tipping her head, trying to catch movement with her small spot of sight. Anybody watching would think she'd lost her mind. There were so many hiding places. The barn, two small outbuildings, the trees, the cornfield. Oh, God, the cornfield. Wind tossed the stalks and kicked up dust, just like footfalls from a person walking through. Grit blew in her face and brought with it the smell of corn and the sickly sweet odor of decay.

Heart tripping in a drum roll, she tried the door. Still locked. *He could have kicked in the back door or broken a window.* She went around the house, peering at windows, bobbing her head like an old lady with new bifocals. Windows all seemed okay from her position on the ground. The rear door was still locked. With a shaky hand, she unlocked it. The kitchen was just as she'd left it that morning.

It was nearly seven and still stifling hot, but she went through the house checking locks. She left the windows closed. All the slips of paper she'd placed in strategic places were just where she'd put them. Except the torn one in the front door. She pulled in a shaky breath.

Despair settled over her like a dirty cotton blanket. She couldn't breathe, or fight her way out. She'd fled halfway across the country and nothing had changed. He was still terrifying her. No matter what she did, she couldn't get free. She might as well just give in now, he was going to win, no matter how hard she fought.

The clock on the wall ticked, the wind moaned, and her heart beat louder than both. Give up. She'd never get away. Why prolong her terror? Why not just open the door and yell, "Come and get me!"

A shot splintered through her fright. *Mitch! Oh my God!* Wildly, she looked around for some place to hide. Maybe she should run. Out the kitchen door. *She could hide in the cornfield—*

A fist pounded on the door.

Ida was rolling through campus when dispatch sent her to investigate reports of a gunshot. Overheads flickering, she drove to the Oliver place and banged on the door.

"Ms. Oliver?"

It took the woman so long to respond that Ida had adrenaline ready to charge, in case Kelby had been shot. When Kelby finally opened the door, Ida pushed through.

"Are you all right?"

"Fine," Kelby said. "Just fine."

She didn't look fine, Ida thought. She looked the color of cooked noodles, and about as sturdy. "We got a report of a shot fired. You hear a shot?"

Kelby nodded. "A shot, yes."

"Who fired it?"

A weird expression came over Kelby's face. Ida didn't know what it meant. Guilt? Fear? "Do you own a gun, Ms. Oliver?"

"No. I—no. I don't own a gun."

"Uh-huh." Then why look so guilty?

"A man was seen here earlier." Ida didn't mention she was the one doing the seeing and she'd only seen him driving away. She wasn't even positive he'd been here. "I want to make sure nothing is missing."

"What did he look like?" Kelby was nearly trembling with terror. Her eyes didn't seem to be tracking either.

Ida repeated the vague description she'd gotten from the clerk at the flower shop. "Sound like someone you know?"

Kelby shook her head.

Ida couldn't tell whether or not she was lying, but the description was so vague it could be anybody. "I'll check out the house. Make sure everything is all right."

"That's not necessary. I—"

Ida was already moving. With Cary like a shadow behind her, Ida went up stairs, looked in all three rooms, went down to the basement and shined her flashlight into dim corners. Something was definitely not right here, but she couldn't see anything that pointed at what it was.

She fished out a business card, told Kelby to call if she needed anything, and opened the door to leave. A big blackbird oozed blood on the porch steps. She squatted over it. Dead, apparently shot. She retrieved an evidence bag from the car, scooped in the bird, and threw it in the trunk with the riot gear. By that time the scorching sun was finally settling down behind the low hills, painting the horizon vivid colors of orange and pink and purple.

As night slowly crept in over the shreds of daylight, Ida made the rounds of neighbors. The closest weren't all that close, the equivalent of a city block spread between Kelby's house and the nearest. Several people heard the shot, but no one had seen anything, or anybody suspicious. Typical.

They didn't seem to know all that much about Kelby either, and that struck Ida as odd. They only knew someone had moved in because they saw the moving van, then lights and the delivery van from

Erle's Market bringing groceries. That was six months ago. When they knocked they got no answer. They watched her drive by now and then, but she never stopped to talk or just be friendly. Lately, she'd changed. Went by on foot sometimes now, always looking around, up and down, like she thinks somebody's hiding in the trees, or she isn't quite all there.

Pearl Wyatt gave Ida the opinion that Kelby was stuck-up. Several times Pearl had waved and Kelby ignored her. The time Pearl made a cake and carried it all the way over there, Kelby wouldn't even answer the door.

"Well that did it, let me tell you. See if I bake that woman any more cakes!" She invited Ida in out of the heat. The house was so cool goose bumps popped up on Ida's sweaty skin.

"Isn't this weather just something awful? I don't know when we had such a hot spell for such a long time. Have a seat, I'll get us something cold to drink." Pearl bustled off to the kitchen, a middle-aged woman, somewhat overweight, who seemed pleased to have company. Pictures of small children—grandchildren, Ida assumed—lined the mantle. An embroidered plaque hung by the door asking God to bless this house and watch over all who lived here. Ida sat on the couch and leaned against the brightly colored Afghan spread over the back.

Pearl returned with two tall glasses of lemonade and handed one to Ida, then plopped down into an easy chair. "I heard the shot. Did old man Lundstrom get away again? Crazy old coot. They really ought to lock him up. He was over that way the last time he got out."

Pearl shook her head. "I saw her—Kelby, you know—lugging stuff around over there. Had a mind to go and see if she needed a hand." After a hefty swallow of lemonade, she went on. "Didn't see her for three or four days or so afterward. I figured he probably scared her to death with all his whoopin' and hollerin' and carryin' on about Nazis."

"Is she a good neighbor?"

Pearl gave a ladylike humph. "Well, doesn't cause any trouble, you know. I introduced myself when she moved in. But let me tell you, there was something real sneaky about her moving in like she did. Middle of the night. Had my own eye on that property, I don't mind telling you. Wanted it for my son. Just waiting till that skinflint Otis came down in price."

Pearl folded her arms across her ample bosom. "And before I know it, she swoops in and grabs it. I was fit to be tied. But what do you expect? She's from Caly-forn-ya."

She shook her head at the unfairness of it all. "That place would have been perfect for Al, and there that woman just goes and snaps it up from right under my nose."

A loss that still rankled.

"I heard she's taking care of Dr. Farley now." Pearl took a swallow of lemonade. "Darla Cleary, over at Erle's Market, told me. Did you know she had a stroke?"

Ida looked interested and Pearl kept going. "I didn't talk to Kelby but the one time. Just seemed to want to be by herself. I see her walking by almost every day now."

"Does she get many visitors?"

"Not that I've seen. I just wonder why she's walking in this heat instead of driving. Once or twice I started to go out and ask if the car broke down and did she need a ride, but she just waved and kept on. So, I guess she didn't want anything."

Ida thanked her for the lemonade and went out to the cruiser. Why did somebody who hid out in the house for six months suddenly start showing herself?

Because the reason for hiding was over. She was grieving over some loss and couldn't face socializing. She was a recluse who didn't want to encourage neighbors. Coming from California, she didn't like the political climate of conservative Kansas. Coming from California, she was afraid a neighbor would ask if she'd found a spiritual home yet.

Or she'd thought the danger was over.

After getting the name of the Realtor from Pearl, Ida couldn't see any harm in paying him a visit. How could asking questions get her in trouble? Laverty Realtors was a husband-and-wife team with an office on Fourth Street. Rich Laverty greeted her with a smile, like she was a real person with real money who wanted to buy a house. What a joke! Her biggest hope was to keep her job so she could make car payments.

"If I can't interest you in a property," Rich scooted back his desk chair, "what can I do for you?" Round, ruddy face with beginning jowls, putting on weight through the middle. Wiry, reddish hair sprinkled with gray.

"The house you sold out by the cornfield."

He nodded. "Applegate place. It's the original farmhouse, you know. Generations of Applegates farmed that land."

Ida knew that Laverty, like a number of people in Hampstead, came from a farming family that no longer farmed. He shook his head sadly. "Farming's never going to be the same. Small farmers are going out of business right and left. It's just too damn much."

"I know a lot of farms are in trouble." Ida sat in a wheeled armchair that was so comfortable she wondered if she could take it with her.

"An understatement. Farmers are trying to sell land. Neighboring farmers don't want it, they can't afford it. Farmers are throwing in the towel. They just can't hack it, or they're going bankrupt."

"It's a sad thing," Ida said. Osey had talked about this as though it was a personal tragedy. Pasture left to grow weeds. In a generation or two, even the landscape will change. The prairie will be lost.

"Tell you the truth, I didn't think that place would ever sell. The house isn't much, and it's way the hell out, isolated and right by that damn cornfield. You can smell the damn corn all the time until the combines come in to harvest. Which should be any day now. They're late this year."

"Something about it appealed to Ms. Oliver," Ida said. "What was it she liked about the place? The isolation?"

"Beats me. I never even met the woman who bought it."

"You never met her? Didn't you sell her the place? Oh, you mean Hattie handled this one."

"Nope, it was me. Only sale I ever made where I never met the buyer." He let his chair tilt back with a squeak. "Say, would you like some iced tea? I can rustle us up some real quick."

"No, thanks. Just tell me how you can sell a house without ever meeting the buyer."

"The Internet. We've been doing that a bit lately. Keep up with the times, you know. We stuck in a picture of that sucker, with all the particulars, on our Web site and, by God, if it didn't pay off. She's the first, mind. But hell, one's all you need, right?"

"Right," Ida said. "Kelby saw the information and . . . ?"

"Yep. Sent me a fax, asked if it was still available. Wanted more pictures. I fired them off. She decided she wanted it. Didn't even quibble over price. Just went with the asking price. I faxed her a contract, she signed and zipped it back by overnight mail."

"Didn't you think that was odd?"

"Hell, Ida, I've been in this business for years. Nothing anybody does makes me think it's odd. There was a little more to it. All kinds of papers back and forth. Inspections, permission for small plumbing repair, stuff like that, all by fax and phone and overnight mail. I did talk with her on the phone. Seemed like a nice woman."

"Did she tell you why she wanted to move here?"

"Nope. And I didn't ask."

"What did she like about the house that made her want to buy it?"

"I didn't ask that either. It's a real personal thing, buying a house. One place just speaks to a person, you know? No rhyme nor reason most of the time."

"You must have seen her when she picked up the keys."

"Not then either. She opened an account at First National on Main Street, had money transferred. She had me make arrangements for her to pick up the keys there. She even asked me to have somebody available to open the house when her furniture arrived. Did that myself. Stood on the porch and unlocked the door for the movers."

Ida thanked him, said if she was ever in the position of being able to afford a house she'd call him, and left, convinced Kelby was running from something, or hiding from something. Or someone. Or she had mental problems. After her shift, Ida went home to the apartment at Vermont and Sixth Street. Two bedrooms and one bath. Second story of an old house with a steep peaked roof. Her living room ceiling went from seven feet at the walls to fourteen feet in the center. The downstairs half of the house was occupied by two guys, a doctor and a lawyer who were rarely home.

She peeled off her uniform and put on a pair of shorts and a T-shirt. This business of not returning calls from a frantic sister was something else that didn't sit right. Of course, she didn't know the situation, and it could be that one sister did something unforgivable and the other one wanted nothing further to do with her. Or something like that. Even she got twisted up in the pronouns, but there was something hinky here and her mind wouldn't let it alone. Even as a kid, she had to pick at knots and untangle them. This was the same. If it didn't make sense, she wanted to know why. Generally, if you figured out the why, the whole thing unraveled and it made some kind of sense, although sometimes weird.

Ida got down the tallest glass in her kitchen, filled it with ice, and poured in Coke from a liter bottle. She shoved the bottle back into her almost empty refrigerator and went to the living room where she'd set up her desk with her computer. Okay. After placing the fan so it would blow directly on her and glugging down a few good swallows, she turned on her computer and searched for whatever she could find under the name Kelby Oliver.

Name, address, and phone number for Berkeley, California. Insurance broker. Divorced. No children that Ida could find. She made a note of address and phone number and kept searching. After three hours, she sat back, rubbed her eyes, and stood up to refill her glass. Kelby had served jury duty on the Lily Farmer case, a young woman raped, beaten, and murdered. The suspect was found guilty and sentenced to prison with no possibility of parole.

Was this connected with Kelby's fear? Did she have doubts about the man's guilt? Feel they had convicted an innocent man? Was he innocent? The guilty man still out there? Could that be what Kelby was afraid of?

It didn't strike Ida as the answer. Kelby was all the time looking over her shoulder, like somebody was coming after her. The guy who committed the murder was behind bars in California, not in Kansas chasing her down. If he was innocent, the guilty party would have gotten away with murder, counting his lucky stars. And why had she moved here? Bought a house without even seeing it, except for pictures on the Internet, moved in and kept to herself. Had her groceries delivered, didn't talk with the neighbors. That said the woman was hiding. From what? Or whom?

Although, Ida might understand Kelby hiding from Pearl. Especially Pearl, mad because she had lost property waiting for the seller to get more desperate and reduce the price.

Something here that Ida was missing. Another hour at the computer didn't get her nearer an explanation. She picked up her phone and dialed Kelby's California number, got an intercept and the recording that the number was no longer in service. She tried information in Hampstead and found out the local number was unlisted. The sister's name was Faye. What was the last name? How the heck was Ida going to find it?

She took a long swallow of the Coke. Well, there was the firm where Kelby had worked. Personnel records might have next of kin. Yeah, but that could get her in serious trouble. She considered the pros and cons. The cons definitely outweighed the pros. What the heck.

By the time she got what she was after, the Coke was down to tiny slivers of ice in a melted puddle. She dumped it in the sink and looked at her watch. Nearly four A.M. What time was it in Pennsylvania? Two hours later? Too early to call. Changing the angle of the fan, she lay on the couch and closed her eyes and slept for three hours. Eyelids at half-mast, she punched in the number for Faye Turney. A woman answered, said she was Faye when Ida asked. Ida explained she was a police officer.

"Oh my God. I knew it. Something's happened."

"Ma'am?"

"I felt it in my bones that something was wrong. I just knew she—"

"Ma'am, if I could just—"

"Oh my God, what was it? Did he kill her?"

"Who?"

"Kelby! Isn't that why you called me? To tell me she's been hurt? Or worse?"

"Nothing's happened to her, ma'am. You called and asked us to check on her."

"Yes, yes. And you said she was all right. Was that a lie? Has she been in trouble all along?"

"Ma'am, if you would just calm down—"

"Calm down! She's my only sister!"

"Yes, ma'am. I just need to ask you some questions." Ida could hear hyperventilation.

"Why? What questions?"

Ida went into some nonsense about needing to know Faye was actually Kelby's sister, that they couldn't simply give out information to just anyone who asked for it. "I'm sure you understand."

"I guess so. What is it you want to know?"

"Why did Kelby move to Hampstead?"

"Where's Hampstead?"

Ida's eyebrows shot up. What the hell? Maybe this woman wasn't a sister after all. "It's in Kansas, ma'am."

"I don't know where she went. She wouldn't tell me, said it was better if I didn't know. All I have is the phone number, and she told me never to use it, that she'd call me. But it's been so long, and I haven't heard, and I just had to make sure she's all right."

Ida heard the woman blow her nose. "She's mad at me, isn't she? That's why she won't call. She's mad at me."

"Uh, why did she move here and not give you her whereabouts?"

"To get away, of course. That awful jury ordeal. Just the most gruesome, awful thing. They had to look at all these pictures and listen to what that awful man had done to that poor girl. It upset her. Gave her nightmares, you know? It got so bad she started seeing a psychiatrist."

"What was the doctor's name?"

"I don't know. Somebody there. You know, where she moved to. What did you call it? Hampstead?"

"You're talking about the Lily Farmer trial?"

"That was it. They weren't allowed to read newspapers or watch the news, but she had me collect all the newspaper articles for her."

"Why?"

"Oh well, I'm not really sure. I never am with Kelby. She does things her way, you know? I think she might have an idea of writing a book about the whole thing."

Ida thought it was too bad she couldn't interrogate the psychiatrist. Well, they always played the confidentiality card anyway. "She left Berkeley rather abruptly—"

"She certainly did. I told her to come and stay with me, but she was afraid he'd find her here. And I have two small children. She didn't want to put them in danger."

"Who?"

"My children? Well, Shelly and Greg, but why—"

An inkling of why Kelby might not have called her sister was becoming clear. Ida'd only known the woman ten minutes and already she was exhausted. "No, ma'am, not the children. Who was Kelby afraid of?"

"Well, the stalker, of course."

Stalker. "Who was stalking her?"

"This man. He kept calling, in the middle of the night. Leaving messages. Threatening her. Turning up wherever she went. Following her. Telling her he was going to kill her. She was terrified."

"She notified the police?"

"Certainly. But they weren't able to do anything. Finally, she decided the only way to be safe was go someplace where he couldn't find her. That's why she just up and moved. She had no ties with anyone in that place. She thought he couldn't find her there and she'd be safe."

"Who was the stalker?"

"She wouldn't tell me. She said I was better off not knowing. That way I wouldn't be in any danger. Or the children. You're not going to tell her I talked to you, are you? She told me never to talk about this."

"No, ma'am, I won't tell her." Ida thanked the woman, hung up, and sat back. A stalker explained Kelby's behavior, looking over her shoulder all the time. She was making sure her stalker wasn't breathing close behind.

Ida brushed her teeth, then got in the shower. Tell the chief? The chief might want to know why Ida was invading the privacy of a citizen. She was pretty sure Chief Wren didn't look kindly on that sort of thing.

Tell Osey? She thought about that as she toweled dry. If she were going to tell anybody, Osey would be the one. He was her partner—for now, anyway, unless he got pissed at her. He wouldn't get all hot about it.

Okay, so tell Osey. And tell him Kelby was scared out of her skin and needed protection. And he'd say, protection from what? And she'd say, the stalker she was scared of. And he'd say how do you know about a stalker. And she'd have to tell him she called Kelby's sister. And how did she find the sister? Well, a little hacking she was sure would be frowned on. And she was kind of sure she maybe should have gotten permission before she started digging into innocent people's lives.

On the other hand, if she did nothing, the stalker might catch up with Kelby.

She stewed about it all during her shift. When she got off duty, she went in to see the chief.

31

At six, when Susan got home, heat still hung in air so thick with humidity that breathing was like sucking through wet wool. Would the damn heat wave ever break? Perissa the cat had left trophies on the kitchen porch steps, a field mouse and what might be the remains of a mole. Tail waving high, the cat came strolling up, enormously proud of herself. Juggling the work she'd brought with her, Susan got the door open and dumped everything on the table. She bent to stroke the cat and praise her for her hunting prowess, then filled the cat bowl with fishy-smelling stuff from a can.

The most important things taken care of, she gathered paper towels and went to dispose of furry little corpses thick with ants. Gingerly grasping the kill, she dropped it in a paper bag and tossed the mess in the garbage can. Two days until pickup. In this heat, they'd be pretty ripe, but she couldn't bring herself to store dead rodents in the refrigerator.

Inside, she washed her hands and headed for the living room. Having baked in the heat all day, the house was like an oven. She turned on the window cooler and was sorting though CDs trying to decide what she wanted to play when the doorbell rang. It was not a welcome sound, and for a moment she considered ignoring it, but marched herself to the door and flung it open.

"Friend." Parkhurst held up a hand. "I come in peace."

"It's been a long day. If you're going to make it longer I'll have to shoot you."

"Just information."

"In that case . . ." She opened the door wider.

"Had anything to eat?" he said as he came in.

She shook her head.

"Pepperoni okay?"

"No anchovies." She went to the kitchen and got a bottle of white wine from the refrigerator and a glass from the cabinet. He went to the phone. She held up the bottle with a questioning look.

He shook his head. "Orange juice?"

She gave him a narrow-eyed look. "What kind of he-man cop drinks orange juice?" She poured a glass, handed it to him, and poured wine for herself. In the living room, she put *The Art of the Fugue* on the CD player, took a sip of wine, and lay down on the couch. "Okay, I'm ready. What have you got?"

"I have to get you some decent music." He sat on the floor with his back propped against the hearth.

"It doesn't get any better than this." Her head ached, her ears hurt like crazy, and she wondered if she'd live long enough until it was time to take more Excedrin. She let Bach filter through her misery.

Twenty minutes later, the doorbell rang. He got up to answer and returned a moment later with the pizza, which he plopped in the middle of the coffee table. "We found the kid who caused the accident." Parkhurst gathered paper towels from the kitchen. "Donnie Jasper. Nineteen years old." Parkhurst peeled out a slice of pizza and handed it to her with a paper towel. "He was racing a buddy."

"Alcohol involved? Drugs?"

"He says not."

"You believe him?" She tore off the pointed end of the pizza slice, popped it in her mouth, and chewed.

"Yeah, I'm inclined to. Twice in the past he was issued speeding tickets. Nothing about DUIs. I don't know about the buddy he was racing. He's not saying." Parkhurst took a gulp of juice, bent one knee, and rested the glass on it. "Strongest rule of teenage ethics: Don't rat out a friend."

"He's facing serious charges. Speeding, reckless driving, accidental death, vehicular manslaughter, probably a few more I could cite if I didn't have a head full of fuzz."

"Yep. Stupid mistake, goddamn adolescent error in judgment, and he could end up in prison for much of his life."

"Is this Jasper kid sorry?"

"Oh God, yes. Wishes it'd never happened, wishes he'd never gotten out of bed that day, wishes he'd never met the friend, wishes he'd never been born."

Susan raised her arm and turned to look at him. "Did you stomp on the kid?"

Parkhurst bared his teeth in a feral grin. "You bet."

"You got him locked up?"

"Yeah. Won't last long. His parents may already have him out."

Susan put her arm back on her forehead and stared at the ceiling. Spider web in a corner with a spider waiting patiently in the center. "Have Demarco talk with him."

"Okay," Parkhurst said flatly. "Why? The kid's scared enough as it is."

Demarco was ex-marine, a poster boy for a lean, mean, fighting machine. He seemed to hate the world, but for some reason she'd never figured out, he could reach kids. He scared the hell out of everybody else just by raising an eyebrow, but kids looked at him and listened. He certainly didn't treat them with kindness; kindness was nowhere in his character. "Have Demarco spell it out. What he could be charged with, what it means in terms of years in prison, what happens to pretty boys in prison, and then give him a proposition."

"Right. Proposition. And that is?"

"Is this kid a loser? Nerd? Loner? What?"

"Football player. Above average student. Competitive. Wanted to go to law school."

"Stupid kid." She pinched the bridge of her nose. That was the nature of kids, stupid. The brain hadn't yet developed enough for thinking.

"Activate Demarco and aim him at this kid. Have him suggest the kid go to the high school and tell his peers what happens if they drive too fast. Demarco will go with him."

"Okay," Parkhurst said in a voice you use to humor the sick. "Could backfire. The kids could be so blown away by Demarco they'll rush out and join the marines and ignore the message Donnie's giving them."

"How bad is it to take Excedrin with alcohol?"

"I'm not sure. I think it kills you."

"Right." She found the bottle, isolated two tablets, and swallowed them with a gulp of wine. "My head hurts. Go away so I can suffer in peace."

After he left, she stayed on the couch listening to Bach. If she had the strength, she'd get up and go to bed. Before she could gather the necessary energy, she fell asleep. In the dream, she walked through tall trees. Wind stirred the leaves. They whispered and sang, the tune tantalizingly familiar. Notes rose to the treetops, tangled with red and gold leaves, then fell to the ground to rot and form nutrients for rebirth. A gunshot shattered the music. Notes re-formed into atonal noise. She woke with a stiff neck. Her watch showed four A.M. Unable to go back to sleep, she took more Excedrin and got in the shower.

Hazel, already at work when Susan arrived, said good morning. Susan gave her a squinty-eyed look. "If it is a good morning, which I doubt."

In the small kitchen, she poured a mug of coffee and went into her office. Paperwork, paperwork, paperwork—the world was sinking in paperwork. She shoved a stack aside and turned on the computer. A search on Lily Farmer got her reams of information. She printed everything, starting with the girl's disappearance. Lily was last seen at a friend's wedding.

She was supposed to drive home with her boyfriend, but they had an argument and he drove off without her. She never made it home. Her father reported her missing. For weeks articles appeared in the newspapers, saying not much more than police were searching and her parents were frantic. As time went on, the articles hinted more loudly of the possibility of tragedy. A man walking his dog in Tilden Park, a vast wilderness area in Berkeley, found her body. Grainy photo of cops at the scene.

She'd been beaten and raped, an attack so vicious it was a toss-up as to what killed her. Autopsy determined death due to exsanguination. Lily had fought her attacker. Skin and traces of blood were under her nails. That was what got him caught. A graduate student from UCLA, he was in Sacramento visiting friends. He'd probably killed three other young women. After a long and arduous trial, he was sentenced to life in prison without possibility of parole.

At ten, eight California time, she figured she had a good chance of finding her former boss in his office. She picked up the phone and punched in a number she remembered. San Francisco PD. If he wasn't in, she'd leave a message.

"Reardon."

"Morning, Captain. It's Susan Donovan." She used her maiden name because that was the name he knew her by.

"Hey! How's it going out there in—Ohio, is it?"

"Kansas."

"Oh, right. Where the sunflowers grow."

"That they do. Emphasis on the sun."

"It's fifty-eight degrees here."

"Eighty-five here, and climbing."

They talked briefly about the people she'd worked with, then she asked what he knew about the Lily Farmer case.

"Not much more than was in the papers. It was Berkeley's, not ours. Why you asking?"

She mentioned some sketchy details about maybe having a stalker after a local woman. "You know anything about Kelby Oliver?"

"Nothing."

She asked who had worked the Lily Farmer case and he told her Sergeant Manfred.

"You know him?"

"Just to say hello to. Berkeley's full of liberal types. Don't associate much."

"If I use your name, will he hang up on me?"

"Naw."

She thanked him, disconnected, punched in the number for Berkeley PD, and asked to speak with Sergeant Manfred. He was busy on current cases, but he remembered the Farmer case because it had been so vicious.

"The parents were at the trial every day," he said. "Apparently, when it ended there was nothing holding the marriage together and they split."

Not uncommon. When a child died, no matter the circumstances, 80 percent of parents got divorced.

"They were upset because the bastard didn't get the death penalty," he said. "You know, why should he be allowed to live after what he did to their only child? Especially the father, Joe Farmer. Did some talking to the press about what a travesty, and not justice, and that kind of stuff. He was really smoked about it. If it were my kid, I'd probably feel the same."

She probably would, too, Susan thought. "You know anything about a jury member being stalked?"

"Yeah. Can't pull her name out right now—"

"Kelby Oliver?"

207

"Yeah." A tighter tone of interest leaked into Manfred's voice. "Why you asking?"

"She moved here. Who was the stalker?"

"Father of the victim. He was pushed pretty far."

"What did you do about him?"

"Talked to him. Went out whenever he violated her restraining order. Hauled him in a time or two. Where did you say you were from again?"

"Hampstead, Kansas."

"Had another homicide with a thin thread to your neck of the woods. Woman beaten to death."

"Tell me about it."

"Arlette Coleridge. Severely beaten, found dead in her home. She was an attorney, so we're looking at disgruntled clients. Family law. Reputation for being the one to hire if you're female and wanting a divorce."

"You looking for a crazed husband legally forced to turn over half his assets to the little woman?"

"And watch her enjoy the fruits of his labors with some clown she's taken up with."

"You have somebody in mind?"

"Can't say that we have."

"There's some connection to Hampstead?"

"Not Hampstead. Kansas. More specifically Topeka. We got a call from there telling us to look at one of our own."

"You think a cop beat this woman to death?"

"Anonymous caller said to take a look at him."

"What's his name?"

"Mitchell Black."

"And did you take a look at him?"

"What do you think?"

"Right. What did you find?"

"Funny thing is, Mitch's wife disappeared a week ago."

That wasn't an answer to her question. Manfred told her of the search for Cary Black. Car found in the parking lot of a shopping center. "She knew the Coleridge woman."

"Any signs Cary Black was abducted?"

Susan heard Manfred take a breath. "Not unless you consider bags of groceries in the backseat and car keys under the car signs."

"Do *you* consider them signs?"

A hesitation, then, "I don't discount them."

"But?"

"But there's a BART station right across the street."

"Meaning she could have gotten on a train and taken off."

"Mitch has a temper, and he's been know to drink a little too much."

Always a potentially lethal twosome. She thanked him, pushed back her chair, and trucked off for more coffee. When she got back to her desk she sat down, leaned back, and laced her fingers behind her head. Arlette Coleridge, homicide victim in Berkeley. Friend of cop's wife. Cop named Mitchell Black. Wife disappeared a week ago. Juror of girl raped and murdered two years ago moved to Hampstead. Maybe to escape a stalker.

Okay, Susan thought, what did she have here? Tangled threads, as far as she could see.

32

$\mathcal{L}$ying in bed staring at the white ceiling, Cary measured her vision against the landmarks, a small water stain in the shape of a star and the light fixture. She closed one eye, then the other. Her tunnel of sight was shrinking and she had nobody to talk with.

Despite her resolve to be matter-of-fact, tears came. Angrily, she rubbed them away. This is just the way it is, so deal with it. It could be worse. You could be homeless and blind. It could be raining. So don't sink into depression. Count your blessings. You're not being used as a punching bag, you have a job, a place to live, food to eat, and you're learning to use a seeing-eye horse. She smiled at what her sister might say to that. Thinking of her sister brought images of her niece and nephew. Would she ever see them again? Rolling onto her side, she reached for a tissue and blew her nose.

Whenever she wasn't with Elizabeth, she was at Ronny's farm learning to work with a guide horse, getting more confident and less scared in trusting the animal. Despite her worries and longings and not daring to hope, she did get paired up with Cinnamon Ginger, the sweetest, most intelligent, most beautiful little horse in the world.

All the time now, she had the panicky sense of being followed. She never saw anybody and—okay, joke. She wouldn't see anybody unless they were wrapped around and around with running arrow lights. How long before Mitch grabbed her? Because he was coming, she knew it. He was out there somewhere, watching her and following, waiting for whatever he had in mind. All the struggle and running and Arlette dying, would all be for nothing. Mitch would get her anyway. Why not just roll over and die?

A few more minutes of wallowing in fear and sorrow and she got disgusted with herself. So, it might happen. He might be out there hiding behind a bush, waiting for the right moment to leap out at her, but until that happened, she was still alive. For God's sake, go with what you've got! She showered and dressed, then went downstairs and stepped out on the kitchen porch. Wind slapped at her face, the hot air heavy with the odor of death. Much stronger this morning.

Somewhere in the acres of corn, something had died. Horror, deep in the pit of her stomach, said Kelby was out there somewhere. Cary bobbed and weaved, trying to determine the focus of the birds. Could it be the barn they circled and not the cornfield? She'd only glanced around inside. Had Kelby gone up to the loft and fallen behind the hay bales? Been laying there this whole time? Oh God, why hadn't she searched every inch? Do it now! She peered in all directions before setting out. She didn't see anything like Mitch carrying a big sign that read "I'm coming to get you."

She rolled the wide barn door aside and stepped in, then waited for light to penetrate the dimness. It was cooler inside. The old stone kept the sun from baking it. Kelby's Honda sat gathering dust. Creeping closer, she peered at the windshield. *Smiley face. In the dust.* Mitch? To taunt her?

Ignoring the urge to rush back to the house and lock herself in, she went into each of the stalls along one side of the center aisle. Two were empty. The third had straw on the floor. She tromped around on it, thinking it would be perfect for Ginger. Across the aisle was a room she knew—after learning a few things about horses and barns—was a tack room. Desk in the corner covered with dust, pegs on one wall, shelving on another, with three cardboard cartons on the bottom shelf. She pulled one out and removed the lid.

Newspaper clippings. All about the Lily Farmer murder and trial. Mitch hadn't worked that case, but he'd talked about it. Everybody talked about it. It had been all over the news and in the papers for weeks. She'd watched news and read articles and was horrified, along with everyone else, at the viciousness of the crime. Why did Kelby have these? Cary glanced at pictures of Lily with her dazzling smile, and saw a shot of the young woman's father with an anguished face.

After the trial, the press had talked with any juror who agreed to be interviewed. Some appeared on *Good Morning America* and *60 Minutes*. Holding a clipping almost to her nose, she read one juror quoted as saying the crime scene photos were very hard to take. One of them, Kelby Oliver, almost couldn't look. Kelby had been on the jury in the Lily Farmer trial.

The other two cartons had more clippings. She put the boxes back on the shelf. A heart-stopping vision of Mitch storming in while she was in the loft filled her mind as she climbed one rung at a time. When her head was just above the floor level, she tilted it this way and that, peering into dim corners.

Bales of hay. And dust. As far as she could tell, the dust hadn't been disturbed in a long time. A small animal streaked across the top of a bale and disappeared behind. Only clamped teeth kept her from screaming. Mouse. Clambering over the last rung, she crept toward the stacked bales and looked over, around, behind, on all sides. Nothing. She drew a deep breath and nearly choked on the dust. There was nothing in the barn. Back out to the hot sunshine, she shaded her eyes as she looked up. No birds.

Veering around behind the barn, she followed a trail to a small, squat building that looked as though only the cracked and peeling paint held it together. The door sagged on its hinges and she had to tug and jerk to open it. All she could see inside was nests of straw. Chicken house, maybe?

Farther along the path, an arched wooden bridge spanned a creek, water rippled along about ten feet below, swirling past large rocks. Tentatively, she took a step onto the bridge, then another. There was no railing to hold onto, but she proceeded carefully up the arch. The wind swirled the shadows cast by the trees, until she could see only movement of light and dark. Inching slowly, she put a foot forward, and then another. Then . . . suddenly there was nothing to step on. Heart hammering in her throat, she knelt for a closer look. Gaping hole. One section of wood had rotted away on the right side of the bridge. She went back to the path. A tall, octagonal building sat at the end, so tall the top was lost in the trees, the crumbling wood had a few flakes of green paint. The sickly sweet smell was almost like a fog she could taste. Silo? For storing grain? There was a small door near the ground. A panel that slid up. Should she open it?

33

---

*E*yes skimming a report, Susan shook two Excedrin tablets into her palm and swallowed them with cold coffee. Her ears crackled. Shouldn't the damn antibiotics be working by now? The phone at her elbow buzzed and, without looking, she picked up the receiver. "Yes, Hazel."

"Hospital called. Jennifer Bryant had an accident."

An icy little worry tapped at Susan's mind as she drove to the hospital. *Oh God, please let Jen be all right.* Sliding doors hissed open as she trotted up. Cool air poured over her when she stepped inside. Strong smells of disinfectant, alcohol and vomit stung her nose. In the emergency room, she found Mary Mason, calm and efficient in the midst of chaos, jotting a note on a chart.

"Jennifer Bryant," Susan said. "What happened?"

Mary's face softened for an instant, then the professional look came back. Fear whispered in Susan's ear. "She took a bunch of pills," Mary said.

Oh Jen. "Is she okay? You pumped her stomach, right?"

"There were complications."

"What kind of complications?"

"Come with me." Mary led her to Exam Room Two and told her to wait.

Five minutes later Susan was talking with Doctor Sheffield, a stocky man in green scrubs, black curly hair, thick chest, and square hands. He crossed his arms and leaned against a metal cabinet with row upon row of drawers. "She was brought in two hours ago. Pupils fixed and dilated."

That was bad.

"No response to pain stimulus, muscles completely flaccid. CT scan showed a subdural hematoma. I called the neurosurgeon and he's operating now."

"A head injury? I don't understand. I was told she took pills."

He uncrossed his arms and rested his palms on the cabinet behind him. "Vicidin, Xanax, Wellbutrin. Maybe a few other things."

"Then how could she have a blood clot on her brain?"

"Apparently, she took the drugs and climbed up to a tree house."

Jen's father had built the tree house when she was little. It was her place of quiet and solitude. Often, she'd climb up there and read.

". . . most likely, she slipped into unconsciousness and fell—hit her head—midbrain. Controls breathing . . ." Doctor Sheffield stopped talking. "You all right?"

"What you're giving me doesn't sound good."

"Yeah." He eyed her with a clinical look. "The neurosurgeon can tell you more after the surgery."

Shivering in overdone air-conditioning, Susan paced a corridor, waited, and looked out a window at the sun blazing from a cloudless sky, and waited some more. She avoided the room where Jen's mother, father, and stepfather sat, isolated in separate misery. Finally, Mary came to tell her the surgery was over, and took her to the doctors' lounge.

Some minutes later, the neurosurgeon came in. Susan was immediately reassured. Gray hair, neatly trimmed beard, crisp white coat, chiseled features. Dr. Phillips exuded competence, an aura of arrogance, confidence that said he could handle anything.

"How is she?"

"I removed the clot. Her brain is very swollen." Calm, soft-spoken, he explained he'd removed a flap of skull to accommodate the swelling brain.

"Will she be all right?" A second ticked by, another, a third. Blood pounded in Susan's ears.

Finally, he said "The odds are very slim."

She wanted to slap him.

"I'd say maybe a three percent chance of survival."

Three percent? No, that couldn't be right. Susan took an elevator to the lobby, went out through the sliding doors, squinted in the bright sunshine as she stumbled across the parking lot to her pickup.

Cary craned her neck. The building—structure—she was pretty sure it was a silo—must be at least forty feet high. She should ask Ronny what it was for. Ronny, trainer of miniature horses to lead the blind, had grown up on a farm and would know about such things. Octagonal in shape, the wood, once painted green, was weathered and crumbling. A rickety-looking ladder went up the side. The wind tossed around the smell of decay.

Kneeling, she leaned close to the door and traced the outline with her fingertips. Not a door, a panel that slid up. With both hands flat against the rough wood, she pressed slightly. Splinters and flaking paint were ready to pierce her fingers, but there was no give, no feel that the old wood would collapse in. She pressed harder. Not a budge. Probably frozen in place by disuse and disintegration.

Most likely nothing inside anyway. She shoved upward. Tiny shift. Grain trickled from the hairline opening near the ground. She shoved harder and got a splinter in her palm for the effort. With repeated pushing, she inched the panel up in such tiny increments she was ready to give up. Except the smell, that awful, sickly-sweet smell of death grew stronger. With everything she had, she managed to move the panel an inch or two upward.

216

The stench made her gag. Grain continued to trickle through the opening. Turning a hand palm up, she stuck the fingertips inside and felt fabric. Holding her breath, she put her face near the ground and tried to see. Whatever, or whoever, was buried in grain.

A scream got trapped in her lungs. She fell backward, fist pressed against her mouth. Scrambling to her feet, she stumbled along the stone path toward the house and heard a car come up the driveway. Her poor sight let her make out the driver as he slid from the car. Tall and thin. That was all she could tell, except he carried a shotgun nestled against his arm, barrel pointed down. A high-pitched buzzing started in her head.

Feet planted wide, he raised the gun and pointed at her. "If you want to live longer than three seconds, just keep quiet and don't do anything stupid."

Whirling, she ran the other way across the dirt road toward the cornfield. The noise deafened her. Fire exploded past her face. She screamed. Hot pain grazed her temple and scalp. Staggering on the hard dirt, she raced into the corn and zigzagged through rows.

Blood seeped down her face. She brushed at it with fingertips and hissed at the resulting sting. She dropped to her belly and slithered along the ground, weaving in and out through stalks. She heard the blades clatter as he pushed through. Terror made her want to jump up and run. *No.* Creep further. Hide. Find a hole and bury yourself. *Creeping and burying made noise.*

Fight! *Bare fists against a shotgun?* Play possum. *That should work. She was paralyzed with fear anyway.* She sat, hugged her knees to her chest, and kept her head bent, hoping he wouldn't see her pale face in the midst of all the green.

The corn stalks swayed as he got closer. The hunter, after a rabbit. How long before he spotted her? When that happened, he'd shoot and she'd be dead. *Think!* Come up with a plan. Her terror-stricken mind saw only two choices. Run, or get the gun away from him.

Sounds told her he was closing in. She concentrated on footfalls.

Three feet away. Two feet. She held her breath. Shifted to a crouch. Tensed. Waited. Now!

Yelling like the damned, she leaped up, grabbed the gun barrel and shoved up with all her strength. It hit his nose. He grunted with pain. His hold loosened. She yanked and twisted. For a second, she had it. Then his hands tightened and he jerked both gun and her toward him. One hand snaked around her neck, and gripped tight, pulling her face against his chest.

She struggled. He was stronger. What little light she could see started to fade. Sounds grew fainter.

Pain. Deep, throbbing pulses in her head, sharp, stabbing bursts behind her eyes, a dull squeezing ache in her ribs. So intense, no other sensations were noticed. Hold on. Don't slide back into velvety darkness. If she wanted to live, she had to concentrate, move past the pain. As she groped toward awareness, consciousness, forcing herself to move through the pain, she realized her body was being shaken and bounced. The movement splintered the pain, sent it like forked lightning along her spine, until it made her teeth ache. Mitch had never hurt her this bad before. What would she tell the doctors? They always looked at her funny when she said she fell down the stairs. What had she done to set him off?

Somewhere in the bottom of her mind, a thought was swimming through the murk. She focused hard, and slowly it connected with other images until she had a string of thoughts. She'd left Mitch, come by a torturous route to Kansas. Other stimuli worked their way into awareness, hands tied, ankles tied. Something thick and vile stuffed in her mouth, tied tightly and cutting into her face. Vaguely medical smell. Panic threatened. She fought it off. A swallow got stuck in her dry throat.

The whooshing sound meant tires on pavement. Car, yes. Fuzzy mat beneath her cheek. Bound and gagged, lying on the floor of a car. She could see only darkness and shadows with an occasional flash of light. Events flooded back. Kelby in the silo. Running, futile fight to escape. No memory of being trussed up like a chicken for barbeque. Despair oozed in. She'd left Mitch, was making a new life, wanted to be whole, and it wasn't enough.

You're alive! She tried to find some comfort in that, but her mind pointed out that if he'd wanted her dead, he'd have killed her while she was unconscious. He had something else in mind. The smell filtered into her nose and down into her throat, making her nauseated and woozy enough that her thoughts were dreamlike instead of sharp. If she was going to survive, she had to be sharp.

He must have lowered a window, because the sound of tires was louder, thumping along on a rutted road. He'd left the main road and was somewhere in the country where there was little chance of anyone else around. It didn't much matter. She was in no position to signal anyone.

The sounds lulled her into a half dream state and she was jolted awake when she thought she might—just might—hear something being added, something in the distance. Another car? She wished she knew what time it was. The middle of the night, when any sensible person was asleep in his bed? Or still morning, when another person out driving might be likely? Hopes soared. Maybe, just maybe, someone else was out here, wherever they were. Elation fizzed through her brain drowning out a small voice somewhere in the murk at the bottom that pointed out it was too much to hope for, and how often had anything she pinned her heart on come to pass?

Suddenly, he was nervous. She could tell, because the leather seat back was swishing with his movement. The sound of another car got louder.

"Damn!"

Ah, he heard it, too. There was another car out there, another person who drove it and—so what? It wasn't as though another car could be any risk to him or help to her. She couldn't send out flares, wave a handkerchief like a damsel in distress, or even scream. She was trussed up on the floor in the backseat and couldn't even move. A whole fleet of cars could drive by and it wouldn't matter. Hope, like a punctured balloon, deflated and dwindled into despair.

But he seemed nervous, squirmed. Did that mean something? He was worried? Like there was someone out there? Someone who might help her? Hope came rushing back, then suddenly she was aware her bladder was uncomfortably full and about to humiliate her.

Jazz was playing on the radio. Mitch liked country and western, she hated it. Whenever she was in the car with him, he'd crank up the volume and she'd listen to betrayal, lovers going away, heartache, and going home to wherever home was. She never complained, otherwise when they got home he handcuffed her to the bed, turned the radio to window-rattling volume, and left her there for hours. The day she was lying there with two broken ribs she'd thought life couldn't get worse.

What a huge, cosmic joke.

This man was going to kill her and she didn't know why or who he was. If she'd known she would die today, she'd have paid notice to everything she'd done for the last time. Last cup of coffee, last shower, last mystery novel, last glass of cold orange juice. She started to cry, tears trickled down her face, her nose ran and she couldn't breathe.

"Coming around, Kelby?"

His voice sliced through her mental fog. He thought she was Kelby Oliver. Relief washed over her. He didn't want to kill her. All she had to do was convince him she was Cary Black, her husband was a cop.

"I know you're awake. I can hear you stirring around back there. Give me a sign. You know, just to let me know that you're still with me in mind and spirit. Kick your feet if you want. Anything, just so I know."

The silence stretched. She lay still. Throat tight with fear, she didn't make a sound. He reached between the seats and backhanded her across the face. Pain flashed across her cheek like fire. Shadows on the edges of her mind threatened to pull her back to unconsciousness. A moan slipped between clenched teeth. Nausea was sticking fingers in her throat. *Don't vomit! Don't vomit!*

"Why did you do it?" he said.

Do what? What was he talking about?

He reached back and yanked on the gag, pulling it down around her neck. It was slimy with saliva. Desperately, she gulped air.

"Aren't you going to say anything, Kelby?"

"I'm not Kelby. She's dead." At least Cary assumed it was Kelby in the silo. "Go back and I'll show you."

"Nice try."

"What do you want?"

"I'm going to do to you what he did to my daughter."

"Please listen. I'm not Kelby. I don't know who you are. I don't—"

"You might as well call me Joe. You can't get much more intimate than killer and victim."

Incipient hysteria was rattling around in her brain. Call him Joe. "I don't know anything about your daughter—"

"Lily! Her name is Lily!"

Lily. Obviously something tragic happened to her, and whatever it was pushed this man Joe over the edge. "What time is it?"

"What does it matter?"

Could she figure it out? It had been about six when she made a pot of coffee, then she'd searched through the barn, checked the chicken shed, and walked to the silo. It took time to push the panel up. She found the body. Joe arrived. He chased her down and tied her up and threw her in the car. How long would that have taken? Two hours? Three?

She didn't know how long she'd been out, but didn't think it was very long. Fifteen minutes maybe? Twenty? Okay, add on the time they'd been driving. At least an hour, maybe more. Her mind was having difficulty keeping track and adding, but eventually she came up with eleven o'clock. Maybe eleven-thirty or as late as noon. When she didn't turn up for work, Stephanie would worry—well, probably not worry, but be irritated—and she could have started somebody looking for her.

He sped up and made turns. Pain battered her everywhere until they jounced onto an unpaved road and he slowed down. "You ever go camping?"

Cary's mind scurried around trying to determine what that question meant.

"Camping," he repeated. "You ever go?"

"Not much." Her voice sounded precise, like a drunk who didn't want anyone to know he was drunk.

"We used to go all the time. Back when I had a family."

"Camping isn't really something I like to do." Mitch liked to go fishing and sometimes he'd make her go along.

"I've rented a cabin for us. A shack, really. But isolated. Nobody will bother us. Or hear you scream. Just like nobody heard Lily scream."

"Kelby is dead."

Joe's voice dripped sarcasm. "Right."

"She's in a building back at her house. I can show you where she is."

"I've watched you going around leading your comfortable life. Buying food, taking care of the sick lady, going to the library."

Nausea sat just at the back of her throat, her head hurt, and she had trouble following a thought. "I'm not Kelby." He was going to kill her because he believed she was Kelby. Maybe that was a fitting fate for having taken over Kelby's life. With her life came her problems. Wherever they were going, when they reached the destination, he was going to hurt her, make her scream and cry and beg him to stop. Then he was going to kill her.

Her full bladder would empty, her bowels would empty. She would be a disgusting heap of rotting flesh when somebody found her. If somebody found her. Would he bury her? Or just leave her for the flies and rats? In a few days, she would end up smelling just like Kelby.

Her head pounded, her hands were numb, she was nauseated and stiff, the carpet on the car floor scratched her face, and she was blind as a bat. The only sensible thing to do was give up and let herself slide down into the waiting cave of unconsciousness. But she fought against it for the same reason she wouldn't cry or beg when Mitch was beating her. Either stupidity or determination.

"Not long now," Joe said.

34

I just want to borrow him." Ida braced herself as the German shepherd barreled toward her. Even so, she staggered back when he reared up and rested his front paws on her shoulders.

"Down, Fergus." Fergus belonged to her friend Bert. The dog lapped at her face, dropped to the floor, raced to the dining room, and snatched a loaf of bread left unprotected on the table.

"No, Fergus," Bert said. "Drop it." The dog shook the bread, tore the wrapper, scattered slices across the floor, and started gobbling.

"Sit." Shoving at the dog, Bert scrambled to gather bread before the dog got it. With all food stashed in the trash, Fergus flopped down and rolled on his back with his feet waving in the air.

"He's not a cadaver dog." Bert rubbed the dog's stomach. "He's not even trained."

"No kidding," Ida said. She explained what she wanted to do.

Bert handed her a leash, then had to be persuaded not to come along. She wrapped the leash around her wrist as Fergus dug in his claws and dragged her toward her car.

"Just calm down!" Maybe this was not a good idea. Another one of those thoughts that seemed brilliant at first, but, past the point of no return, started looking like a mistake.

Fergus, excited about going for a ride, but nervous that he might end up at the vet, panted and drooled on her seat covers, occasionally on her arm as she drove out to Kelby Oliver's house. Something was dead out there, probably in the cornfield, and she wanted to find it. Even though his pedigree was dubious, he had a German shepherd's nose, and she thought he could take her to the source of the smell. He stuck that nose she was counting on out the window and panted. As she rolled into Kelby's graveled driveway, the dog crouched on the seat and flattened his ears. Ida climbed out and opened the rear door. Fergus looked up at her with mournful eyes.

"Come on, dog. Out." She tugged on the leash. Fergus slunk from the car, belly hugging the ground. This wasn't going as planned. Ida thought the dog would smell the odor and take her to the source, but he dropped and wouldn't move.

"What's the matter with you? Don't you want to find the funny smell?" She tugged on the leash and managed to get the dog into a sitting position.

"That's better. Now, let's go, find it."

The dog threw back his head and howled. The mournful sound sent shivers along the back of her neck. With words of encouragement, coaxing, and disgusting baby talk, she urged him toward the cornfield. He wanted to go off to the right, toward the outbuildings. "Not that way, you dumb dog. This way."

She tugged. Fergus would have none of it, and kept scrabbling toward the barn. "No, this way. Come on. Don't you want to see what it is?"

Apparently not. The dog kept straining the other way. She gave up and followed. They went toward the barn. Fergus stopped, put his muzzle in the air and sniffed, then took off like a shot. She had to sprint to keep up with him. He ran around behind the barn, stopped to sniff the air, and galloped along a stone path, choking himself against the collar.

"Slow down!"

He dragged her to an old wooden silo at least forty feet high. She heard a buzzing sound. At a small panel door, he snuffled along the crack at the bottom where grain dribbled out, then threw back his head and howled again. She squatted and tried to see inside. Flies. Oh God. Millions of flies. She kept shoving the dog aside, he kept scrambling back. She could make out the back pocket of blue denim.

Whoever was buried in the grain had obviously been dead a long time. Ida jerked on the leash to take Fergus back to the car. Now he didn't want to leave, and she had to drag him, toes digging in, all the way back and hoist him in. She went to the house, up on the porch, and banged on the door. "Ms. Oliver? Kelby?" Nothing. She banged again. No response.

Should she go in and see if the woman was okay? Would that compromise the crime scene? What if Kelby were hurt? Lying on the floor bleeding, and speed was necessary. She started in, then stopped and called it in.

Reaching for the phone when it rang, Susan knocked over a mug of coffee. "Damn it!" Receiver tucked between ear and shoulder, she snatched tissues and blotted furiously before papers got swamped by the spreading puddle. "Yes, Hazel." She tossed soggy tissues in the trash.

"Ida just called in to report a dead body."

"Oh, Lord, did she get somebody killed?"

"Apparently, this one's been dead for some time."

"Who is it?"

"Unknown."

Susan got location and directions. "Where's Parkhurst?"

"In his office."

She picked him up on her way out.

* * *

He pulled the Bronco into the gravel drive and parked behind a Jeep with a huge German shepherd inside, head out the window, barking furiously. Ida, standing beside the car, had a hand on the dog's collar trying to shut him up. And, by God, if that wasn't a guilty look on her face. What had she done now?

"Your dog?" Susan said.

"Belongs to a friend." She explained she'd borrowed him to find the reason the crows were circling. "The body's back this way."

Susan, Parkhurst at her heels, followed Ida past the barn and along a path to a hugely tall structure—crumbling wood with a perilous-looking ladder going up one side. The air was thick with the odor of decay. The loud buzz meant swarms of flies.

Osey, squatting near a small opening by the ground, stood when they approached. "Been dead a while." A wooden panel had been removed in pieces and grain had spilled out. Gunner, their Emerson student who moonlighted taking crime scene photos for the PD, snapped away.

Parkhurst grunted. "In this heat, decomposition wouldn't take long."

When Osey stepped aside, Susan took his place and tried to make out details. She couldn't see much. Buttocks, clad in blue denim. Female, apparently. Completely buried in grain, millions of maggots wriggling away at their work. Killed first and the body shoved in here? Pushed in and the grain released to kill her? Susan hoped that wasn't the case. If she was buried alive, she suffered an agonizing slow death.

Susan turned to Osey. "Who is she?"

He looked at her in his deceptive, slow-witted way. "Don't know. No way to tell what she looked like."

"Have you talked to the owner of this . . . this . . . ?" She waved a hand up the crumbling building.

"Silo. Applegate sold out and went off and just left the wheat." He scooped a handful of kernels and rolled it in his hand. "I'd say that's criminal."

He let the grain trickle through his fingers, then brushed his hand against his pants. "Whoever she is, she's a city person. Farm people know to stay away from a silo. They'd never go in a rat hole."

"Kelby Oliver owns the place now," Susan said. "What do you know about her?"

"Not much. Moved in and kept the doors bolted."

"Uh . . ." Ida took a step nearer.

Susan switched her attention to Ida, who quickly erased a guilty look. "What?"

"She has a stalker. Kelby. Ms. Oliver. I talked with her sister."

"Who was stalking her?"

"Her sister doesn't know, but Kelby moved here to get away from him. He threatened to kill her." Ida related what she'd learned from the real estate agent.

"Is this Kelby?" Susan gestured toward the body.

Ida shook her head. "Can't be. Whoever this is has been dead a while. I saw Kelby yesterday."

"Where is she?"

"I don't know. I called where she works, but she was a no-show this morning."

If a stalker was intent on killing Kelby, but Kelby was still alive, who ended up dead in the silo? A mistake? An accident? Practice?

Suddenly Ida gasped and reached for her gun. Susan turned to see what the problem was. Inside the silo, a huge black snake was gliding its way over the grain.

Osey, with a "what's your problem" look, pushed Ida's gun gently down. "Rat snake. Good guys. Good to have around. They keep the rodent population down. Probably wouldn't be a kernel left if it wasn't for these guys."

Maybe not such a bad deal, Susan thought, then they wouldn't have to remove it grain by grain. She and Parkhurst went through the house but found nothing that gave away who Kelby Oliver was. No letters, no snapshots, no address book. A woman with no clutter of identity. Had she killed the person in the silo? Who was the dead woman, and why was she killed?

"Two people were living in this house," Parkhurst said. "Clothes in one bedroom, personal things. Shoes, jumble in drawers, chest with socks and underwear. In the second bedroom, an item or two hanging in the closet, meager pile of clothing in a drawer. Stacks of books by the bed."

Susan agreed. "Two toothbrushes in the bathroom. So, who is the second person?"

"Female. Friend, maybe?"

"Kelby wouldn't even let in visiting neighbors. It would have to be someone she knew. Maybe the guest is dead in the grain."

"She's been dead for some days," he said. "Why didn't Kelby report her missing? Wouldn't you go looking for your visiting friend if suddenly she didn't show up for dinner?"

"Unless the friend had told me she was leaving, packed up, and then was killed by someone lurking in the bushes."

"Or because Kelby Oliver killed her."

Susan had a bad feeling about this. "We need to find Kelby."

35

Cary bobbed along like a swimmer just under the surface, until a shift of her body shot her to the surface. Her eyes opened to darkness. Blind, totally blind! What little vision she had, gone. A sob caught in her throat. The car made a turn and she rolled to her side. Shadows, she saw shadows. Not blind, getting dark.

"She was beautiful," Joe was saying. "And smart. We got her first camera when she was twelve. Carried it everywhere, snapped everything. Started winning prizes. Then she wanted a place to develop the film. Nagged until I wanted to yell at her. She said the garage wasn't used much anyway. She spent hours making prints."

Nausea tickled at Cary's throat. A thought crossed her mind. Throw up on him. That triggered another thought.

"I remember the night she was born like it was yesterday. The nurse put her in my arms, this warm little bundle all wrapped up. She was covered with chalky stuff and screaming her head off. I held her and looked at her and knew what pure love was. You know what I mean?"

Cary didn't. She'd loved Mitch before they'd married, but she'd never experienced anything like what Joe was talking about.

"That son of a bitch, that animal, killed her. Tortured her and killed her. Oh, God, he—" Joe's voice broke and anguish spilled through. "I hate to go to sleep. I hear her screaming. Calling to me." His pain was so raw, the air was thick with misery.

"I went to the trial. Every damn day, I sat in that court room and listened to what he did to her. That monster! He sat there looking like a clean-cut college kid."

His voice took on a thin edge. "Why'd you do it! Because you *could?* A power thing?"

Power? She'd never had any power in her life. She'd been a mouse who tried to be good, wanted people to like her. If he'd studied the jury, why couldn't he see he had the wrong woman?

"You were the only one. When it was over, I talked to the jury members. One woman cried. She apologized, said they tried to make you see, convince you to do the right thing." He smacked the steering wheel. "You wouldn't."

Ah. Now Cary understood. Kelby had been on the jury. "If you went to the trial every day, you saw the jury. Look at me. Can't you see I'm not Kelby?"

He grunted. "You tried to look different. I'll give you that. Did something to your hair. Lost some weight. It didn't fool me."

She wouldn't even die under her own name.

"If you'd voted for the death penalty like all the others, we wouldn't be here."

Cary nearly choked, on a sob, or a bark of laughter, it wasn't clear which. She was getting the death penalty for using a dead woman's identity. Kelby must be buried in all that grain. Who killed her? Obviously not Joe. Mitch? Why? He didn't even know her. Unless he thought she had helped Cary get away.

"Arlette?" she asked. Had Joe killed her?

"I didn't mean to hurt her. I'm sorry. She wouldn't tell me where you were."

230

"My husband's a cop. He'll find us."

"You're not married."

Joe couldn't let it go. He'd invested too much of himself in revenge. Maybe, before tragedy struck, he'd been a nice, ordinary man, but his mind snapped when the jury didn't vote for the death penalty. California had a two-phased system, first the trial, then, if the defendant was found guilty, a second phase to determine sentencing.

"What about my body?" she said.

"You'll be beyond caring."

She struggled to change her position, the pain in her left hip was becoming unbearable. Ha. If she couldn't even stand to lie on her side for any length of time, how did she expect to suffer torture?

"I have a sister. I don't want to simply disappear and have her wonder for the rest of her life. Her name is Sybil Pernich and—" The car hit a bump and she bit her tongue. "Please let her know I'm dead."

"Shut up! Just shut up!"

She twisted and wriggled and struggled to hoist herself up on the seat. Breathing hard, ignoring the pain in her head, she got her feet under her and forced her knees to lift her. Falling forward against the seatback, she flung her arms over his head, taped wrists around his neck. She dropped to the floorboards, letting all her weight pull against his throat. He made a strangled yell. Clawed at her hands. The car swerved erratically.

He stomped the accelerator. The car screamed in a turn, skidded, and rocketed forward. Brush scraped the sides. The car hit something that sent it flying. It landed with a thud and kept going. He squealed around turns. She saw flashes of fencing, green pastures, dark sky. Crossroads. Oncoming car. She tensed. The car passed. How long, she thought desperately. How long does it take to strangle someone?

Forever. She was tossed from side to side, getting battered and more nauseated at each screaming turn. The car slid onto an unpaved road, skidded with a cloud of dust toward a parked car. Kaleidoscope of pain and colors. Tortured shriek of crushing metal. Huge black pain filled her mind.

The next thing she knew, Joe was crouched over her with a knife.

At four o'clock, an ominous dark twilight wiped out the afternoon sunshine. Susan, working at her desk, looked up with a start when the overhead light flicked on.

Parkhurst came in and set a laptop on her desk. "Weather."

Oh-oh. That had a tone she didn't like.

He raised the lid and turned on the laptop. She watched a forecaster with a pointer touch a map with lines all over it. ". . . cold air dropping down from Canada and moving across a section of the Great Plains . . ."

"It's finally going to cool off?" she said.

"More than that."

". . . fine particles of dust picked up by rising air. Dust storm warnings for western Kansas . . ."

Hampstead was in the northeastern section of the state.

"Coming this way," Parkhurst said, as though he'd read her thought.

". . . the cold front saturated with dust will mix with the hot, dry air that has been suffocating the area for so long . . ."

Oh, shit.

". . . cause a low-pressure system . . . whirling counterclockwise . . . warm air rising from the ground mixing with the cooler mass above."

She looked at Parkhurst. He nodded. Oh shit.

". . . indicating heavy rain, large hail, high winds, and tornadoes. Since midmorning, the National Weather Service has been tracking this system with radar and satellite. Dust storms and thunderstorm bulletins, at this time, are upgraded to include tornado watches. Local authorities are advised of the need for emergency situations."

Just great. A homicide and now a tornado.

". . . winds reaching eighty miles an hour and three- to four-inch hail . . ."

Her phone buzzed.

"Yes, Hazel."

"Dr. Fisher just called. He's ready to do the autopsy on the silo victim."

In the hospital basement, she walked a long, empty corridor with harsh overhead lights, cement walls painted white. The morgue had stainless steel cabinets, stainless steel tables, and a drain in the tiled floor. The body lay on a table, in such a state of decay, it wasn't recognizable as human. A mass of rotting flesh, greenish black, abdominal area distended, skin and hair missing, fingers, hands reduced to bones, facial area so bloated features were missing. Clothes had been removed, shreds of a yellow T-shirt and blue denim jeans. The smell was almost more than Susan could bare.

Dr. Fisher, in hospital scrubs, handed her a mask and she put it on, not that it did anything to dilute the smell. He grinned at her behind his mask. She wondered, as she had before, if he had some deficit in what he could smell. Nothing seemed to bother him. Floaters, bloaters, putrefaction, all seemed a puzzle he was privileged to solve.

"Looks like we're in for some weather." He walked around the table and studied the body from all sides.

"How long has she been dead?" Susan asked.

He shot her a glance, the same one he always gave her when she asked that question. "Given the heat we've had, and the humidity, and the extent of decay, I'd guess at two weeks, give or take." He turned on the microphone hanging over the table and stated the date, his name and qualifications, then her name and position, as being present. "The body is that of a female in a state of severe putrefaction . . ."

He made the Y incision through the rotted flesh and opened the chest. Susan had, long ago, stopped thinking of the individual on the table as human, only the focus of her job. He spoke for the recorder as he poked through shreds of muscle. Susan tried to breathe through her mouth. The last thing he did was remove the top of the skull. Goose bumps broke out on Susan's arms at the shrill shriek of the saw.

When he was finished, he stripped off his latex gloves and washed his hands in the deep sink. He ripped paper towels from the dispenser, turned to face her, and leaned against the cabinet as he dried his hands, then pulled down the mask until it rested under his chin.

"Only thing I can tell you for certain is the body is female. Cause of death . . ." He shrugged. "Too much putrefaction. I didn't find anything obvious, like a bullet. Close examination of the bones might show something like a nick from a stab wound, but I doubt it."

He balled up the towels and tossed them in the trash container. "My guess is she died of asphyxiation. Not enough left of the lungs to tell. Poor lady. Terrible way to die. The pressure against her chest made it increasingly impossible to breathe. She couldn't expand her chest to pull in air. Slow death. Her last hours were excruciating."

"How long did it take?"

"Four or five hours."

Just thinking about it had Susan pulling air deep into her lungs. That brought in the heavy stench of decay and set off a fit of coughing.

"You don't sound so good. Maybe you ought to see a doctor."

"Very funny. Send me a preliminary report."

36

Knife in one hand, shotgun barrel in the other, Joe bent over her. To see if she was still breathing, Cary supposed. He moved from her sight. A moment later she heard the trunk lid slam. When he returned, he leaned the gun against the fender and sliced through the cord around her ankles. He yanked her to a sitting position and dragged her from the car. It was smashed up against a boulder in an empty field. Black clouds piled up in the sky, turning day into night. Wind tore at her hair and flung grit in her face.

He grabbed the gun—a rifle! He'd exchanged the shotgun for a rifle. What did that mean? Hand like a vise on her elbow, he jerked and shoved her up a slope. Two small cabins sat at the top, one on each end of the ridge, surrounded by trees whose branches whipped and twisted in the wind.

Hands still tied, Cary stumbled along on numb feet, her balance precarious. Grassy fields stretched away on both sides. Across a hill, she could see another cabin. Too far to hear a cry for help, even if someone were there.

He staggered as the wind hit him, then leaned into it. She planted her feet. He shook her until her head wobbled, sparks of pain sizzled behind her eyes. Arm around her shoulders, he propelled her through dead leaves and rotted vegetation. A piercing cry, like a woman screaming, rode on the wind. She froze.

"Bobcat," he said. "Just like the sounds in my dreams."

The cabin's two windows faced a rutted dirt driveway, a tattered screen dangled from one, a pane was missing from the other. He kicked open the door. The small room was grungy, walls of unfinished pine, an unscreened fireplace, sagging, lumpy, gray couch with two grimy pillows, easychair in the same dilapidated condition. Musty smell.

He hauled her to the chair and tossed her in. "Don't move or I'll start hacking off fingers." Breathing heavily, he backed to the couch, leaned the rifle against the arm.

Wind howled in the chimney and rattled the windows, sweeping in through the missing pane. He took a lantern from the mantle, lit the wick, and replaced the glass globe. The soft glow showed marks in the dust like the floor had been recently swept.

"Kelby is dead," she mumbled through dry, cracked lips.

He took out a knife. Air got trapped in her lungs. Heartbeat pulsed in her ears. She was going to die. Not at some distant future. Now. She'd be tortured and killed.

Wind slammed the door open. Startled, he turned to look. Screaming like the bobcat, she jumped up and swept the lantern to the floor. Glass shattered, oil ignited, and fire spread. She gave Joe a shove that sent him sprawling and darted for the door. In an instant, he was after her. She stumbled onto the porch, down the rickety stairs, and hit the driveway running. She fell against the car, rebounded, and kept going.

Running, stumbling, falling, she rolled downhill. She struggled to her knees and he snatched her arm and yanked her to her feet. His precarious balance brought him crashing into her. She tumbled sideways and he fell over her. Scrambling, he got to his feet, raised a hammer and slammed it down. She rolled. The hammer caught her hip.

Pain streaked along her leg. His hand closed around the back of her neck and he raised the hammer again.

Wind hit the cruiser broadside. Ida fought the wheel as she fumbled with the mike. "Just got word," Hazel said. "All of Fredericks County has been placed under a tornado warning until midnight."

"Okay," Ida said, not sure what she was supposed to say.

"This should be a bad one. Winds over two hundred miles an hour. You need to take a swing through the northeast section of town and make sure people are aware."

"Right." Ida dredged her mind for the procedure. First warn the citizens. Anybody in the elements should be taken to shelters.

She wished she had rain gear. When she came on this afternoon, it was a hundred and two degrees. Who needed a raincoat? Flashers blinking, she rolled.

Mike in hand, she spoke slowly: "This is the Hampstead Police. A tornado warning has been declared for Fredericks County. Repeat, a tornado warning has been declared for all of Fredericks County. All citizens are advised to take shelter immediately. Enter a concrete-reinforced building, or go below ground. Stay away from windows and doors. Repeat. A tornado warning has been . . ."

She didn't see a single soul as she cruised the area. Anybody who lived here would know better than she what to do. The closest she'd ever come to a tornado was watching news clips taken by idiots who tracked them. Residents were all probably inside finding candles, checking food supplies, and rounding up kids. Not that she wanted anything to happen, but she must admit, she felt a thrill that raised her pulse.

The sky was black. The wind blew dust and debris, plants, small tree limbs and fast-food wrappers across the street. A tornado could be right next to her and it was so dark she wouldn't see it. She'd been told they sounded like freight trains. How close before they could be heard?

The windows of the Coffee Cup were steamy bright through the gloom. She angled into a parking slot and got out of the squad car. Wind, howling in fury, tore at her pants legs, and damn near blew her into the street as she fought against it. The air smelled of sulfur and dust. Grit and torn plant life peppered her face. Everybody looked up when she pushed through the door.

"We got a tornado coming," she said. "Everybody should get home and find shelter. Weather bureau is saying we could have tornadoes reaching force three." She didn't know what that meant, exactly, but she knew it was potential disaster. She'd never heard Hazel have that tight sound to her voice. If unflappable Hazel was concerned, it was serious.

Ty Baldini, reporter for the local paper, looked up from the counter. "Get an identity on the woman in the silo?"

Ida could see his mind thinking headline: WOMAN IN SILO. Everyone in the place read it as though it hung in the air. Even killer tornadoes weren't as interesting as a homicide victim buried in grain.

One whiff of the odor, they'd have skedaddled.

"We're working on it."

Ty snorted. "Sure sure. Blah-blah-blah."

"I can only tell you we have new evidence."

Ty shot to his feet. "What evidence?"

Oops. She should have kept her mouth shut. "Nothing I can talk about."

He took a step toward her, and by God if it wasn't menacing. The jerk. She could break him in two. Not that she would. Mangling members of the press probably wasn't a good idea, since she really really wanted to keep this job.

"What would it be, if you could talk about it? Where's the chief? I haven't seen her around anywhere."

"She's making progress, and when—"

"What kind of progress? The citizens of this town have the right—"

Without warning, Phyllis, who had been a waitress here for probably as long as the place existed, came from the kitchen. "Knock it off, Ty. She's trying to do her job."

"But Phyllis, I'm just trying to—"

"Well, stop trying. She came in to tell us there's a tornado on the way. You all get yourselves out of here so I can get the windows shuttered and head for the basement. The lot of you, if you have any sense, had better do the same."

"Right," Ida said. Running procedure from the manual through her mind, she gave the group a stern look. "Go to the basement and get under something sturdy. Stay away from windows. Take water, food, flashlight, radio, and extra batteries. The warning is in effect until two A.M. Listen to your radio to learn if it extends longer."

The handful of customers got up and trooped out. Ty gave her a dirty look as he went past. "The citizens have a right—"

"Yeah, yeah, yeah. Go."

Phyllis crossed her arms. "Pack of idiots. Don't know enough to come in from a storm. Ty's a good kid. Except he takes this reporting stuff too seriously. I don't know if it means anything with the storm coming and all, but Kelby Oliver called earlier and ordered some hush puppies to pick up, then she never showed."

Ida didn't say that Kelby, most likely, had killed an as yet unknown woman and hightailed it for parts unknown. "When did she call?"

"Around seven. Said she'd pick them up on her way to work. I'm just a little worried, you know? She's taken to stopping by and getting things Dr. Farley likes. She's never failed to pick them up."

"I'll look into it. Maybe she's busy getting herself into shelter, which is what you should be doing." Ida helped Phyllis put shutters over the windows, then got in the cruiser. As she was pulling away, her radio crackled. It was Hazel, with a report of an accident on Larsen Road, telling her to investigate. Ida hit the overheads, gave the siren a whoop, and went into a U-turn. Larsen Road. West. Right.

Wind buffeted the cruiser as she sped through town and bumped into a turn onto an unpaved. Might as well be midnight, she thought as she turned on the headlights and tried to identify landmarks that looked completely different in the dark. Just ahead, past a dip in the road, light glowed. At the top of the rise, she saw an SUV, headlights on, parked by the side of the road. She stopped behind it and got out. Wind hit her so hard she got pushed several steps. The driver of the SUV was the concerned citizen who had reported the accident. She thanked him for calling it in and told him to find shelter.

A car missed the turn, hit a parked car, rolled down the embankment, smashed through the barbwire fence, tearing out the fence post, and came to an abrupt stop, front end mashed up against a boulder in the middle of a grassy field. Two shacky cabins at the top of the slope two hundred yards apart, trees behind, trees along the right edge of the field. A man was dragging what appeared to be an unconscious woman toward the cabin on the right.

Ida yelled, "Don't move her!"

Switching on her flashlight, she made her way down the hard dirt of the embankment, sliding and nearly landing on her butt at the bottom. Staggering against the wind, she stepped over barbwire and tromped across uneven ground.

"Any closer and I'll kill her!"

She froze. "She's hurt. She needs medical attention." Ida took a step.

Muzzle flash and the zing of a rifle shot. She switched off the flashlight so she wasn't such a clear target. Talk about dark. Headlights from the cruiser provided the only source of light. How badly was the woman hurt? Who was this creep? And what the hell did he think he was doing?

Wind howled so loud she couldn't hear anything else. Even as she struggled toward the trees on the right edge of the field, she was talking into her shoulder mike. She explained where she was and described the situation, requested backup and an ambulance.

"Help on the way," Hazel said. "Wait for it."

The cabin on the slope above had flickering light inside. A couple football fields across an empty pasture, the cabin she'd glimpsed earlier was lost in darkness. She considered running for it, but didn't know where the sniper was. Creeping up on her?

Hairs prickled on the back of her neck. Shrieking wind made so much noise, she wouldn't hear him sneaking up until he stuck the rifle in her face. Maybe he'd gone for the cabin. Or slipped away. Simply left the woman and taken off. Slowly, she shuffled across the field, stumbling on the uneven ground, to the row of trees along the right.

Suddenly, with no warning, hail pounded down. She crossed her arms over her head. Lightning split the sky. Whoever lay on the ground was getting pelted with golf-ball-size hail. Where was the jerk with the gun? How long before backup got here? She held up her wrist to peer at her watch, but it was too dark to see her hand, let alone the hands of her watch.

Rain poured down in buckets. Wind whipped tree branches in a frenzy. Lightning crackled. Hail battered her from all sides. She had a stray thought that standing under a tree in a lightning storm was not a good idea. Probably also a bad place to be when the tornado roared through. Oh boy. An injured woman couldn't be left out in this deluge. Unlit flashlight in one hand, gun in the other, she started toward the middle of the field with a mental picture of where the woman should be.

Wind and hail wiped out all sounds. She curled her index finger around the trigger of her gun and held it straight down alongside her leg. Taking in a breath, she kept her eyes focused on the spot where the woman should be, alert for any hint of the man with the gun appearing through the rain.

The storm battered her. Tree branches moaned and lashed. The wind howled, hail beat down, rain drummed against the ground. Unless he yelled through a loudspeaker, she couldn't tell where he was or what he was doing. A denser shadow seemed to separate from the darkness below and flutter in the wind. Then the shadow melted again into the black night. *Wait! Was that him?*

As loud as she could, hoping her voice would carry over the storm, she yelled, "Police! Drop your weapon!"

Lightning crackled, flooding the field like a stage. Then darkness. In the brief glimpse, she'd seen only an empty field. He wasn't anywhere. Nor was the woman.

In the dying echo of thunder, she heard another shot. "Police!" she shouted again. "Surrender your weapon!"

Desperately, she wished for better visibility. A solid curtain of rain fell. Lightning splintered the sky. For an instant, she thought she saw a face, white with pain and twisted with rage. The eyes were those of the mad, or the damned. *Great*, she thought. *Now I'm hallucinating.*

She heard screaming, something unintelligible, coming from the deep rage, something dark and unreachable. He was coming toward her!

Wind penetrated her wet clothing. Icy rain blew against her face, blurring her vision. She blinked, saw nothing but a faint flow from the headlights of the cruiser. She raised her gun, held it ready. She waited, watching. Heard something.

So dark, so dark; if only she could see. A misstep could send her headlong into the mud. A shadow loomed out of the dark. Her finger curled around the trigger.

The shadow hurtled toward her.

37

Ida strained to see through the pounding rain. Her finger tightened on the trigger.

The apparition fell against her. She staggered back, dropped the flashlight, grappled with the weight clinging to her.

"... help ..."

Lightning splintered the black sky. A shot boomed through the rumbling thunder.

"... kill me ..."

A split second passed before Ida realized the weight clutching at her was the injured woman. Another shot was fired.

Gun in her right hand, left arm supporting the woman, Ida half-carried, half-dragged her over the field. Wind hit her with staggering force, pushing her at an angle. She fought to stay on her feet. The uneven ground, soggy and slick, tripped her repeatedly. She stumbled, nearly fell, and lost her grip on the woman she carried. Hail pelted her. Lightning zigzagged through the dark. Ida glimpsed the woman's face. *Kelby*.

The rifle cracked. Thunder tumbled. With an instant's thought of causing further injury, Ida holstered her gun and yanked Kelby to a sitting position. *Hurry hurry hurry.*

Arm around Kelby's waist, Ida slogged toward the other cabin, the one on the left, across the field. Slipping, sliding, feet getting tangled in soggy grass, she dreaded the next lightning flash that would spotlight them for the sniper. She ran smack into barbwire and punctured her arm and the back of one hand. Gently lowering Kelby to the soggy ground, Ida wriggled under, then pulled Kelby through after her. Howling wind tore at her clothes and blew rain in her face. Where the hell was the backup?

Lightning flared and she saw crumbling porch steps. Stumbling under Kelby's weight, Ida struggled to the steps. Fearing the weathered boards would cave under her feet, Ida got herself and Kelby up onto the porch. Blessed relief. Hail battered the roof making it even harder to hear anything, but they were sheltered from the rain.

Lowering Kelby to the warped floorboards, Ida swiped water from her face and knelt. "Kelby?"

She picked up a limp hand and squeezed it. There was no responding squeeze. Placing icy fingers against Kelby's throat, Ida felt the pulse beat thin and fast. She pushed hair away from Kelby's face. A tornado was about to blast in and here she was with an injured woman on a flimsy porch and a creep with a rifle out there.

Crouching beside Kelby, gun in hand, Ida strained to see through the darkness. The drumming against the roof meant the sniper would have to make noise louder than a marching band for her to hear him. *Wait . . . Was that a footfall on the porch steps?*

No. Wind whipping tree branches against the house. Wasn't it? She stared into the pounding rain. Blinked and saw something move. The sniper! She raised her gun. "Police! Put down your weapon!"

No response. At least none louder than her pounding heart. *Noise? A shout? Was it him?*

She yelled again. "Police! Put down your weapon!" Rain poured down in a heavy curtain. Lightning forked across the sky. For an instant she saw, thought she saw, a face frozen in a grimace of rage.

"Drop the gun! Hands on your head!"

Another jagged streak of lightning. She saw him again. Closer. Features twisted. Mouth opened. She strained to hear. No words. Only a scream. Of rage and grief and despair and menace. A guttural noise mixed with and nurtured by the storm.

Rain on the porch roof sounded like rapid gunfire. Shaking with cold, she yelled, "Hands on your head!"

Oh, Jesus, the lightning had let him see where she was. Worried about Kelby in danger of a bullet, Ida yelled again, "Drop your gun! Hands on your head, or I'll shoot!"

Thunder mingled with the pounding of her heart. Was that a response? *Oh God.* "I will not hesitate to shoot! Lay down your weapon and put your hands on your head!" Should she fire? Desperately, she wished she could see more clearly.

A strong gust of wind tore a hole through the curtain of rain and for a moment, she thought she saw a pale oval with hair plastered down, the entire face twisted into a mask of rage.

She imagined eyes that glowed with demonic fever. Fear slipped in along with the icy damp air she breathed.

The horrible mask faded, then appeared again, mouth open. She strained to hear words, a raging curse that would tumble from that distorted devil face. Rain, wind-whipped into pounding fury, dissolved the image. Hesitantly, she raised the hand that held her gun, listened, raised the gun slightly higher. She could hear nothing but hammering rain.

She blinked, she waited. Still hesitant, she raised her gun higher yet. Way in the distance, through the murky blackness, she saw a weak glow. *That had to be high enough.* Anxiety knotted her gut.

She squeezed the trigger. The shot was lost in a clap of thunder. *Surely that was high enough.*

Another shot, the muzzle flash closer. Aiming high, she squeezed her finger.

The blast blended with thunder as it rumbled through the pounding rain. Kelby stirred. Ida crouched and trailed gentle fingers across her face. "It's going to be all right," she whispered. "Help is on the way. Just hold on."

Whether Kelby heard her or not, Ida had no idea. She stood. Another rifle shot. Thunder echoed in her ears. She returned fire. Pounding rain and howling wind made hearing anything else impossible. Had her shot discouraged him? Was he getting away? Waiting out there in the dark? Moving closer? Waiting for another flare of lightning to get a fix on her? Muzzle raised, finger on the trigger, aimed at the porch, ready?

She struggled to see through the blowing rain. How critical was Kelby? Lying on the porch floor in wet clothes wasn't helping. What further damage had Ida done by dragging her across the pasture and up the steps? Would a twister wipe them both out before help arrived? *Where was he?*

Keeping her gun ready, she moved slowly to the steps and started carefully down. The decaying wood was slick with rain and her hard-soled shoes slid. Grabbing at the railing to keep from falling got her a handful of soggy splinters.

Down toward the road, two football fields away, she thought she saw the glow of headlights through the rain. Backup finally here? The glow disappeared. Simply a motorist slowing to pick out the road? When her foot felt squishy ground, she backed up against the house and waited, listening. She needed another flash of lightning to spot him. After sweltering for days, she was now freezing and couldn't feel her toes in her wet shoes.

Finally, a siren wailed in the distance. She wished for a flare. How the hell were they going to find her? Her flashlight was lost out there somewhere, dropped when Kelby collapsed against her. Ida did the only thing she could think of. Pointing her gun straight up, she pulled the trigger. After what seemed an interminable time, a squad car, lights flashing and siren wailing, jounced into the field. It was followed by another squad car and then an ambulance.

Relief wormed its way through her cold, wet body and threatened to buckle her knees. With cops swarming across the field, they should scoop up the sniper. He'd be collected, cuffed, and shoved in the back of a squad car. Paramedics could get to work on Kelby, get her in the ambulance and to the hospital. Doctors, nurses, dry clothes.

Ida yelled, hoping to be heard over the storm. Someone must have heard something, because cops moved toward the house. Wind impeded their progress and blew them off course as they staggered in her direction. The glow of flashlights bobbed through the dark.

White and Brennan stomped up on the porch shaking water like wet dogs. Two paramedics followed. One crouched over Kelby, wrapped a blood pressure cuff around her arm and pumped it up, listened and murmured to his partner, then listened to her chest and murmured again. Quickly, they loaded her on a stretcher and carried her to the waiting ambulance.

White gave Ida a hard look she didn't understand and muttered about setting up parameters. He disappeared into the wall of rain.

Brennan scrubbed rain from his face. "What a friggin' mess. First all the endless heat, now this. God sends devastation. You okay?"

Ida was so cold she had trouble making her throat muscles respond to a simple yes. She nodded.

"Osey's on the way. He said you weren't to say anything until he got here."

What? "Did you catch the guy?"

Brennan gave an ambiguous dip of his head and clambered down the porch steps. Ida tried to flex her toes inside her wet shoes, but it only made them hurt more. What did he mean by devastation?

Why were White and Brennan acting so squirrelly?

38

$\mathcal{R}$ain hammered like a mad drummer against the roof of the squad car. Parkhurst slid out and crouched, then braced himself as a gust of wind flattened him against the door. "More light!" he yelled at Osey. Howling wind tore the words from his mouth. "Lose the fence!"

"Right," Osey yelled back. He snipped strands of barbwire, then he and Demarco peeled them aside. Osey clambered up the embankment to the road and used his flashlight to wave two more squad cars onto the field. Four cars parked at angles, with headlights on, made sickly tunnels through the dark and sparked against the pounding rain.

Not much help, not nearly enough light to penetrate the wall of rain. They needed a helicopter. Hell, it couldn't fly in this shit anyway. Parkhurst hoped the cruisers wouldn't get bogged down. A tornado on the way and four vehicles out of commission, mired in mud. Just what they needed.

When the next jagged streak of lightning forked across the sky, he took note of the cabin on the rise above. Seconds later the sky blacked out and thunder rolled. Flickering light glowed from the cabin interior. Flashlight or lantern. Candle maybe. He had a snarky feeling about this. One of those situations with everybody keyed up, fingers too quick on the trigger. He hoped one of the good guys didn't put a hole in another one of the good guys.

A shot rang over the field.

Parkhurst keyed his radio. "Osey?"

"Yeah, Ben?"

"Send Yancy and Quince to the left. Tell them, move slowly up toward the cabin. Don't get tangled in barbwire, and for God's sake, don't shoot each other."

"Right."

"You and Demarco come up the middle."

"Got it."

"Try not to kill him. We need this guy in cuffs. He has questions to answer."

"Do my best."

"And keep talking to him. Keep his attention focused on you." Parkhurst moved up the right of the field, keeping low, and getting buffeted by a wind so strong at times that he staggered and nearly fell. A bright flash of lightning lit up the sniper standing fifteen yards above, legs planted wide, rifle raised. Parkhurst dropped to the muddy ground, scrambled to his feet when the sky darkened.

"You're too late!" the sniper screamed.

"Drop the gun!" Osey yelled.

Parkhurst could barely hear him over the shrieking wind. He rubbed at the rain on his face.

"She's dead!" the sniper screamed.

"Put down the gun! Hands on your head!"

The wind howled down from the north with icy fingers, tore at his wet shirt, whipped his dripping pants legs, and fluttered the ballooning back of his jacket.

"Why'd you kill her?" Osey was following directions, keeping the sniper's attention focused down the slope.

The noise of the storm covered any sound Parkhurst might make creeping up behind. The trick would be to disarm the suspect before he whirled and reflexively pulled the trigger, thereby blowing Parkhurst's head off. He sincerely did not want that to happen. Through the two front windows in the cabin, he saw light burst up. Flames licked out the broken pane. Oh, Christ, the place was on fire. What other disaster could occur on this beastly night?

An unexpected depression in the ground had him coming down hard on one foot, splashing through two inches of standing water and twisting an ankle. Damn. It would help if he could see where he was going. Keeping a straight course in the dark, with nothing to guide him, was difficult. He hoped he didn't angle too far to the right and get impaled on the barbwire fence on that side of the field.

He heard Osey yell again, but couldn't make out the words. At the next burst of lightning, he waited for the resulting thunder and scuttled toward the row of trees circling the rear of the cabin. Air wheezed in and out his lungs. He had no idea what obstacles were in his way back here. Any number of discarded junk items could be littering his path. Hell, he could cut himself on some rusty farm implement and end up with tetanus.

When he heard Osey's voice again, he listened intently. A response, even though the words were undecipherable, told Parkhurst the sniper was still in front of the cabin. He turned on his flashlight for a moment. Uneven muddy ground up against the cabin, and beyond that tall weeds battered down by the rain. Being careful to avoid the mud, Parkhurst moved in a straight line across the rear of the cabin. When he reached the far side he waited again and listened. Osey yelled, the suspect replied.

Parkhurst used his flashlight to check the terrain along the side of the cabin. Rougher here. Areas of depression like basins filled with water. Hard rain pounded the puddles and splashed back with a bounce. Flames licked through a side window. He murmured in the radio for Osey to make his move.

"Put down the gun!" Osey yelled and shined his flashlight at the suspect.

While the suspect was trying to decide whether to shield his eyes from the light or shoot, Parkhurst rushed at him from behind. Even with the storm covering any noise, the sniper must have sensed something. He whirled and fired. Parkhurst dropped, landing in a hollow full of water. He rolled and splashed and scrambled out. Osey tackled the suspect and grappled with him on the soggy ground. Parkhurst threw himself into the tangle and grabbed at arms and legs. The suspect's clothes were soaked, and with mud added, he was slippery as an eel. Parkhurst felt him wriggle free. It took Demarco and Parkhurst to hold him down while Osey cuffed him.

Once the cuffs were secured, the suspect was a pussycat, wet and miserable and all fight gone. Parkhurst grasped an arm and helped the man to his feet. Osey shined his flashlight in the man's face.

"What's your name?" Parkhurst said.

"Joe Farmer. You're too late. I shot her."

"Shot who?"

"Kelby Oliver."

"Anybody in the cabin?"

Farmer shook his head. Parkhurst handed the suspect over to Demarco with instructions to take him in. Parkhurst was wondering what to do about the fire, when flames shot through the cabin roof, only to be quenched by the rain. More water pouring down on it than the fire department could provide. He keyed his radio and asked dispatch to send out the firefighters. There might be evidence inside that needed preserving.

"Uh, Ben," Osey said. "We really should get everybody into some kind of shelter. This tornado's supposed to be a bad one."

"Yeah. Go talk to Ida."

Ida waited, miserable, soaked, and shivering cold. Jesus, what she wouldn't give for a hot bath. Finally Osey, flashlight in hand, came loping up on the porch.

"You got him?" Ida said.

Osey held his flash pointed down. "Did you fire your gun?"

"Yes."

"I'm going to need it."

"Right." Her hand went toward the holster on her belt.

"Easy."

What was the matter with everybody? You'd think she shot some-one the way they were looking at her sideways. Oh God, surely, she hadn't. The first time she'd fired, the sniper had fired back. The second time, she wasn't aiming to hit, only let them know where she was. With thumb and forefinger, she clasped the grip, slowly removed the gun from the holster. She dropped it in the evidence bag he held. What was going on? Nervousness pulled her mind from cold and wet.

"Tell me what happened here," he said.

She related events, beginning with Hazel's sending her out to warn the citizens about the coming tornado and ending with drag-ging Kelby up to the porch. "Is she seriously injured? Is that why you're questioning me like a suspect? Did I do some serious damage by moving her?"

"When you started toward the injured woman, the sniper fired at you."

"Yes," she said.

"You turned off your flashlight so he wouldn't be able to pinpoint your location."

"Yes."

"Then the hail and rain started."

"Yes." She was beginning to lose patience. She wanted to get off this damn porch and into some dry clothes. She wanted to get to the hospital and find out how Kelby was.

"You fired at the sniper. One shot."

"Yes."

"The woman, unconscious woman, suddenly leaped out of the rain and fell against you?"

"More or less."

"Did you shoot at her?"

Ida took a breath to spread calmness over her rising temper. "I was expecting the gunman. She startled me. I nearly shot her, then realized it wasn't the creep with the rifle. What's going on?"

Osey looked at her long and hard, then he shook his head. "You shot the chief."

"*What?*"

39

———

 $\mathcal{P}$ arkhurst shucked wet clothes, bundled them in a plastic bag, and took out the extras he kept in the locker. "Where is he?"

"Interview room," Demarco said.

"He give you any trouble?" Parkhurst pulled on dark gray pants and a white shirt.

"None. Except talking. He wanted to confess, wouldn't shut up. Said his name was Joe Farmer and he did it for Lily."

"Any ID on him?"

Demarco nodded. "Driver's license with an address in Palo Alto, California."

"He ask for an attorney?"

"Nope. Said he didn't want an attorney. Signed a release to that effect."

"Been read his rights?" Parkhurst put on dry shoes, put a foot on the bench and tied the laces, put the other foot up and tied laces.

"Yes."

Parkhurst went down the hallway to the interview room. Joe Farmer sat in the center of the long table. Forties, thin face, with the tight drawn look of someone who's been sick a long time. Dark hair and dark eyes with the intense stare of a fanatic. Someone had taken his wet clothes and given him an orange jailhouse jumpsuit. Demarco stood by the doorway, Parkhurst sat across the table from Farmer and turned on the tape recorder, stated the date and time and mentioned the names of those present.

"I had to do it," Farmer said. "Kill her. Kelby Oliver. She deserved to die."

"Why?"

Farmer talked about Lily, his daughter, how beautiful she was and how smart and how talented as a photographer, how her pictures won awards, then he talked of her brutal death and the trial. "Kelby was the only juror who voted against the death penalty. My Lily is dead but that animal is still alive because of her."

"You killed her and put the body in the silo."

"Silo?" Farmer looked confused. "No. I meant to torture her, so she would know what Lily went through, but then . . ." He shook his head and glanced at Demarco, at the bare wall behind Parkhurst, and then at Parkhurst. "She ran so I shot her. A police officer—she came and dragged her away. I tried to shoot her, too. But the dark and the rain. The wind."

"Who is the woman in the silo?"

"I know nothing about silos, or any woman in one."

"How did you find Kelby Oliver?"

"Her friend—Arlette Coleridge. I—uh, persuaded her to tell me."

"Persuaded her so hard she died."

Farmer studied the scarred tabletop. "I'm sorry about that. I never meant to hurt her. She wouldn't tell me what I needed to know."

"Why'd you set the cabin on fire?"

"That was Kelby. She knocked over the lantern."

"Torture," Parkhurst said flatly.

"You don't know what it's like." Farmer leaned forward. "The dreams . . ." He tapped fingertips against his forehead. "The dreams, and Lily crying, calling to me, help, and I can't and . . ." Farmer looked up, face anguished. "I knew if I did to Kelby what that sick bastard did to Lily, the dreams would stop. I could sleep." He put his palms on his temples and squeezed. "I had to do it. She kept saying she was Cary Black, but she didn't fool me. I knew who she was. She was Kelby."

Cary Black, Parkhurst thought. The missing wife of police officer Mitchell Black.

Osey guided Faye Turney along the hospital corridor with gently nudging progress. Mrs. Turney, Kelby Oliver's sister, was a woman who couldn't talk and walk at the same time, and she talked a lot. She had blown into the police department and demanded God knows what all. Parkhurst had explained the situation. Sort of. When he'd said Kelby was in the hospital, Mrs. Turney had fits and that's when he'd handed her over to Osey with instructions to take her to see her sister.

"I just knew it." Mrs. Turney stopped and looked at Osey. "I just knew it. I've been so worried."

Osey was worried about Ida and what was going to happen to her. She'd probably get fired. You couldn't go around shooting the chief of police and not have serious consequences come down on you. Even if it was an accident.

". . . and when Kelby didn't call me for so long, I just knew something had happened to her. She wouldn't let me help her, you know. She was worried he might do something. Harm us. And, of course, there are the children to think of. That awful man. He stalked her, you know. She lived in terror. Thank goodness it's over. Now maybe she can get back to her life and live like a normal person again. It's been hard for her, you know. I hope she's going to be all right." The last was said with a rising inflection making it a question.

"Dr. Gordon seems to think she'll make a full recovery. It's just going to take a little while."

"Thank goodness for that." Mrs. Turney laughed. "Oh well, I mean about the recovery, not that it will take a while. I'm going to take care of her. This time I'm not going to take no for an answer. She's my only sister. I'm going to be there for her."

Osey thought that would probably double the recovery time. "She's in this room right here."

Mrs. Turney rushed in with a big smile, then stopped and looked at Osey. "Oh," she whispered, "you got the wrong room. This isn't Kelby."

"Are you sure?"

"Certainly, I'm sure. I guess I know my own sister. Who is this person?"

A very good question. Osey hustled Mrs. Turney out of there and, with repeated coaxings and nudgings, got her on the elevator, up a floor, and into the small chapel.

"What's going on?" she said. "You said Kelby was going to be all right. Where is she? Why did you take me to that woman? I demand that you take me to see Kelby this instant!"

Osey very much thought he knew where Kelby Oliver was. In the cooler down in the basement. And he very much doubted Mrs. Turney could recognize that decomposed, rotting corpse as human, let alone as her sister. He asked her to wait, he'd be right back.

"I will not wait! I want to know what's going on!"

"You have every right to know. I'm going to tell you. In just a few minutes."

Mrs. Turney sank down in a pew, her expression a mixture of anger and fear, and an overall growing awareness that the explanation was going to be bad. Osey backed out, then loped to the nearest nurses station and had them page Dr. Gordon. Using his shoulder mike, he called in and asked dispatch to send him the watch and ring found on the body in the silo. Cooling his heels in the lobby, he hoped Mrs. Turney would stay put. When Ida pulled up at the entrance with the overheads flashing, he dashed out.

257

"What's going on?" Ida handed him an evidence bag with the items he'd requested.

"I think I've identified the body." He signed and dated in the required spot, dashed back inside, and took the stairs two at a time.

Mrs. Turney popped up when he came back. He showed her the watch and ring. She identified them as belonging to her sister. Despite strong discouragement from him and the doctor, Mrs. Turney insisted on seeing the body. When she saw the black bloated corpse, she freaked, had to be admitted, and screamed until the sedative took effect.

Cary floated in silence on a soft cocoon of black water. Whispery voices were calling to her. She drifted on. The voices got louder, insistent. One higher voice. Shrill. Hysterical. She tried to make out the words. They had no meaning. When she opened her eyes, light rushed in and pain splintered through her brain. Cautiously, she reached up to touch her head. Gauze. Bandages. Why did she have bandages wrapped around her head? A wave of sleep rose up and washed her away.

The voices were back. She clung to the tattered edges of sleep. The voices prodded. Eyelids raised a tiny bit, she saw blurry shadows. White jacket. Doctor? Saying someone was very lucky. It was good that someone was lucky, but she thought she'd just go back to sleep.

"Lucky?" Another voice. Talking with the doctor.

She moved her head a fraction, trying to get her small section of sight to center on the second speaker. The effort was exhausting and made the pain worse.

"From a medical standpoint she's very fortunate." The doctor again.

She wished they'd discus this somewhere else.

"Broken ribs knit fairly quickly. The collar bone will take time, but should have no problems healing. Compound fracture of the left radius. Is she left-handed?"

Talk somewhere else. If they didn't go away, they would tear through the sleep and let the pain in.

"What about the head injury?"

"Concussion. We wait and see. Her vitals are strong."

The next thing she knew, someone was thumbing her eyelids up and shinning a light in her eyes. "How do you feel?"

With great effort, she raised one hand and did a thumbs up.

He laughed and patted her shoulder. "It will get better. Just give it time."

He disappeared from her sight and she felt herself drift along toward the black ocean where there was no pain.

Voices again. The doctor and—no! Not Mitch! No!

Machines beeped. "What happened? She was fine a second ago. Why has her pulse shot up like this?"

Fear faded along with the voices and she rode on blue velvet.

"Cary Black . . ."

Cary licked her lips and mumbled, "Go away."

"I need to ask a few questions, but first I need to read you your rights. You understand?"

"Yes . . ."

"You have the right to remain silent. Anything you say can and will be used against you in a court of law. You have the right to an attorney . . ."

Osey watched her as he recited the Miranda warning. Face and right arm scraped raw and crisscrossed with scratches, left arm bandaged and immobilized in a sling. Deep cut on her upper arm, stitched with black thread and oozing fluid. She looked small and vulnerable, battered by someone much stronger than she was.

"If you cannot afford an attorney, one will be appointed for you free of charge before any questioning, if you want. Do you understand?"

A long second's wait, then a slight nod.

He couldn't see this woman getting in a rage and pushing Kelby Oliver into the silo. Cary Black didn't seem capable of pushing a kitten into anywhere, but he wasn't seeing her at her best. Maybe it wasn't rage, but cold-blooded calculation. Kill the Oliver woman, assume her identity, and take over everything that was hers.

Well, it wasn't up to him to make the big decisions. He just followed orders. When a machine started beeping, a nurse came in to check and threw him out.

40

After three days in the hospital, Susan was more than ready to go home. While the tornado was roaring into Hampstead, an ambulance was screaming to the emergency room. The twister touched down in two places, uprooted trees, flattened houses, twisted cars, and downed power lines. Eight people injured, two seriously, fortunately no deaths. While George and Parkhurst dealt with the aftermath, she languished in a hospital bed.

Dr. Sheffield snapped on latex gloves and eased the bandages from the wound on her left hip. "Looking good," he said.

"Easy for you to say." Lying on her right side, she craned her neck to see what damage Ida's bullet had done.

"No signs of infection." Doctor Sheffield prodded and squeezed and tapped. "You're fortunate the bullet missed the femur."

She gritted her teeth as pain zinged through her entire left side. He dropped bloody bandages in the hazardous material receptacle, applied clean gauze, and taped it securely. She felt better having the wound covered up.

"Another day and you should be able to go home.

Susan looked up at him. "I need to leave now."

"Another day," he repeated. "To make sure you don't do any more damage to that leg. That you stay off of it and keep it dry."

Susan opened her mouth to protest, then said, "How's Cary Black?"

"Feeling miserable, but coming along."

"I need to question her."

Head lowered, he peered at her, then gave a short nod. "Okay. You can have a few minutes." He paused to make sure she understood. "If she gets agitated, you'll have to stop."

He got busy scribbling orders on the chart. "You lost a lot of blood. We need to keep an eye on you."

"I need to get back to work."

He said no, she said yes, they argued. Finally, despite her weakened condition, she managed to convince him to discharge her. Flush with success, she rolled out of bed and nearly screamed at the pain. She picked up the phone, got an outside line, and asked Hazel to send her Parkhurst. A nurse brought her a set of scrubs and a pair of crutches. By the time she got the scrubs on, Parkhurst was striding in with a bouquet the size of Montana.

"*What were you thinking?*" He banged the vase down on the bedside table.

"That it was time to get out of here."

"You need rest." He crossed his arms.

"There's no rest in hospitals. They're loud. Someone is always drawing blood. They send in the kitchen help for the practice." With a great deal of awkwardness that necessitated much muttered cursing, Susan managed to get herself and the crutches to the elevator. Parkhurst thrust the flowers at a nurse, told her to keep them, and followed Susan.

In the second-floor room, Cary lay motionless, eyes closed, bruises vivid purple against her pallor. A nurse adjusted the clear plastic tubing sending oxygen to her nose and hung a new bag of fluid on the IV stand. She patted Cary's hand, gave Susan a cautionary look, and left.

"Cary Black? I'm Susan Wren, police chief. This is Lieutenant Parkhurst."

Cary looked so battered and frail, Susan wondered what a defense attorney could do with any statement she might give. Susan hobbled to the chair balanced on her good leg, propped the crutches against the wall, and dropped to the seat. "I need to ask you a few questions."

"What questions?"

Susan knew Osey had Mirandized her, but she did it again, then said, "Do you understand?"

Cary pushed herself higher in the bed. "Am I being arrested?"

"We're just asking questions." Parkhurst stood inside the door-way.

"Was it Kelby in the silo?"

"It appears so." Susan rubbed the top of her good leg in a failed attempt to ease the pain in the injured one.

"What happened?"

"We're working on that. How well did you know Kelby Oliver?"

"I didn't know her. I never even met her."

"You were pretending to be her. Living in her house. Using her ID, her money."

Cary scrunched in on herself. "Was she murdered?"

"We don't know that yet." Susan wondered where the woman's husband was. He came to see her when she was first brought in, but the visit seemed to cause so much stress the doctor wrote orders he shouldn't be allowed back. Nobody'd seen him since. He checked out of the motel he'd been staying in, and so far they'd been unable to locate him. Had he gone home?

"Where is Joe Farmer?" Cary had the taut, skin-too-tight look of someone who'd recently lost weight.

"He's been arrested." Right now, he was in a cell talking to his dead daughter, crying and carrying on, apologizing all over the place

263

because he'd let her down, was unable to save her from the sicko who hurt her. Susan didn't know what would happen with him. Padded cell, most likely. He'd obviously slipped off into the ether somewhere.

"He came to the house. He had a gun and . . ." Cary related what had happened, but it was apparent there were gaps in the memory, or she deliberately left a lot out.

"Why does seeing your husband upset you?"

A small sound, like a resigned breath. "If he knew where I was, he'd kill me."

"Your husband." Susan loaded the two words with sarcasm, but years of being a cop made her aware of the dynamics in a "battered wife, abusive husband" situation. They needed to double their efforts to find him.

"How did she—Kelby—die?"

An attempt to sound innocent by showing she didn't know the manner of death? "Grain pressed against her chest so she couldn't take a breath. She suffocated."

"Am I a suspect?"

"Not at this time." This was a lie. Cary Black was their best suspect.

"Maybe . . ." Cary paused, like she had to search around in her head for the words. "Maybe Joe Farmer pushed her in there. And when he saw me maybe he thought she got out somehow."

Was that possible, Susan wondered. "How did you know it was safe to use Kelby Oliver's name?"

"I don't think I want to answer any more questions," Cary said. "I'm very tired. Please leave."

Susan looked at Parkhurst, he raised an eyebrow.

Out in the hallway, he said, "You didn't arrest her."

"We don't have enough evidence."

He started counting off on his fingers. She was living in the dead woman's house, using her name, using her money, using her ID, writing checks on her account. How could she expect to get away with that unless she knew Kelby Oliver was dead? And she knew the woman was dead because she killed her.

Susan nodded at all that. "Let's talk with the DA, see what he thinks."

"Right. Let's get out of here."

"There's something I have to do first. I'll meet you in the lobby."

She took the elevator up a floor and went to a room at the end of the corridor. Jen lay on the white sheets unmoving, looking small and blank. Somebody, probably her mother, had pinned a pink bow in her hair. She would hate it. All the fire and spirit and wide-eyed eagerness, all the special qualities that made Jen such a neat individual were gone. All that was left was the hiss and thunk of the respirator keeping air in her lungs

Susan picked up her hand, surprised at the warmth. Somehow she'd expected it to be icy cold, but it was warm and pink, and completely flaccid. She curled Jen's fingers around her own, held them a moment, then put Jen's hand back on the bed. From the box on the bedside table, Susan tore out a tissue, wiped her eyes, and blew her nose. She met Parkhurst and hobbled out to the Bronco. At home, she hobbled inside.

"Yank the phones," he said. "Take your drugs and crawl in bed. I'll come back later with soup."

"A cane would be more useful." She swallowed the magic pain pills and went to bed, drifted in and out, dreamed about corpses on the autopsy table. Sometimes her own face looked up at her, sometimes Jen, sometimes a stranger, sometimes the badly decomposed woman from the silo. What had happened to her?

Yellow, a voice explained. The voice was familiar. Whose was it? She slept fitfully, dreamed, heard the voice again. Ah, she thought, that's it, that's—

Pounding at the door shattered the dream. She woke.

41

$\mathcal{S}$usan propped the crutches under her arms, swung into the living room, and answered the door. Parkhurst came in with a container of minestrone soup. He poured out a cup. She sipped and swallowed, took more pills, drank a few gallons of water, went to bed, and dropped off the edge of the world. Hours later she opened her eyes, groggy from drugs and too much sleep.

Sunlight bashing through the open curtains made her squint. The clock said twelve. Not dark. Had to be noon. She inched herself from the bed and stood to see if she could manage that Herculean feat without falling down. Yes.

She pulled in an invigorating breath that was going to allow her to leap tall buildings and stop locomotives. The leaping and stopping idea lasted until she took a step and pain buzzed through her leg. Okay, tall buildings were out. However, she was alive, she was awake, and life was good. That lasted until she remembered she couldn't take a shower. Okay, she was alive and awake and life had a few drawbacks.

She brushed her teeth, washed her face and slathered soap and water around, trying not to get bandages wet. By the time she was dressed and slipping on shoes, Parkhurst was at the door.

"There's no reason you can't stay home today," he said.

"No reason I can't go to work."

"Right." He opened the passenger door, then went around and slid in under the wheel. "What's a little gunshot?"

Hazel looked up when she came in. "You sure you should be here?"

"Yes." Susan hobbled toward her office. As soon as she got settled behind her desk, Parkhurst came in with two mugs of coffee and handed her one. He planted his rear in the visitor's chair and slid down so he could rest his mug on his chest.

"Anything more from Joe Farmer?" she asked.

Parkhurst took a cautious sip of hot liquid. "He's still claiming he shot Kelby Oliver in that field. I questioned him again. Osey had a go at him. Farmer's slipped over the edge and there's no hauling him back. He admits to all kinds of things. The problem is about half of what he says is completely wacko. He talks a lot to his dead daughter, and she tells him things like 'Kelby should know what it was like. If she did, she would vote for the death penalty.' Times are mixed up in his head. He apologizes to the daughter for not torturing Kelby. She was getting away so he had to shoot her."

Parkhurst lifted the coffee mug. "From what I can gather, the dead daughter is irritated about it. He says killing Arlette Coleridge was an accident. Claims he didn't mean to, didn't want to. She wouldn't give him Oliver's address and so he hit her. Apologizes all over the place for slapping a woman, says he's never done that before."

"How did he know Arlette had that information?"

"He'd been stalking Kelby Oliver for months, following her around, calling, threatening. He saw them together numerous times."

"Slapped her," Susan said. "The woman was beaten so severely she died."

Parkhurst nodded. "I've hammered at Farmer, and each time he comes back with a different story. Sometimes he just slapped her, sometimes he hit her over and over until she talked, sometimes he shot her."

"Shot her." Susan's head was starting to ache. "Autopsy show any bullet wounds?"

"No."

She massaged her temples. "Is it possible he didn't kill Arlette?"

"He's so out of it anything's possible. Innately he feels you don't hit a woman, so he's changed beating her severely to a slap. Or maybe he did just slap her and then someone else came along and beat her to death."

"Anything point to that?"

"Nothing to say either way, according to Sergeant Manfred in Berkeley. She was a defense attorney. Could be somebody wasn't happy with his defense."

"And came along just after Farmer left?"

"Possible. Not likely." Parkhurst sipped at coffee. "He admits to killing Kelby Oliver, but thinks he shot her, and denies shoving her in the silo."

"If he didn't kill her, who did?"

"We have a dandy suspect lying in a hospital bed."

Susan massaged her temples. "Cary Black exercised her right to keep her mouth shut."

"Sounds like guilt to me," Parkhurst said.

"Yes," Susan said, drawing out the word. "Cop's wife. She knows a thing or two about how the system works."

"She moved in, took over Kelby's name, her house, her money."

"True." Susan hoped the caffeine would get rid of her headache. "I got the impression Mitchell Black slaps her around."

"Sweet fellow."

Something flickered way down in the murky bottom of Susan's

mind. She couldn't get it to float up where she could grab it. "Where is he? Why can't we find him?"

"He moves around. By the time we find the motel room he rented, he's checked out."

"Why?"

Parkhurst shrugged. "Something to hide."

"What?"

"When we find him, we'll ask."

Her dream from last night swam around and floated slowly up. The voice in her dream was Jen's, telling her about a yellow shirt. "Find something of an evidentiary nature and we'll arrest somebody."

Parkhurst stood up. "Do my best." He gave her a sharp look. "You okay?"

"Yeah, I'm fine." She buzzed Hazel and asked her to have Osey come in, then she took a folder from the teetering pile, moved it to the center of the desk, and opened it. As she read about the devastation caused by the tornado, she tried to tease loose the rest of the dream. Just as she grabbed it by the tail, Osey came in and it slithered away.

"You wanted to see me?"

She nodded. "Have a seat."

In his loose-jointed, ambling way, he folded himself into the chair Parkhurst had vacated.

"How's it going with Ida?"

Osey grinned. "She's a mite subdued."

"What about Kelby Oliver's sister? She tell you anything that might help us?"

"That woman sure does talk, that I can give you. Enough to cause a headache. She was in Berkeley trying to find her sister. Talking to police and people who knew her. At her job, and like that. There's some gaps in her story. I've been checking airlines."

Susan rubbed her right leg, because rubbing the left made pain shoot everywhere. "Was there any friction between Kelby and her sister?"

"I don't know about that, but I did learn that Kelby Oliver was a rich lady by most standards. Seems she owned a house in Berkeley that she sold for over two million, and she had money on top of that. Who pays two million for a house?"

"Someone who wants to live in Berkeley."

"Faye, the sister, inherits everything, and she can use it. She's married to a man who can't keep a job. When he gets one, it isn't right, or the boss is stupid and he says so to the boss's face and gets fired. Never finds anything he likes, or a place where he's appreciated. Faye's been supporting the family working at the phone company. I can see him drooling over the fact he'll be able to get his hands on Kelby's money."

"Anything on his whereabouts during that time period?"

"Yeah. He was away on a camping trip. Somewhere in the wilderness, all by himself."

"What do you have on Cary Black?"

Osey repeated what he'd put in his report, essentially that she was a friend of the woman in Berkeley that Joe Farmer either killed or didn't kill. Cary Black left California without telling anyone, even her husband, making it look like she was a victim of foul play. *Big search for missing wife of police officer.*

"She had to know about the search," Osey said. "She bought San Francisco and Oakland newspapers. Lots of articles about her disappearance. Her picture all over."

"You suggesting she planned it? She left home and came here for the express purpose of killing Kelby Oliver?" That said premeditation.

Osey sucked in a breath and let it out on a sigh. "Well, ma'am, I'm not sure. She sure did leave home for some serious reason." He frowned. "The dead woman was too badly decomposed to tell much, but this Cary Black isn't very big. How'd she get Oliver in the rat hole?"

"Kelby Oliver wasn't very big either. They were roughly the same size."

"Driver's license says five-two, a hundred and thirty-five pounds. If she was banged on the head—"

Susan looked at him. "What did you say?"

Osey eyed her like maybe she'd get dangerous any second. "A hundred and thirty-five pounds. Cary could have knocked Oliver unconscious first."

"Before that."

"Uh . . ."

"Getting Oliver in the silo."

"The rat hole?"

"Why did you call it that?"

Osey shrugged. "That's just what we always called that door. It's used to get the grain flowing down, if it's not coming. Every kid who grows up on a farm knows to stay away from silos."

Susan rubbed her leg again, then reached for the phone. "Hazel, would you please send Ida in."

Shit, Ida thought, *oh shit, this is it.* This is where the chief says pack your bags and get the hell out of Dodge. I shot the chief of police, for God's sake. How am I going to get another job with that on my résumé? She hesitated at the doorway when she heard Osey's voice. Had he made a complaint?

Deep breath. Chin up. Get in there. *Ida Rather get it over with.* Osey got up to offer her the chair. Did he think she couldn't take this standing up? She ignored the chair and stood at attention.

"Sit." Susan couldn't take all that rigid discipline. "Tell me about Cary Black."

Ida unbent enough to perch on the chair, mentioned the poor eyesight, the fear, the reluctance to call her sister. "Of course, Faye isn't her sister, but I didn't know that when I urged her to call."

"What did she say about her ordeal with Joe Farmer?"

Ida repeated everything she'd put in her report.

Susan shifted, trying to find a position that would ease the pain in her leg. "Anything you can add?"

"No, ma'am, not really. Except Pearl Wyatt, a neighbor. She was really mad at Kelby, because Pearl wanted to buy the place and she feels Kelby snuck in and stole it away from her. She wanted it for her son. She told me she was so mad she could spit. But nobody would kill over something like that, would they?"

People kill for all kinds of reasons. Susan had known a homicide to result over two quarters.

By the late afternoon, Susan's leg throbbed with such vengeance she propped herself on the crutches and hobbled to the pickup. On the way home, she stopped off at Doctor Eckhard's office to have the wound checked and the bandage changed. China said it was bleeding again and she should stay off of it, gave her another prescription for pain pills, and told her to go home. Wobbling with an unsteady lurch, she climbed back in the pickup and took herself home.

She swallowed pain pills with a gulp of water, oozed herself down on the couch, and floated away on chemically induced sleep. No dreams disturbed her. She slept through the night, woke at five, drank a large glass of water, and basically drifted in and out of sleep all through Wednesday.

When she finally surfaced, at nine o'clock in the evening, she realized her ears weren't crackling. *She could hear!* That called for a celebration. She picked up a handful of CDs and looked through them, but before a decision could be made, the doorbell rang. She let Parkhurst in.

He looked at the CDs in her hand and grimaced. "Bach, I presume."

"A little Borodin, I think, for a change."

"Some change," he said.

She stuck the CD in the player, turned the volume low, and went to the kitchen for two glasses of orange juice with ice. She gave one to Parkhurst. He sat on the floor, back propped against the hearth, legs straight out. She slouched in a corner of the couch, pillows stacked behind her, closed her eyes, and listened to the nocturne from String Quartet no. 2.

"We still haven't found Mitch Black," he said. "Anybody who takes such precautions to keep his whereabouts unknown has got to have something to hide."

"No doubt, but he didn't arrive until Wednesday, August twenty-seventh. Kelby died on Monday the eighteenth."

Parkhurst raised an eyebrow. "You know what day she died? Even Doc Fisher doesn't know that. Okay, if Mitch Black didn't kill her, what about Faye Turney? She's rich now."

"She didn't do it."

"Okay. We still have Faye's no-good husband. He's rubbing his hands together at the thought of putting them on all that money."

"Not him either."

"I strongly doubt Pearl Wyatt shoved Kelby in the silo in a fit of pique because Kelby bought the house. Which brings us back to Cary Black."

"Cary got here on Wednesday the twentieth. Kelby was killed on Monday."

"There you go with Monday again. Why are you so sure she was killed on Monday?"

42

"So what's with Monday?" Parkhurst said.

Susan captured an ice cube and crunched down. "I think it went like this: Kelby Oliver had a stalker. We know now it was Joe Farmer. He terrified her. He sent notes, innocent words with an underlying flavor of menace, left messages on her answering machine, turned up wherever she went, followed her, overtly threatened when nobody could overhear. Said what happened to his daughter would happen to her. She fled, bought a house without even seeing it, and came here. She hid away, seldom went out."

"Yeah, so?"

"On Monday she was outside when she saw a man with a shotgun."

"If she was holed up in the house, what was she doing outside?"

"I don't know. But for some reason she went out . . ."

. . . *and lugged the cardboard box to the barn, stashed it on a shelf in the small of-ficelike room, and dusted her hands on the seat of her jeans. Why, Kelby wondered, had she agreed to this? The entire morning cleaning the guest room and getting it ready for Arlette's friend, she'd felt serious misgivings. She didn't know this Cary Black and she certainly didn't like the woman knowing where she was. What if this Cary let slip to a friend or relative that she was here living with Kelby?*

It was a mistake, it was a mistake, it was a mistake. Kelby knew it. By letting Cary come, the danger doubled. Now two people knew where she was. Tucking in her yellow T-shirt, she went from the dim light of the barn out to bright sunshine. She blinked.

Man with a shotgun! He raised the gun. Boom! She ran.

Boom! She raced to the open shed that sheltered a tractor. Ducking inside, she crouched by one large wheel. How had he found her? Slowly she rose, peered around the side of the shed. The harsh sunlight was dazzling. Shot pinged against metal.

"Got ya!"

She ran, stumbled, recovered, kept running. Lungs on fire, breath coming in short gasps, heart hammering, she pounded toward the cornfield. The wind picked up. The great stalks rustled like a live thing just coming awake. Was he hiding in there? Stalks eight feet high. She'd never see him.

Sweat stung her eyes. She swiped the back of a wrist across her face, stumbled again. Heat lightning flickered in the distance. Heavy smell of dust and corn mingled with the sweet scent of flowers.

At the last second she shot off to the right and ran along the flagstone path toward the cottonwood trees. Slipping on fallen leaves, she skidded around a tree and squatted, leaning against the trunk, trying to quiet her breathing. Leaves blew in her face. She pawed at her hair to get it out of her eyes.

Ears straining, she waited. Where was he? She heard the crackle of dry leaves. A footfall. Faint. To her right. She froze, strained to see. The wind sighed, the cottonwood trees murmured back. Carefully, she rose, waited.

Boom! She took off, hoped she wouldn't fall. The air was alive with sound, whispering grasses, swaying leaves, creaking branches. Hearing a thud, she whirled. Behind her! Coming closer! A scream bubbled in her throat. "What do you want?"

He raised the shotgun.

She pulled out more speed. Fighting hard for air, she pushed on. Relentless footfalls behind her crunching on dry leaves. Coming closer. Closer. She heard his breath laboring through his lungs.

"You won't get away!"

The sudden shout, too near, sliced her with terror. She spurted ahead. His thudding footsteps grew closer. Wait. Car. On the road. She skidded, slipped, put down a hand to save herself and raced into the road, yelling in mad panic. Screaming, she waved her arms in a futile attempt to get help. Her shouts faded along with the sound of the car disappearing. She stopped, beaten, bent, and clutched her stomach, felt as if her lungs would tear.

Finished, done, over. She was tired of running, of hiding. She waited for him to raise the gun and tighten his finger on the trigger. The wind excited the cottonwood trees, tossed the branches. A moment passed before she realized, she couldn't hear him. She looked around. Where was he? Gone? Scared away by the car?

Coughing, lungs grabbing at air, she stared wildly around, unable to believe he'd simply left. Half-stumbling, half-running, wheezing as she tried to breathe, she started back to the house. Call the police.

A triumphant yell. He angled toward her from her right. She spun. Run! Don't look back. Run! Faster! She ran and ran. She stumbled, fell. She rolled and came to a stop at the base of the tall wooden structure. Scrabbling at the panel near the ground, she shoved it up and tumbled inside.

She closed the panel and stood in dim light. Air wheezed in and out through her mouth. Dust stung her eyes and threatened to make her cough. Heart pounding, she pressed her back against the door. Had he seen her go in?

Smells of mold and rust and long unuse. A wall of something, grain of some kind, filled the space in front of her. It was nearly in her face. If she reached out, she could touch it. Claustrophobic panic scratched at her throat.

She listened, trying to hear if he was coming, was trying to get inside. Back hard against the panel door, she heard nothing but the thudding of her heart. Seconds crept by. She stopped taking in great gulps of air and turned

her head to put an ear against the door. Not a sound. Was he waiting for her
to come out? Would he blast away at the door?

She stood motionless. After a time—she had no idea how long—she was
aware of something slithering across her shoes. It stopped. Heavy. Moved
slowly. Slithered again. She stared at her feet. A big, thick, black—

Snake! Oh my God, snake! Huge snake! Kicking and stomping, she
whirled around, flung her arms, waved her hands. It slid away.

Oh thank God. The damn snake was gone. Had it bitten her? She didn't
feel anything. What does a snake bite feel like? Surely you'd feel fangs sink-
ing into your skin.

Wait. What was that? Whispery, slithery sound, trickling. Sinister.
Snake coming back? No. The grain. It was moving, shifting . . .

. . . and somehow she dislodged the grain. It came down and
buried her." Susan took a sip of juice and swallowed. Halleluiah, no
pain.

Parkhurst, skeptical eyebrow raised, rattled the ice in his glass.
"And the guy with the shotgun?"

"Monday, Simon Lundstrom got his hands on a shotgun and fired
at her."

"Simon Lundstrom? Whose mind has softened to the point
where he's back in World War II keeping us all safe from Nazis?"

"Jen said yellow clothing set him off, had him ranting about
yellow-bellied cowards. Kelby was wearing a yellow T-shirt. Osey and
Ida both said he yelled about shooting the Nazi rat who escaped down
a rat hole."

"You think he meant Kelby Oliver diving into the silo?"

"I've tried to interrogate him, but it's hopeless. He slips away to
the horrors of his incarceration and torture." She stopped to listen to
the end of the Borodin nocturne.

"What are you going to do about Ida?" Parkhurst asked.

"That's a hard one. Next time she might hit some more vital piece of my anatomy." Susan shrugged. "I could see how she works out and hope she doesn't get anyone killed."

"You could. Is that what you'll do?"

Before she could respond, the phone rang and she went into her office to answer.

"A hysterical call from Cary Black just came in," Hazel said. "She said somebody was trying to kill her. The call got cut off or she hung up."

43

Cary leaned against the side of the hospital bed and tried to read the instructions she needed to follow after being released. With the paper nearly against her nose, she moved it into her small spot of sight. The effort made her head ache. She coughed, which made everything ache. Never mind, the nurse had explained it anyway. Mainly, don't take anything except Tylenol. Nothing else, because of the head injury.

Right. Tylenol was what she'd been given all the time she'd been here, and she could tell anyone who asked that it didn't do much for pain. On top of a broken wrist, broken collar bone, cracked ribs, concussion, and no place to go when she was released except Kelby's house, her period had started. She was beginning to feel decidedly sorrier for herself.

Considering the circumstances, it was generous of Kelby's sister to extend an invitation. How she might get there was a problem, because she had no money. She could walk, of course. Would she survive that? A soft knock on the open door made her look up.

"Hi." Ronny Wells strolled in, tucked a loose strand of gray hair behind an ear, and plunked herself down in the only chair. "I hear they're kicking you out of here. I came to give you a ride home."

"How did you know I was leaving?"

"One of my trainers has a sister who's a lab tech here. I know you can't drive, so I thought I'd come fetch you. Ready?"

"I guess so."

A nurse brought in a wheelchair. Cary got in and was pushed to the elevator and through the lobby to the front door. Ronny pulled the van up. Cary, shaky and weak, got herself inside.

"You brought Ginger." Cary reached back and gave the little horse a pat.

Ginger, standing calmly in the back, tossed her head.

"I thought you could use some company," Ronny said.

That was true enough, but how about Kelby's sister? The house might feel like Cary's, but it wasn't. When they pulled into Kelby's driveway, Faye came out to greet them.

"Thank you for letting me stay," Cary said.

"Tell you the truth, I'm glad for the company. What's that you got?" Faye watched Ronny unload Ginger. "You brought a pony?"

"She doesn't have to stay, if you don't want her to. Ronny can take her back to the farm. Right, Ronny?"

"Why, it's just as cute as a button. I don't mind at all, just so long as I don't have to take care of it."

"I can do that." Cary hoped she could. She was feeling a little light-headed and her cough was getting worse.

Ronny told her to go on in the house, she'd see Ginger was settled in.

"Won't she be lonely here all by herself?" Cary worried that Ginger would miss the other horses.

"She'll be fine."

Faye fussed around making sure Cary was comfortable on the sofa, brought her pillows and water, made sure the Afghan was available if she got cold. The constant chatter made Cary's headache worse. At lunchtime, Faye brought in a tray of pasta salad, a bowl of sliced fruit, and iced tea. She sat in the easy chair by the fireplace while they ate and kept up the constant stream of talk. Cookies and chocolate ice cream followed.

"There now," Faye said. "I'll just clean all this up in a jiffy and you rest. You need anything?"

About thirty minutes later, Faye came back. "You know? I don't think there's any reason why I need to stay any longer. I think I'll just take off this afternoon. I was going to wait a few days. Take care of some loose ends, you know? But I don't really think that's necessary, do you? And I would like to get home. I'm missing my children. And my husband, too, of course. And I know there's a million things piling up at home I need to tend to. So it seems to me it just makes sense that I get all my things gathered up and packed in the car and I'll just take off."

"Oh " Cary started to get up.

"No no, that's all right. Don't you move. You are perfectly welcome to stay just as long as you like. Probably better that way, you know. Somebody here."

Ah. That explained the invitation. Faye wasn't comfortable leaving the place empty. She needed a house sitter.

"When you do leave, just lock the doors and take the keys to the Realtor. I put his card on the mantle. Do you have anyone to call if you need anything?"

"Yes. Ronny, the woman who brought me here and uh, Elizabeth, Dr. Farley, the woman I work for."

"You'll be all right then? Because I can stay, if you like, I don't want to abandon you. You being under the weather and all. So just say the word and I'll stay."

"No," Cary said. "I'll be fine. You just go ahead and leave."

"Well, if you're sure."

"I'm sure." With her head pounding the way it was, Cary was more than sure.

When Faye finally left, the silence was so light and lacy that Cary thought it was better than a basket of sparkly diamonds.

Two hours later, that very same silence began to feel oppressive. The house groaned in the wind and tree branches tossed outside. When she could stand it no longer, Cary got herself up and followed the stone path out to the barn, telling herself Ginger must be lonely. She brought the horse in to share some microwave popcorn and an old Jack Lemmon movie on television.

Cary coughed, clicked off the television, and switched on the table lamp. The mantel clock read ten-fifteen. Despite her pain, she'd dozed off trying to watch the movie. Her vision being what it was, she mostly just listened. Ginger, dozing by the arm of the sofa, shook her head as though relieved the movie was finally over.

Carefully, Cary pushed herself to a sitting position, rested a moment, and then stood. With her left arm in a cast, her right shoulder in a sling to allow the collar bone to mend, her cracked ribs ready to shriek at deep breaths or sudden moves, Cary felt she was in danger of shattering at the touch of a feather. She put a hand on Ginger's halter and they went through the kitchen, across the screened porch, and down the steps. Feeling with the toe of her shoe, she found the stone path that led to the barn. In city terms, it was a block from the house.

She needed to find another place to live, with a shed or barn for Ginger. Even though Faye said stay as long as you want, Cary felt uneasy. Because of all that's happened, she told herself. She was traumatized by all she'd gone through. A nervous, tight feeling of eyes watching her made her look around. Not that she could see anything. The night was black, overcast with clouds that covered the stars and moon. Fortunately, she had Ginger and could feel the flagstones beneath her feet. If she felt grass she'd know she strayed from the path.

Where was Mitch? At home? She'd had a dream in the hospital that he'd come to see her. Don't worry. He didn't know where she was. She'd be fine. Wind brushed her face with a strong smell of corn. The stalks whispered and rattled. Just one night, she promised herself.

She'd be okay for one night. If she was still jittery tomorrow, she'd figure something out. Call Ronny, talk with Stephanie. Stephanie owed her some money for the days she took care of Elizabeth. Surely enough for a motel room for a few days.

Maybe Mitch understood everything was different now, that she wouldn't go back with him. What a fairy tale. Much as she wanted to believe it, she knew that wasn't like him. I can survive, she told herself. Broken bones and bruises would heal. I'll miss Arlette, and think of her always, but I'll live.

She rolled the barn door open, reached inside, and turned on the switch that flooded the outside area with light. The stall was all ready for Ginger. Ronny had seen to it that fresh straw was on the floor and hay in the manger. Ronny was turning into a friend. When Cary found a place of her own, she'd ask Ronny about a companion for Ginger. Used to being with a herd, Ginger couldn't help but be unhappy all by herself.

Ronny needed an accountant. When she discovered Cary was a CPA, she'd offered Cary the job, as soon as she recovered from her injuries. That meant money enough, she hoped, to pay back Kelby's sister for all that she'd taken and get a place to live. She could do the accounting and still take care of Elizabeth.

"Hello, Cary." The words snapped like frost in the still air.

She whirled, heartbeat rushing in her ears. She couldn't see him. His voice came from the direction of the house. She hadn't heard a car come up the driveway. Had he been here for some time, hiding and waiting?

"Aren't you going to give your ever-lovin' man a big hug and a kiss?"

"Mitch . . ." She stood frozen outside the barn door, one hand on Ginger's halter. Where was he?

"You don't seem so thrilled to see me." His foot crunched on gravel.

She could barely make out his dark shape on the driveway next to the house. "Don't—"

"*Don't?* Don't what? Tell you how worried I've been, how I'm going half crazy wondering what happened to you? How could you do that to me, Cary? Let me think some sick bastard grabbed you and killed you?"

"Everything's changed, it's not—"

"What's that? Got yourself a dog? Sure is ugly. Stinks, too. It'll have to go back." His voice sounded closer.

"Just let me go, Mitch."

"It must be the concussion talking. You know I can't live without you."

"I'm not coming back." She could tell from his voice he'd been drinking.

"Well now, that's where you're wrong, darlin'." His voice got a hard, quiet tone that raised the hairs on the back of her neck. "You're coming home with me. You belong with me."

"No. Not any more."

"We're going home and we're going to talk about what you did."

She bobbed her head, trying to see where he'd gone.

"Didn't I tell you I didn't like it? That time before, when you took off? I guess I'm going to have to tell you again." He sounded closer.

She flipped off the barn light, plunging the area in darkness. Holding Ginger by the halter, she tried to run. She stumbled along the stone path toward the silo. *If she could just get to the bridge.* Ginger, thinking this was a game, trotted easily along.

"Cary! Don't be stupid!"

She heard him thudding after her. Maybe she could lose him in the dark. With no light, he couldn't see. She couldn't either, but she had Ginger. Her breath came in short gulps, pains stabbed her chest. An ankle twisted as it came down on a loose stone. Mitch's footfalls got closer. The dark shape of the tractor shed was just ahead. Hide there?

"You can't get away!"

284

The open shed had nowhere to hide. She stumbled, shaking pain through the broken arm pressed against her stomach. She labored to pull air in her lungs.

"Cary! God damn it! Stop this!" His voice sounded right behind her. "If you don't stop right now, I'm going to make you wish you had."

Keep moving. He can't see in the dark. Ginger can get us out of this.

Finally, the silo, tall and ominous, loomed in the black sky. Cary doubled over, unable to pull in enough air. Ginger nuzzled an arm, uncertain what was expected of her.

"Forward," Cary whispered. Ginger trotted on. They stayed on the path, moved around the silo, and kept going. It couldn't be far now. Cary pressed against the horse, holding the halter tight.

"The harder you make it, the sorrier you'll be."

He was so close, she heard his breath rasp as he sucked in air. What if Ginger couldn't get them around the rotted section? What if she jumped over it? What if she'd never been taught what to do if a great big hole suddenly appeared in the surface she was racing across?

Cary felt rough wood beneath her feet. They'd reached the bridge. A click to Ginger. They raced up the curve.

Footsteps thumped behind her. Too close, too close. They'd never make it.

Faster! Blood rushed in her ears. She was almost to the top of the crest. The rotted area was just below the highest point. Hurry!

"Cary! Stop!"

Such was his hold over her that she nearly obeyed. She was only making it worse for herself. When he caught her, he would hurt her more. Unbearable pain grabbed her chest as she struggled over the highest point. Momentum hurled her downward.

She stumbled and fell against Ginger. The horse missed a step but recovered and kept going. *Just ahead. Careful.*

"Cary!"

Oh, God, two more steps and he'd have her. Run! Run!

Could Ginger maneuver them past the gaping hole? Keep them safe on the thin strip that wasn't rotted? Would their combined weight be too much, cause the bridge to crash into the creek?

Ginger daintily moved to the left without hesitation and trotted steadily on. They were going to do it, they were going to make it. Cary tried to take in gulps of air and set off a coughing fit.

Mitch grabbed the back of her shirt. She jerked away.

He stumbled. She ran, urging Ginger on faster.

"Cary!" His voice sounded hollow, and far away.

She spared a glance over her shoulder.

"Help me! I can't hold on!"

Where was he? She spoke a command to Ginger who stopped. Cary looked back.

"Cary! I'm hanging by my hands!"

He had fallen through the gap where the bridge had rotted. Had he really? His voice was coming from below. She hesitated. "I'll get help."

"It'll be too late. I'll fall."

A trick?

"You want me to die?"

No, she didn't want that. She only wanted to slow him down so she could get away. Now she'd gone too far. She shouldn't have tried such a dangerous ploy. Standing close to Ginger, she nudged the horse nearer the rotted section.

"Cary! Don't let me die!"

She inched another step. "Hold on. I'll—"

He grabbed an ankle.

No! No! He was pulling her in. She'd fall. Please, no! Shaking her foot to get free, she accidentally kicked Ginger. The horse circled, trampling on his hands. His hands slipped. He yelled.

She heard a splash and then a thunk, like a ripe watermelon hitting the ground.

Gasping in air, she clutched Ginger's halter, turned carefully, and made her way to the house. Pain spread out through her entire body. By the time she reached the house, she could barely breathe.

In the kitchen she fumbled for the phone and punched in 911. She said something, she knew she did, but she couldn't make it clear, and then she felt herself sliding down to the floor.

44

Susan grabbed the cane and hobbled as fast as her injured leg would allow. Though she needed the cane more than she liked to admit, it wasn't as awkward as swinging herself along on crutches. When she was belted in, Parkhurst turned the ignition, hit the overheads, and stomped the accelerator.

At Kelby Oliver's house, he zipped into the driveway, scattering gravel. As she climbed from the Bronco, she gritted her teeth against the pain. He took off, his gun held alongside his leg. At the screened porch, he proceeded more cautiously. She was behind him when he went into the kitchen.

Abruptly, he stopped. "Pony in the house. One down."

Cary Black lay slumped in a corner, propped against the cabinet. The phone receiver dangled, making the beep-beep-beep noise as a reminder to hang up. The horse nuzzled Cary's cheek, then raised its head and looked at them. They did a quick run through, room by room. No one else inside. Where was Faye Turney?

Parkhurst slipped his gun back in the shoulder holster and radioed for an ambulance. Susan knelt and put her fingertips against the corner of Cary's jaw. Pulse rapid, but strong.

"Cary?" No response.

He went outside to check the area. She waited with Cary. What the hell had happened? Did someone hurt her? Was she released from the hospital too soon and had some kind of relapse? Did concussion victims have relapses? Where was the ambulance?

Five minutes later, a siren screamed its way toward the house, up the driveway and got cut in midwail. Two young males in navy blue jumpsuits came in and stopped at the sight of the horse.

"Why is there a pony in the house?"

She told him to look at the victim. "Her name is Cary Black."

One paramedic knelt and put a stethoscope to Cary's chest, the other slapped a blood pressure cuff on her arm and pumped it up. Plastic tubing went around her neck to administer oxygen.

"Ma'am? Cary? Can you hear me?"

Cary's eyelids fluttered. "Mitch . . ."

"Just take it easy. Don't try to move."

She struggled. "Mitch . . . fell . . ."

"Just relax. You had a fall."

"Hurt . . . Mitch . . . fell . . . creek . . . help . . ."

Susan knelt beside her. "Did Mitch hurt you?"

"Creek . . . help . . ."

"Take it easy," the paramedic said. "We're going to help you." He lowered his voice and said to Susan, "We need to get her to the hospital."

Cary clutched Susan's hand. "Creek. Help him."

The paramedics loaded Cary on the gurney and rolled her out to the waiting ambulance. Susan, one hand on Ginger's halter, led the horse out and to the barn.

She was headed back to the house when Parkhurst trotted up. "Did you see a creek?"

"I saw a bridge and heard water trickle."

"Cary was saying her husband fell in the creek."

He handed her his flashlight and went to the Bronco for another one. "Take it easy." He shined his light on the uneven stone path. "Good place to twist an ankle."

He took off. She followed more slowly.

"Somebody's in the water!" he called a moment later.

Carefully, she made her way to the edge of the bridge, shined her light down at the water, then up at the underside of the bridge. Old wooden bridge, but she couldn't tell much more. Too dark.

Parkhurst clambered down the bank and splashed over to the body that was facedown in the water. Mitch Black, Susan assumed.

Placing his flashlight on a rock, Parkhurst squatted beside whoever it was. She dropped her cane and picked her way down to the creek, grabbing at low-growing vegetation to keep from falling. When she reached the water's edge, Parkhurst was doing chest compressions. She waded toward him. The water wasn't deep, only five or six inches. She took over the chest compressions to give him a rest.

He shined his light on the victim's face and then out over the creek and along the bank. "Another ambulance on the way. But . . ." He shook his head, then resumed CPR. She went back to the house to show the paramedics where to go.

Cary Black was admitted to the hospital for observation and it was the following afternoon, Sunday, before Susan was allowed to question her. Cary explained why she was running and hiding, told of the bus ride, getting to Hampstead, Kelby missing. "I didn't know what to do. If I went to the police Mitch would find out where I was."

"You assumed her name."

"I didn't intend to, it just happened." Cary explained her need for books and getting a library card in Kelby's name, getting the job of taking care of Dr. Farley. She asked about Ginger.

Susan assured her Ginger was fine. Ronny Wells had the horse at the ranch. Susan asked about Faye Turney and Cary said Faye had decided to leave early.

"Mitch?" Cary said.

45

$\mathcal{O}$n Monday morning, feeling very much an intruder, Susan slipped into the small room where Jen's mom waited with her new husband, Jen's dad, a social worker, and a nurse. The result of Jen's latest cerebral flow study showed no blood flow to the brain. She was pronounced brain dead. Terry made the agonizing decision to remove all life support keeping her daughter alive. "You were her friend," Terry said to Susan. "She'd want you here."

Susan wanted to be anywhere else in the world. She expected Terry to fall apart, sob and scream about the unfairness and how she couldn't go on without her daughter, but when she was pushed against it, Terry came through with dignity. Pale, hands clasped so tightly the knuckles were white, her eyes were dry and her voice quiet.

"I have to be proud," she whispered. "Hold my head up high. For Jen's sake. I don't want her to be ashamed of me. I want her to know I love her. She'll always be with me." Terry touched her chest with a clenched fist.

A social worker led them to Jen's room. "If there is anything I can do, if you need anything . . ."

Susan felt numb, movement was difficult, like she was wading through wet cement. The minister from Terry's church was there and he hugged her. A nurse rattled the curtain closed around the bed. Cables and wires connected Jen to machines that beeped and flickered, the ventilator pushed air in and out of her chest. She looked young, and peaceful.

With icy fingers, Terry took Susan's hand and drew her close to the bed. She picked up one of Jen's limp hands and placed it in Susan's. Terry went to the other side of the bed and picked up Jen's other hand. She nodded to the minister.

In a quiet, resonant voice, he said, "Jen, your job here is finished. You're going to leave this earth and go to a new school far greater than any you could choose. To keep you safe on the journey, we send with you our blessings and all our love."

Terry said, "I love you, Jennifer. I'll always be your mother. I'm releasing you. I'll always love you with all my heart."

Pain squeezed the air from Susan's lungs. Softly, she stroked Jen's cheek with fingertips. "Good-bye, Jen. You're a great kid. I love you."

Terry rested her cheek against Jen's chest, as though listening to the heartbeat for one last time. She straightened and walked away. Susan kissed Jen's limp fingers and gently put Jen's hand back on the bed.

One week later, Susan stood on the crumbling wooden bridge. Mitchell Black had fallen, hit his head on a rock, and drowned in five inches of water. A flock of crows rose from the field filling the silence with jeering calls. She could imagine Jen saying something silly like, "Too many rooks spoil the croft."

That night Susan dreamed, not the dream filled with dread and gunfire, but a dream of Jen on the bridge with her legs dangling through the hole in the rotted boards. Jen smiled. Feeling a great surge of joy, Susan smiled back and started to run toward her. With a shake of her head, Jen slipped through the hole and sat cross-legged on a boulder in the creek. She said something important that Susan didn't understand, because trickling water distorted her words.

Finally, Jen covered her eyes with her hands and Susan understood what she was saying. Blindness comes in all forms. Blindness where your eyes don't function, where you can't understand, where you look the other way, where you jump to the wrong conclusion.

But the very worst was promising to help a young girl and not seeing the disastrous outcome of a promise not kept.